ADVANCED PRA[ISE]

"Refined by Fire" was absolutely superb. "Trailblazers" takes it up a notch. The characters are so realistic and the settings in Europe so familiar, I felt as if I were living the moment. This series paints a vivid picture of the competence, character and chemistry of the brave young women who led the way for others to follow as the military integrated women into previously all male formations. Their leadership continues today. Can't wait for book three in the Guardians of Peace Series.

—Major General, U.S. Army retired, Robert D. Shadley, author of "The Game"

Trailblazers is an attention grabbing read that I couldn't put down. Having attended and graduated from West Point in 1977 and served in the Army during this period, the imaginary characters all ring true and this historical fiction series offers accurate insight into the way things were. I can't wait to read the next volume in the series.

—Major General, U.S. Army retired, R. Mark Brown

"Trailblazers" and "Refined by Fire" are written from the perspective of the small group of female Army lieutenants and cadets who were integrated into the active duty Army and West Point, during the 1970's. Their motivation to join and serve varies by individual to include service to the nation, educational opportunities, unit cohesion, travel and friendship. These reasons are still relevant today. Having served in the Army during this period, the series expertly captures what it was like to be a cadet/young officer in an Army that was struggling with massive organizational and social change. I look forward to the next book.

—Colonel, U.S. Army retired, Mary Brown

YVONNE DOLL | RUTH VANDYKE

a novel

TRAILBLAZERS

BOOK TWO *in the*
GUARDIANS OF PEACE SERIES

This book is a work of fiction. Names, characters, businesses, organizations, places, events, and incidents are either a product of the authors' imaginations or are used fictitiously. Any resemblance to actual persons, living or dead, events, or locales is entirely coincidental.

Published by Dog Ear Publishing
4011 Vincennes Rd
Indianapolis, IN 46268
www.dogearpublishing.net

Copyright ©2015 Yvonne Doll & Ruth VanDyke

All rights reserved.

No part of this book may be reproduced, stored in a retrieval system, or transmitted by any means, electronic, mechanical, photocopying, recording, or otherwise, without written permission from the copyright holder.

This book is printed on acid-free paper.

Printed in the United States of America

Distributed by Dog Ear Publishing

Design and composition by Dog Ear Publishing

Cover design by Dog Ear Publishing

Cataloging-in-Publication data

Print ISBN: 978-1-4575-3911-4

First Edition

Other Edition(s):
eBook ISBN: 978-

PREFACE

THE GUARDIANS OF PEACE series begins in 1976 because that was a watershed year for the changes the military would make over the next thirty-nine years regarding women in the military. The impetus for our historical fiction series was our desire to entertain readers while providing an accurate depiction of women in the Army.

Volume I, *Refined by Fire*, recounts the experiences of Amelia, Maura, and Anne as they transition from college students to newly commissioned second lieutenants with initial assignments in Germany, along with the trials of Lori, Cate, and Trish, three of the first female cadets to attend the United States Military Academy (USMA) at West Point, New York, and become members of the Long Gray Line.

Volume II, *Trailblazers*, starts in the summer of 1978, as Lori and Trish experience the "real" Army at Cadet Troop Leadership Training (CTLT) in West Germany, with Maura and Anne assigned as their sponsors and culminates with their USMA graduation in June 1980.

For our readers who do not have a military background, we have provided a glossary of military terms and jargon in Refined by Fire and on our website, for you to refer to as needed.

We hope you'll visit our website (http://ydoll8.wix.com/guardians-of-peace) and our Facebook page (https://www.facebook.com/GuardiansofPeaceMilitarySeries) and share your thoughts with us and our followers.

1

COOKE BARRACKS, GÖPPINGEN, GERMANY, MONDAY 12 JUNE 1978

LOUD BANGING ON HER BOQ door jolted Lori out of a sound sleep. Startled because she had lowered the metal window shutters to keep the early morning sun from waking her up prematurely, Lori fumbled around in total darkness, until she found the light switch on the lamp beside her bed. Seeing the time on her alarm clock, she muttered, "Crap!" as she realized she had inadvertently overslept.

After jumping out of bed, Lori opened the front door. At the sight of Maura standing there, Lori exclaimed, "Uh, sorry, ma'am, I don't know what happened!"

Maura put her hand up. "It's okay. You arrived here exhausted, and jet lag can be pretty rough. Can I come in?"

Lori motioned Maura to come in, closing the door behind them.

Turning the foyer light on, Maura pointed to the bathroom. "Get dressed. I'll get you a Tab and banana to get you through until lunchtime. Can you get dressed in ten minutes?"

As she walked into the bathroom, Lori said, "Yes, ma'am!"

Locking her BOQ door a few minutes later, Lori followed Maura down the hall, taking a large gulp of Tab, hoping the caffeine would kick in quickly. She was perturbed that she had overslept and now had a blistering headache. This was not how she had envisioned her first day on the job.

Walking out of the BOQ, Maura pointed to her car. "I'd planned to walk to the brigade headquarters, but with 0900 staff call and a few things to do before then, we need to drive."

They pulled into the brigade headquarters parking lot and got out of the car just as Lori finished off her can of soda. Maura pointed to a light green truck parked near the entrance of the brigade headquarters. "That's the roach coach. If you need a bit more to eat, we can stop on our way in."

"I'm fine, ma'am. The Tab and banana'll hold me 'til lunch."

After entering the headquarters, they jogged up the stairs to the top floor. Maura punched in the entry code on the keypad to the right of the red metal door and entered the ops center yelling, "Uncleared personnel in the area!"

"Morning, ma'am!"

"Mornin', Master Sergeant Smith," Maura replied cheerfully and turned to Lori. "Cadet Nelson, this is Master Sergeant Smith. He's the Operations Sergeant. He'll help you get started with your in-processing paperwork. I'll return in a few and take you to staff call." Turning to Master Sergeant Smith, she added, "Take good care of her. I'll be back at 0845."

"Check, ma'am. C'mon, Cadet Nelson. There's some paperwork I need you to sign before you go to staff call."

★ ★ ★

AS MAURA WALKED INTO the fire support section, the major queried, "Where's our cadet, LT?"

"Master Sergeant Smith is getting her to sign the nondisclosure and other security paperwork so she can attend staff call this morning, sir."

Looking irritated, the major growled, "Who'd you coordinate that with, LT?"

"The G-3, sir."

The major snorted disapprovingly and went back to reading the document in his hands. Maura knew this was his way of indicating the conversation was over, so she sat down at her desk to review the staff duty log and her notes for the morning staff call before returning to the Ops center.

★ ★ ★

MASTER SERGEANT SMITH LOOKED up as Maura approached the counter. "Okay, ma'am, she's signed the paperwork we need to allow her access to classified materiel up to Secret, on a *need-to-know* basis. When staff call is over, bring her back here to finish her in-processing."

"WILCO," Maura replied as she motioned Lori to follow her.

Walking down the hall, Lori queried, "Ma'am, that NCO seems awfully gruff and bossy. Why did you let him talk to you that way?"

Maura smiled. "Lori, senior NCOs like Master Sergeant Smith and Sergeant Major Atkins, who you'll meet at staff call, only tolerate junior officers. You're a cadet and I'm a lieutenant. My granddad served in World War II, and the only piece of advice he gave me was that officers make decisions, but NCOs run the Army. He told me that if I wanted to be a good officer, I'd have to earn the respect of and learn from my NCOs."

Maura stopped in front of a closed heavy wooden door. "This is the G-3's conference room. We have staff call every Monday morning at 0900, and that is the only time we can walk in unannounced."

Maura opened the door, and they walked into the empty conference room. "I wanted to get here a bit early so you wouldn't have to walk into the gaggle I encountered on my first Monday. You'll probably be ignored for most of your time here. From the sounds of some of your experiences at West Point, I'm comfortable you can handle that, but if you were expecting to be welcomed with open arms here, it just ain't gonna happen. You're here for such a short time. I doubt any of the guys will even give you the slightest notice, after an initial introduction and assessment of you. Lieutenant Colonel Connolly is the G-3. He or I will introduce you."

Maura pointed to a row of chairs along the wall. "Sit in the last chair near the window. I sit at the far end of the table; that way, you'll be right behind me."

Lori had barely sat down before a few of the staff officers came in. They nodded at Maura and sat down in their assigned seats. Within a few minutes, everyone except the G-3 and sergeant major had arrived. Most of the staff were busy looking at notes they had made for the morning meeting. Maura turned her chair around to face Lori's and was telling her the names and positions of the officers as they arrived. She had just finished when Sergeant Major Atkins opened the private door that led into the G-3's office suite and bellowed, "At ease!"

Everyone stood up and came to attention. The G-3 walked in behind Sergeant Major Atkins and casually announced, "As you were." Everyone relaxed but waited for the G-3 to be seated before they sat down again. LTC Connolly looked around to ensure that the entire staff was there before telling Maura, "LT, introduce our cadet."

"Yes, sir." Maura motioned Lori to stand up. "This is Cadet Lori Nelson. She's a West Point cadet and is assigned to the brigade for her Cadet Troop Leader Training rotation. Because the brigade receives a West Point cadet every year, most of you are familiar with this program. I'm her sponsor and responsible for ensuring she has a productive and positive learning experience. I coordinated the training plan with the FSCOORD, who up until this year has been the primary sponsor for the cadets, and appreciate his assistance. LTC Connolly approved the training plan last week that identifies the dates Cadet Nelson will be in each of your respective sections. I've put Cadet Nelson's bio and a copy of the training schedule in your in-boxes. I need your assistance in ensuring you have a training plan set up before Cadet Nelson arrives in your sections. This is her first and only experience with the active-duty Army before she graduates from West Point. I know you will make this a positive experience and ensure she is afforded every opportunity to learn from you." Maura paused. "Sir, subject to questions, that's all I have."

LTC Connolly turned to face Lori. "Cadet Nelson, being a grad myself, I'm committed to ensuring you have the best experience possible. Normally, you would have been assigned to a grad, but in this case, the commanding general and I feel strongly that the best sponsor for you is Lieutenant Collins. You could not have a better sponsor, and I know you'll learn a lot from her." Looking at Maura, he continued, "I'm going to amend your schedule today, Maura. I want to talk to you and Cadet Nelson privately at the conclusion of staff call."

"Okay," LTC Connolly continued, "Ops, brief me on the upcoming Operational Readiness Test."

At the end of staff call, LTC Connolly gestured for Maura and Lori to follow him into his private office and motioned both of them to sit down in the chairs in front of his desk. Lori was immediately transfixed by his trophy wall, which was filled with unit plaques and awards. Sitting down, she was awe-struck by the massive window overlooking the Swabian Alps. It was a sunny day, and the view was compelling.

Chuckling, the G-3 addressed Lori directly. "Pretty impressive, isn't it?"

Nodding, Lori quietly replied, "Yes, sir."

Turning his chair around to look out, he added, "I don't get much of a chance to remember to enjoy the view." After a few seconds, he turned back around, asking, "Were you able to get a good night's sleep?"

"Yes, sir, perhaps too good," Lori added a bit sheepishly. The G-3 looked at Maura questioningly. Maura shook her head, indicating he didn't want the details.

The G-3 addressed Lori. "Okay, the reason I wanted to talk to both of you privately is because I want you to know that if the staff is unprofessional or uncooperative in any way, let me or Lieutenant Collins know immediately. I will ensure it is rectified and you will not be negatively impacted. I don't know if Lieutenant Collins shared her experience with you, but her welcome was not what it should have been, and even though she's been accepted as a valued member of the team, there's still significant resistance to any female being assigned to this or any other combat brigade. Having said that, Congress and senior military leaders have decided women will have a larger role in the military, and it's my responsibility to ensure I train and treat every soldier the same, regardless of personal views. Do you have any questions?"

"No, sir!" Lori replied crisply. Lori was surprised the G-3 had taken the time to talk to her about this, and she wanted to talk to him about his experiences at USMA but was too afraid to ask for more of his time and attention.

"Okay," LTC Connolly added, "That's all I have for you, except my wife reminded me that whenever a West Point cadet was assigned to our unit, we had him over for a meal to relax and ask us questions about life in the Army.

She has informed me that this year will not be any different." LTC Connolly turned to Maura. "LT, get with household six, and figure out a night that works for dinner at our house. The sooner the better, got it?"

"Yes, sir." Maura stood up, and motioned Lori to do the same. As Maura and Lori walked out of the G-3's private office into his reception area, Maura saw Sergeant Major Atkins sitting at his desk pretending to read a manual. She knew he was pretending to be busy, because she had seen him look up briefly before dropping his eyes back to the document he'd been reading when they came out of the office.

"Sergeant Major, do you have a minute?" Maura asked.

Looking up, Sergeant Major Atkins feigned surprise. "Sure, ma'am, whatcha need?"

"I'd like to introduce you to Cadet Nelson."

She turned to Lori. "Sergeant Major Atkins and Master Sergeant Smith are the only reason I survived my first month in the brigade. None of my fellow officers would talk to me, let alone help me. Sergeant Major Atkins and Master Sergeant Smith made it clear to me they weren't happy to have a woman in the 3-shop but had a responsibility to me and told me that if I would trust them, they would guide me and ensure I didn't step all over my wing-wang."

Sergeant Major Atkins laughed heartily. "Shit, ma'am, you don't got no wing-wang to step on!"

"Yeah, I know, but that's exactly what you said to me."

Sergeant Major Atkins looked at Lori. "Welcome." Pointing at Maura, he continued. "You can learn a lot from her, but try to be a bit more lady-like. She came here as a sweet, normal young lady about eighteen months ago, but somewhere along the line, she turned into one of the guys. I don't consider it an improvement, but she didn't ask my opinion."

Surprised by the sergeant major's candor and casual attitude, Lori stiffly replied, "Thank you, Sergeant Major."

Having returned to the Ops center, Maura handed Lori off to Master Sergeant Smith. "Okay, I'm going to get some work done while Master Sergeant Smith helps you finish in-processing. Come to my office when he releases you for lunch." Nodding to Master Sergeant Smith to indicate that Lori was now his responsibility, Maura walked away.

The major looked up as Maura walked into the FSCOORD's office. "You didn't have to tell the G-3 that I helped you with the training schedule."

Maura replied, "I know, sir, but I wanted him to know that you helped me and I appreciate it."

Ignoring that comment because it made him uncomfortable, he asked, "So, whaddya think of her?"

"She's a cadet, sir. A clueless, idealistic cadet." Maura instantly regretted that characterization. "She's sharp, sir, just what you would expect of a West Point cadet. She has some notions about interactions between officers and NCOs that surprise me, but otherwise, I think this will be a good experience for everyone."

The major replied curtly, "She's a West Point cadet, LT. It's up to you to help her see the rules they teach at West Point are guidelines, not immutable standards."

Maura nodded as she walked over to the small safe behind her desk, sat down, and spun the combination dial to open it. She was frustrated because she felt Lori's sponsor should have been a grad, but once again, her being female took precedence. Unsure about how best to handle the situation, Maura turned her attention to one of the documents she had taken out of the safe.

THE SOUND OF LORI'S voice startled Maura. "Ma'am, can you break for lunch?"

Maura looked up to see Lori standing in front of her desk. Instinctively looking at her watch, she put her document down and stood up.

"Gosh, sorry, I lost track of time. Are you hungry?"

Lori emphatically replied, "Yes!"

"I'll take you to the German *kantin*a for a schnitzel sandwich and the best fries you'll ever eat."

As they walked out of the brigade headquarters, Maura stopped, "Say, I know you're hungry, but right now there'll be a long line at the *kantina*, so being as we didn't get to walk up here from your BOQ this morning, can I show you a shortcut that takes about five minutes off your walk up here, before we go to lunch?"

Lori nodded yes and followed Maura across the parking lot, stopping between two large office buildings. Maura pointed to the BOQ, which was about a quarter of a mile away. "If you walk around behind the BOQ and take the shortcut through these two buildings, you'll be at the headquarters in less than five minutes."

Turning around, she added, "Just to the left of the brigade headquarters is the gym. Half a mile down the road in the opposite direction is the shopette. If you take a right out of the BOQ and walk about half a mile, the O'Club's on your right. I'll show you where the commissary is at the end of the day. It's near the class VI liquor store, in case you want to buy some beer to keep in your room, but you can walk to all the conveniences on post in just a few minutes."

"Thanks, ma'am. What about the chapel and theater?"

"Sorry, forgot about them. The chapel is about a mile away, and the post theater is near the front gate."

"Great, ma'am."

"Okay, let's head to the *Kantina*."

Lori followed Maura, mentally noting landmarks so she could find things when Maura was not around. They walked in a comfortable silence until they got to the *Kantina*.

"You're gonna think you died and went to food heaven," Maura said as they walked into the small, dark restaurant. "Lunch is my treat today." Pointing to a black chalkboard, Maura added, "There's today's options, the special is *Hirsch Gulasch Suppe*, which is a wonderful stew with mushrooms and a local noodle called spätzle. Hirsch is German for deer, so if you like venison, you'll love it."

The smells emanating from the kitchen were tantalizing. "I'm famished. The gulasch sounds great, how long will it take?"

Maura who had been looking for an empty table in the crowded room, laughed. "Long enough for Hannelore to throw it in a bowl. You'll actually get it quicker than the schnitzel sandwich and fries. C'mon, those guys are getting up, and I don't see any other open tables."

Lori followed Maura to the table and sat down. "A large bowl of stew and some bread sounds great."

Maura went to the counter, ordered their food and sodas, and returned to the table a few minutes later, with two steaming bowls of gulasch, dark bread, salads, and two large glasses of a drink Lori didn't recognize.

Lori took a sip of her drink. "What is this?"

"It's *Spätze*."

"This is really good! Much better than plain Coke. Can we get this in the States?"

"Nope. I'm not sure why, but the Coke and orange Fanta here tastes different, so enjoy it while you're here."

Lori sighed disappointedly, consoling herself by taking another sip of *Spätze* followed by a large spoonful of gulasch. They ate in silence for a few minutes, before Maura asked Lori if she wanted another *Spätze* or some dessert. When Lori said no, they got up and headed back to the Ops center.

2

GÖPPINGEN, MONDAY AFTERNOON, 12 JUNE 1978

BACK AT HER DESK, MAURA decided to call Anne to see how things were going with Trish. Maura had met Anne on the plane to Germany and they had become fast friends. After a number of rings and no answer, Maura was just about to hang up when she heard, "Lieutenant Devereaux."

"Anne, how's it going with Trish?"

"Pretty good. Trish got her TA-50 this morning. I showed her around and we had lunch at the snack bar. She's doing her security in-processing now. How 'bout you?"

"Good. Lori's getting her TA-50 issued as we speak. I told her to give me a call when she's finished. I'll drive down to load everything in my car to take to the BOQ."

"So what's the plan for the rest of the week?" Anne asked.

"I'll go to dinner with Lori at the O'Club tonight, see what questions she has, then tell her to meet me at the office at eight tomorrow morning." Pausing, Maura chuckled. "Lori either forgot to set the alarm this morning or slept through it. When I got to the parking lot and didn't see her, I went into the stairwell. When she wasn't there, I went up to her room. It took some prolonged and heavy pounding on the door before she woke up and let me in."

"Oh, too funny!"

"Yeah, but I felt bad for her. She was embarrassed and apologized, saying that she doesn't usually do things like this. She's nice, but a bit tightly wound. What about Trish?"

"Well, she was waiting for me, and no mishaps today, but yeah, she's pretty intense. It's like having a two-year-old following you around, asking incessant questions. Don't get me wrong, she's no bother, and it's natural for her to have lots of questions; it's just really a lot of work to make sure she stays on schedule and knows where to go. I'm hoping by the end of the week, I'll have explained enough that she can work on the project I'm going to give her tomorrow, with just a bit of supervision."

"Yeah, I guess I didn't think about how much work it'd be, to keep her busy. When I looked at the training schedule I devised for Lori, I realized she'll probably have a lot of questions this first week and I won't get much work done, which is a bit problematic, because we're doing an ORT next week and I've never done one, so I need to bone up on a few things to make sure I don't screw up."

"Yeah, It's difficult for me to find things for Trish to do here. I wish I were still a platoon leader. I've talked to the current commander and he may be able to get her into a platoon. We'll see."

Maura sighed, "In the past, the cadets spent all their time in one of the infantry platoons, but because she's a female, that isn't an option. I'd like to think that if someone had taken the time to look at it, they would have realized they should have sent the few female cadets to Division Support commands, where at least they could be with soldiers instead of being on a staff."

Anne suddenly interrupted, "Maura, sorry, just realized I have a meeting in fifteen. Thanks for calling. It'll be interesting to compare notes this weekend. Trish and I'll see you guys at the *Volksmarch* registration area, on Saturday morning."

★ ★ ★

MAURA WAS IN THE middle of a Nuclear Release Authentication System inventory when the phone rang.

Maura lifted the receiver. "LT Collins."

"Hi, ma'am, it's Lori, I have my combat gear."

"Okay, take everything outside and wait for me. I have some classified out, so it'll take me a few minutes to secure everything."

As Maura approached the CIF a few minutes later, she saw Lori sitting on one of her duffle bags, chin cupped in her hands, staring at the nearby mountains. Maura realized with a start just how young and vulnerable Lori looked, and she reminded herself that Lori was still just a college student. Her next thought was, *Do I look that young and vulnerable as well?* After all, she was only four years older than Lori, but now she was responsible for nuclear material codes, ensuring the brigade was prepared to fight and survive in a nuclear, chemical, or biologically contaminated battlefield, and a number of other readiness activities.

Hearing the approaching vehicle and recognizing Maura's car, Lori waved and stood up.

After loading the first duffle bag in the trunk, Lori walked over and picked up the other one. "Thanks so much for helping me get this stuff back to the BOQ, ma'am. I coulda gotten it there, but I'd have to make two trips and these duffel bags would get heavy after about a block." Lori stuffed the second bag in the backseat because Maura's trunk was too small to fit both duffel bags.

Maura grimaced. "Oh, I know. That's what I had to do. Luckily, it wasn't too cold or icy. But I was foolish enough to think I could carry both duffels at the same time. I put one on my back and carried the other. I had to stop about every five minutes to take a break, and my shoulders and arms were killing me when I woke up the next morning."

A few minutes later, Maura pulled into the BOQ parking lot. Lori got out first. "Thanks again, ma'am. I can manage from here. I'm sure there's a bunch of stuff you need to get done."

Maura got out of the car. "I'll grab the duffle in the backseat. You pull the one out of the trunk." Maura continued, "I toyed with the idea of going back to the office, but by the time I get back, I'd only get about thirty minutes of work in before calling it a day, so decided I'd take a run and shower at the gym, then come back here to take you to dinner at the O'Club."

Closing the trunk and putting the duffle bag on her back, Lori interjected, "A run sounds great, ma'am. Do you mind if I join you? You're welcome to change and shower at my place."

Maura suddenly realized she was so used to being by herself that it had never occurred to her to ask if Lori wanted to join her. "Of course, Lori. Sorry, I should have thought to invite you. I guess not really having any friends here, I've just got used to doing things solo, which when I think about it is pretty sad." Seeing the dismayed look on Lori's face, she added, "It's cool; I'm used to it."

Walking into the BOQ, Lori began to get an inkling of how lonely and tough it had been for Maura. "Wow. Ma'am, I don't mean to pry, but you really don't have any friends here?"

Maura grinned wryly. "Yeah, it does sound pretty bad when I hear it from you, but actually, no. There are two other female officers in the brigade, but we don't really have anything in common and I sorta pissed them off at the last PT test. I pal around with some of the single schoolteachers, but I don't really have a lot in common with them either."

Lori nodded knowingly as she turned right at the top of the stairs and headed down the hallway to her suite. "Yeah, just because we're all women doesn't necessarily mean things are going to work out. Luckily, I met Trish and Cate plebe year and we've been friends ever since."

"Yeah," Maura acknowledged. "It was great when Anne and I were both in Stuttgart; we were inseparable. We met a few other women officers and had a small group to do things with and go to for advice. Anne and I get together almost every weekend, but during the week, it's me, myself, and I. Quite honestly, between work, PT, and getting a few personal things done, I don't really mind or notice being alone."

Lori reached into her fatigue jacket pocket to pull out her door key. She unlocked and opened the door, walked into the kitchen/living room area, and put down the duffle bag along the wall, motioning Maura to put her bag right beside it. "I'll put everything together later and store it in the closet here."

Maura said, "That's one good thing about living in the BOQ; you have lots of closet space. I really like living on the economy but miss having real closets."

Lori looked at Maura questioningly. "You don't have any closets?"

"Nope. In Europe if you build a closet, it's considered a room and subject to an additional tax. Europeans pay some pretty heavy taxes, so to minimize costs, Germans have these huge wall units called *Schränke* that take the place of closets, but they're not nearly as spacious. When you come over to my place, I'll show you the ones I use. Luckily, my apartment came furnished, so while I don't have the greatest stuff, it's good quality and fairly nice." Switching gears, Maura motioned that she was going into the bathroom to change. "If we're going to get a decent run in, we need to get going."

Maura met up with Lori in the foyer, and they headed outside. After stretching for a few minutes, Maura said, "Cause the back gate leading to the forest and up the *Hohenstaufen* is closed, we'll have to go out the front gate. After about a mile, we'll veer off into the forest. How long we run depends upon how far you want to go today."

Lori thought about it for a few seconds. "Would five miles be okay?"

Maura smiled. "Perfect. You set the pace. You don't know the route and I don't want to exhaust you."

Lori immediately retorted, "I'm a pretty good runner, ma'am, so likewise, if my pace is too fast, just let me know and I can throttle down."

Maura had originally planned on a leisurely jog at a pace of about eight minutes per mile so they could enjoy the scenery and talk. Amused that Lori had perceived her effort to be considerate a challenge and being a bit competitive as well, she couldn't resist upping the ante. "Don't worry about me. We can run as fast as you like."

Lori started out at a reasonable pace, but after about five minutes, she picked up the pace. Maura smiled as she recalled her first run up the *Hohenstaufen*. She hadn't realized how long and steep it would be to get to the top, but seeing the captain and other officers on her run, Maura hadn't wanted to show any signs of slowing down. By the time she had gotten to the top, she felt as if her lungs were going to explode and had been relieved that the run back was mostly downhill. That might be the case today as well, if they kept this pace up.

Maura realized Lori was a good, efficient runner, but Maura had the psychological advantage of knowing the route and more importantly, Lori would not realize until they returned back to the front gate, that the last half mile leading up to the BOQ was a steep uphill climb.

They had not spoken a word since the initial turn off into the woods, and were both breathing hard as they came out of the forest and headed home. Just over a mile from the BOQ, Lori picked the pace up a bit more. When they made the left into the *kaserne* and Lori saw the long steep hill leading to the BOQ, she involuntarily slowed down.

Secretly amused, Maura decided to test Lori's mettle by picking up the pace for the final uphill sprint. Lori was determined not to be left in the dust, and even though her lungs were on fire and her legs felt like petrified tree stumps, she managed to catch up with Maura about half way up the hill, and stayed with her until they stopped in front of the BOQ to cool down and walk it out.

Neither of them spoke for about a minute. Then Maura looked over at Lori, smiling. "Good run. I could have given it a bit more, but not much." Showing Lori the timer she'd taken on the run, Maura added, "We ran about five miles in 36:36. That's just a bit faster than a seven-minute pace. Don't know 'bout you, but that pretty much maxes me out."

Lori grinned sheepishly. "A'yup, especially that long hill at the end. Wow, I knew we were going downhill on the way out but didn't really give it much thought. Just about crashed when I came around the corner and saw that hill!"

Both of them spontaneously burst into laughter. Lori suddenly realized that although she had initially been disappointed that her sponsor was not a grad, spending the summer learning about and experiencing the real Army with Maura instead of some male grad who resented her was going to be a lot more worthwhile and fun.

Lori was a bit embarrassed and nervous about sharing her thoughts, but decided to give it a try. When she told Maura what she had been thinking, Maura nodded in agreement. "Yeah, they haven't really discussed it with me, but I've occasionally come up on a group of the grads talking. They're not happy you're here and wonder what they did to get a girl."

Lori bristled. "You know, that just pisses me off. I mean, when are they gonna get over it? Those of us who made it through Beast have proven we're just as capable as they are. Sure, they're stronger, but it's not like the days of the Civil War, when you had lots of hand-to-hand combat and needed brute strength!"

"I hear ya, Lori, but it's just like when we were little. Boys roughhoused and girls played with tea sets and dolls."

Lori grimaced. "I played baseball and gave up dolls when I was six."

"Yeah," Maura rejoined. "My mom bought me a Barbie one year for Christmas. I was so disappointed. I'd wanted a chemistry set, and when I realized she hadn't bought me one, I thanked her and asked if we could return it so I could get a chemistry set."

"What'd she say?"

"She looked at my dad and started crying!"

Lori and Maura spent the next fifteen minutes stretching and cooling down, and talking about how they had each been sort of normal girls, but different too.

"Okay, enough of memory lane," Maura announced finally. "Let's shower and head to the O'Club for a drink and some chow. I've got a few things I need to get done at home, and I'd like to settle in around nine."

Lori exclaimed, "You go to bed at nine?"

Maura cracked up. "Not since I was nine years old! No, I settle in with a good book or a magazine and read for a few hours. I usually fall asleep around eleven, unless I get really interested in a book and can't put it down. Whenever that happens, I'm a mess the next morning when the alarm goes off at six."

"You have to get up at six to get to the office by eight?"

"Nope, I'm usually in the office at seven, but you don't need to be there 'til eight."

"I can show up at seven; it's not a problem."

"Nope, don't come in until eight. That'll give me a few minutes to get things ready for you and see what happened overnight. Because I'm the NRAS custodian, I have to check the staff duty log to see what exercise message traffic was sent the night before, what actions were done, and whether or not I need to follow up with the Corp Ops center. If you show up when I do, you'll be sitting around twiddling your thumbs. Sleep in a bit and have a decent breakfast."

"Sounds good." Lori pointed to the bathroom. "In case there's not a lot of hot water, I'll give you first dibs on the shower."

"Thanks, I'll take you up on that."

About an hour later, both of the women walked into the O'Club. Because it was a Monday night, there were only a few customers in the dining room, but they could see a bunch of the guys in the bar area drinking and playing pool and foosball. Maura asked the hostess to seat them outside on the patio.

En route to the patio, Lori asked, "Do they ever invite you to join them?"

Maura smiled wryly. "Nope, and actually, I'm sorta glad they don't. One woman with a bunch of drunk, stupid guys isn't such a great idea."

As they stepped outside onto the patio, Lori exclaimed in delight, "This is really neat!"

The sky was a brilliant blue and almost cloudless. The early evening sun provided plenty of bright light and warmth but was low enough so as not to be blinding. The flagstone patio enabled a view of the verdant fields and the nearby Swabian Alps. Sitting down at one of the black wrought-iron tables, they took in the relaxing, beautiful views that nature provided from their vantage point on the top of the hill at the foot of the *Hohenstaufen*.

It didn't take long for the waitress to return with a gin and tonic for Maura and Weizen beer for Lori. Maura held up her glass, saying, "*Zum voll*, Lori."

Lori clinked her beer glass and took a healthy gulp. "Aaah," she sighed contentedly. "I'm so glad the waitress suggested this wheat beer with a slice of lemon. It's so refreshing and light."

"Glad you like it. I'm purely a gin and tonic or wine girl."

"I've never had hard liquor or, for that matter, a mixed drink. What does it taste like?"

Maura motioned the waitress to come over. "Could you bring us an empty shot glass?" When Lori looked at her quizzically, Maura said, "I'm going to give you a taste."

The waitress returned, and Maura poured a bit of her drink into the shot glass, handing it to Lori, who cautiously took a sip, grimaced, and started coughing. Maura burst into laughter. "Guess it's an acquired taste. You can leave the rest; I just wanted to give you a chance to taste it."

Lori pushed the glass away and reached for a large gulp of beer to take away the burning sensation the gin had produced.

When the waitress came back to take their dinner order, Lori ordered a *ziguener* schnitzel with *spätzle* and Maura ordered grilled smoked trout, with julienned vegetables. Lori's schnitzel arrived first. Maura explained to Lori that counter to the American habit of waiting to eat until everyone had their meal, European convention was to start eating a meal while it was hot. Lori was really hungry but was uncomfortable eating while Maura was still waiting for her meal, but when Maura insisted she start eating, she relented with almost no resistance.

When Maura's meal came, Lori involuntarily dropped her fork and knife when she saw the complete fish, head and all, on the plate. Maura explained that was the way Europeans served their fish.

Lori asked querulously, "You eat the head, eyes, and all?"

This sent Maura into another paroxysm of laughter. "No way, goofball! You just cut it off and set it aside, just like you debone the body before you eat it."

"Ish!" Lori exclaimed, still disgusted by the fishy eyes looking up at her. "My dad is a fisherman, but we don't eat fish like that!"

Maura picked up her knife and fork, then announcing, "*Guten appetit!*" as she put the first bite of fish into her mouth.

After dinner, they passed on dessert but Maura told the waitress they wanted to sit and relax a bit longer. Both of them sat quietly, enjoying the view and relaxing, until Maura broke the silence. "You're welcome to stay and enjoy another beer or just sit here, but I need to get a few things done tonight, so I'm gonna head home now."

Not quite ready to go back to her BOQ, Lori said, "I think I'll have another beer before I walk back. See you in the morning, and thanks for a great first day."

Maura smiled as she picked up her bill. "I was initially a bit nervous about being your sponsor, but I'm glad we got this experience and promise to give you as realistic an experience as possible. I think we have a good training plan and with the help of the G-3, Ops NCO, and sergeant major, you'll learn what it's like to be an Army officer in a combat brigade over the next six weeks."

As Maura walked off, Lori motioned the waitress to get her another beer. She'd been sitting alone for about ten minutes when she heard a heavily southern accented male voice say, "Hi, can I join you?" Looking up, she saw a nice-looking first lieutenant.

"Uh, sure," Lori replied raising her eyebrows, too surprised to say anything else.

Putting his half-filled mug of beer on the table, he sat down, announcing, "Hi, I'm Del."

"Nice to meet you, Del."

"I'd say the same thing, but I don't know your name."

Unprepared for the encounter, Lori slowly said, "Uh, Lori."

"Nice to meet you, Lori. I gather you're new here."

"Yup, got here a few days ago."

"What unit are you assigned to?"

"I guess the brigade, but I'm not really assigned here. I'm a West Point cadet. I'm here for CTLT."

"Oh, yeah, now that I think 'bout it, I sorta remember a bit of a hullabaloo about women going to West Point and Annapolis. ... So, you're one of them, huh?"

Not amused, Lori replied cautiously, "Uh huh."

"Cool. Now that I think 'bout it, really cool."

Relieved, Lori relaxed, but an uncomfortable silence set in because she didn't know what to say next. Apparently, neither did Del, as he took a gulp of his beer and pointed to hers. "What kinda beer ya drinkin'?"

"Weizen."

"Hmm, I'm a Pilsner man, myself. ... You oughta try one. Would you like another beer?"

"That's really nice, but this is my second and I already have a decent buzz, but thanks for the offer." In an attempt to keep the conversation going, Lori quietly asked, "Where do you work?"

"The S-4, in 1-26th Infantry. They call us the Blue Spaders."

"So, you're an infantry officer?"

"Nope, quartermaster," Del replied.

"What made you choose that branch?"

"Well, I got drafted in '71 and they sent me to supply school at Fort Lee. I did pretty well there, and with the bad economy and all, when my time was up, I talked to my company commander about possibly staying in and he suggested I apply to OCS and get my commission. I decided what the heck. I got accepted and went to the Benning school for boys. Luckily, 'Nam was over, so I wasn't forced to go combat arms and decided to be a quartermaster officer."

"Do you like it?"

"Yeah, it's pretty easy, and most times I can get off work at 1600 and head over to the club to play pool or foosball, have a few beers, eat, and call it a day. Göppingen isn't exactly a hoppin' party town, and I don't speak German, so trying to date the local girls is a problem."

Lori nodded as she took a sip of beer. Del said a bit nervously, "I saw you walk in with that lieutenant who's assigned to the brigade and thought you were really cute." Looking a bit sheepish, he added, "I mentioned something to the guys, and they dared me to invite myself to sit down with you. I was too scared with the LT around—rumor is she's a real hard-ass—but when I saw her leave, I decided to give it a try. Thanks for letting me sit down with you. I woulda taken some serious shit if you'd told me to blow off."

Amused, Lori responded, "Always glad to help, but I really should go back to the BOQ. I've still got some unpacking to do and have to iron my uniform for tomorrow." Standing up, she held her hand out. "Nice to meet you. I'm sure I'll see you around later."

Del stood up. "I live in the BOQ too. Would it be okay if I walked home with you?"

"Sure."

They paid their bills and walked the short distance in an uncomfortable silence. When they got to the stairwell, Lori stopped. "Well, this is where we part company."

"Sure, see you later. Perhaps some other time when both of us are at the club."

"Sounds good. ... Night." With that, Lori walked up to her dark BOQ room, poured a glass of cold water, and sat down on her Army issued couch. At first she thought about Del and how hard it was for American soldiers to meet dating partners. As Lori's thoughts meandered into tangential areas, she reflected on her first few days in Germany. Then, without warning, a gnawing, gripping feeling of homesickness began to set in. Trying to stifle her feelings, something she was adroit at doing from her first two years at West Point, Lori decided to take action and write an upbeat letter to her parents.

Dear Mom and Dad,

Well, my first day at work was interesting and busy. I'm really struggling with jet-lag, but my sponsor Maura said I'd adjust after a week. You're probably as surprised as I was, that they didn't pair me up with a West Pointer, but I'm really glad I've got a female sponsor. Maura seems nice and takes her responsibilities seriously. She made sure I got in-processed today, took me to a great little German place for lunch, and took me on a run after work. We just finished dinner at the O'Club.

The O'Club is nice. They have a great patio, sorta like the one from the castle in the Sound of Music. But instead of looking out on a lake, we have some nearby mountains, called the something or other Alps, and on a sunny day, it's beautiful! I'll take some pictures over the next few weeks so I can send some home.

Promise to write more later, but figured a short note would be better than nothing. Don't worry mom, they're taking really good care of me and I just LOVE it here! It's so cool, I mean, I never even considered the possibility of living in Germany! Love, Lori

3

GÖPPINGEN, FRIDAY 16 JUNE 1978

MAURA'S FRIDAY-MORNING STAFF duty officer debrief went longer than usual because there had been a Corps-wide telephonic alert and several NRAS exercise messages had been processed the night before. "Good morning, Cadet Nelson," Maura said as she entered her office to find Lori sitting at her desk. Lori looked up, and Maura pointed to the empty desk across from hers. "The major is on leave today. You can sit at his desk, until sergeant major comes to take you to the battalion."

Standing up and waking over to the nearby empty desk Lori remarked, "I really enjoyed the assistance visit and trip to Neu-Ulm yesterday. Are we going to do any more unit assistance visits while I'm here?"

"Sorry, the next one isn't scheduled until sometime in August, but I'm glad you got to experience one of them."

Yesterday Maura and Lori had driven to Neu-Ulm to for an assistance visit with 2nd Battalion, 33rd Artillery. Maura had explained that all of the units had annual command inspections and would typically ask for an assistance visit about three months before their scheduled command inspection.

"How do you determine what to inspect?" Lori asked as she sat down.

"All specialties have manuals governing what standards and activities the unit has to meet. G-3 training uses those to develop the checklist we used yesterday."

They'd spent the entire day inspecting the unit's training records, nerve-agent antidote inventory, masks, and overgarments (called CPOGs, short for chemical protective overgarments). They had finished their inspection around 1600 hours, changed into civilian clothing, and driven the short distance from Wiley Barracks to downtown Neu-Ulm, to eat dinner and see the *Ulmer Dom*.

"Is there anything you want me to work on until sergeant major comes by to pick me up?" Lori asked Maura.

Maura felt a combination of guilt and frustration that she had not had time to figure out something for Lori to do until sergeant major took her to the battalion. She had suggested that Lori not come into the office until nine that morning, because there really wasn't anything she could dream up for Lori to do for an hour; but she also understood Lori's desire to take advantage of every single moment she had to learn more about what would be expected of her, when she graduated and was assigned to a unit of her own.

"Sorry, no. I guess if you want, you could grab one of the manuals in our reference library and look at it for an hour. Otherwise, I'm fresh out of ideas." Maura said apologetically.

"I understand Maura. I know it's a lot of work to keep me occupied and learning and I really do appreciate it. Would it be okay if I wrote some letters home, while I wait for sergeant major?"

"Perfect!" Maura said with obvious relief, as she reached in her desk drawer to pull out a pen and fresh pad of paper. Getting up from her desk, she handed both to Lori. "Will this do?"

Lori nodded, taking the pad and pen, as Maura returned to her desk to finish the reports that had to be completed by the end of the day.

Dear mom and dad,

Hi from Germany! Maura and I inspected a field artillery unit yesterday. It was cool to see real nerve and blood agent antidote vials. I hope we never have to use them, but it's comforting to know that if we need them, they're there and we'll be trained on how to use them.

We finished around five and went downtown Neu-Ulm to see the Ulmer Dom, which is this huge cathedral. Maura told me it took almost 500 years to build and was financed mostly by private donations. It's the tallest church in the world and we walked about 800 steps to get to the viewing platform. Maura pointed out some mountains in the far distance and told me that we had gotten lucky, because it was such a clear day, that she was pretty sure that one of the peaks in the far distance was the Zugspitze, but she didn't really know which peak it was. I took some pictures, but it's just not the same as being here. You can't imagine the beautiful stained glass windows, massive wooden doors, and amazing carvings inside the church.

After that, Maura asked me if I wanted to dine alfresco. I asked her what that was, and she laughed, telling me it was a fancy way of asking if I wanted to eat dinner outside on the terrace. We found a really nice restaurant on the square and had just ordered when the chimes of the cathedral rang. They were so beautiful. As usual, it was a great meal. We didn't get back to my BOQ til almost nine-thirty, but after a full day of work and walking all those steps, after taking a shower and getting ready for the morning, I think I fell asleep instantly.

Okay, the sergeant major will be here in a few to take me to an infantry battalion, so I'll close for now. Love, Lori

Lori put down her pen and started folding the letter up. Looking over at Maura, she asked quietly, "Sorry to bother you Maura, but do you have an envelope I can put this in?"

Maura looked up and pointed to a metal file cabinet in the corner. "That's our supply locker. I think there are some on the second shelf." Feeling a bit guilty that she had left Lori to fend for herself, she asked, "Do you mind my asking what you wrote about?"

Walking over to get the envelope, Lori replied, "Nope. I told them about what a great day we had yesterday. I hope you don't mind, but told them about you asking me if I wanted to dine alfresco. I think they'll get a good laugh out of that."

Maura grinned and playfully asked, "Did you tell them that you had two large beers with dinner?"

"Absolutely not! Lori laughingly replied. "Not sure I could, or want to explain that walking all those stairs made me really thirsty!"

MAURA AND LORI'S LAUGHTER was cut short by Sergeant Major Atkins bellowing from the doorway, "Good morning, ma'am. Is Cadet Nelson ready to go?"

"Almost, Sergeant Major, Maura replied in a businesslike tone. Turning to Lori, she added, I know you'll have a great time with Sergeant Major and the Blue Spaders. I think he arranged for the battalion motor officer to let you shadow him for the day, so you'll get a better idea of some of the PMCS responsibilities you might have as a platoon leader."

"That's correct. I also got him to agree to take you out on a short ride in one of the new infantry fighting vehicles." Sergeant Major added.

"Thanks, Sergeant Major. It's exactly the kind of experience I was hoping for," Lori said excitedly.

"Lori, I've got to write a report on the assistance visit we did yesterday and have several very boring meetings today. I've also got a few things to do tonight, so when you finish at the battalion this afternoon, you're on your own until I pick you up tomorrow morning for the Volksmarch. Any questions?"

"No, ma'am. See you tomorrow morning."

4

SATURDAY 17 JUNE 1978

MAURA AND LORI PULLED into the parking lot at the small park where the Volksmarch up the *Hohenstaufen* started. It was already crowded, but after a few minutes, they found a parking space. Scanning the crowd for Anne and Trish as they walked up to the registration area, Maura stopped, looked at Lori, "Don't think we missed them; guess they're running a bit late. Maura pointed to a small clearing that gave them a good view of the registration area and the path leading up to it. "Let's hold off on signing in and stretch."

A few minutes later, Lori stopped stretching as she exclaimed, "I see them." Walking toward Anne and Trish, waving her hands, Lori yelled, "Trish!" Trish looked toward the sound of the familiar voice and, recognizing Lori, waved, and started jogging toward Lori and Maura. Maura waved to Anne to join her as she told Lori and Trish, "You guys catch up while Anne and I get us signed in."

"So, what's new with you?" Lori asked Trish.

"Man, am I beat. I've been learning so much stuff about the Army. I've got a cool master sergeant showing me the ropes. Anne's been great about making sure I don't mess up too bad. What about you?" Trish asked.

"Yeah, I know the feeling, so many new things to learn and figure out, but I love it! I went to one of our infantry battalions yesterday. I spent the morning in the motor pool and just before lunch, got to ride in and actually drive one of the new infantry fighting vehicles for a few minutes!"

"Wow, Trish whispered. Wish I could have done something like that, what was it like?"

"Pretty cool. It was a bit awkward at first, because the soldiers were really nervous around me and kept calling me sir; but they calmed down and when we finished the ride, they asked me if I had any questions. You should have seen the look on the vehicle commander's face when I asked him if I could drive it for a few minutes!"

Lori and Trish started laughing. "But they said yes, obviously." Trish replied.

"Not at first," Lori answered. "The sergeant had to ask the platoon leader if it was okay for me to drive it and the lieutenant told me that if I agreed to do a unit run with them next week and promised not to fall out, he'd let me drive it."

Trish hissed, "What did you tell him?"

"I told him he'd fall out and die before I did and that I'd check with my sponsor and let him know when I'd be there next week."

Trish gave Lori a hearty shoulder slap. "Good job!"

Yeah, I think I surprised him. After we were finished, he told me he was class of 75 and after telling him that I was on the basketball and volleyball teams and my run times on PT tests, I got a bit of credibility with him and he invited me to join him and the other battalion officers at the club for happy hour on Friday evenings."

"Did you go?"

"Yeah, had a good time and ran into Del, this officer I met the other night at the O'Club."

"Well, my week was nowhere near as fun as yours, but an odd thing happened to me at the snack bar this week," Trish said. "A female sergeant walked up to me and told me she really liked the khaki uniform

I was wearing and asked where she could get one. When I told her the uniform is West Point unique and only cadets are authorized to wear them, she was bummed."

"Yeah, I really like our khakis," Lori replied.

"So, what's this about meeting a guy the other night? Is he cute? Do you like him?" Trish asked, happy for Lori, but feeling a bit envious as well.

Before Lori could respond, Anne and Maura returned from registration. "Okay, you two, let's get goin'," Anne announced with a bit of her Cajun drawl coming out. "You'll have plenty of time to catch up on the walk."

Maura handed them their passbooks, explaining, "There'll be several checkpoints along the route, and you'll need the proctor to stamp your booklet so you can get your pin at the end of the march."

"How long is it?" Trish asked.

"Ten kilometers, or 6.2 miles," Anne responded.

They spent the next hour walking at a brisk but comfortable pace through the woods and surrounding farms as Maura and Anne pointed out some of the local plants and an occasional passing rabbit or other woodland creature. It was a beautiful day, and as they passed locals walking in a leisurely fashion, Maura would gaily bid them, "*Grüß Gott,*" to which they would smile and return the greeting. Lori and Trish asked about the traditional garb the Germans were wearing, and Lori, who because of her Swedish and German heritage, knew that *Gott* meant God, asked Maura, "Why do you use that greeting?"

"This particular greeting is common in Southern Germany and Austria, and while the locals will respond to the traditional *Guten Morgen,* or *Guten Tag,* the local vernacular is, *Grüß Gott.* The outfits they are wearing are called *Trachtenmode.*" Maura replied adding, "It's a Bavarian folk dressing tradition that goes back to the 1800s and nowadays is worn and used as a way of maintaining some old folk traditions. The best way I know how to explain it, is to compare it to the practices of some small rural groups in the Midwest that get dressed up in dirndls and do folk dancing. Does that make sense?"

Already having lost interest in the subject, Trish nodded and asked Anne, "How many Volksmarches have you been on?"

"This is our first one. We wanted to give you as many experiences as possible, so we decided to give it a try," Anne answered.

Trish replied, "Thanks!"

The route was a maze of interconnected footpaths that wound through a small patch of forest, leading out to a large field just below the town of Hohenstaufen, that provided stunning vistas of the Swabian Alps and the surrounding valley. At one point, Maura stopped and pointed to some ruins to the west, "That's the original Hohenstaufen castle, called Burg Hohenstaufen. It was built in 1070 and destroyed in the Peasant Revolution in the late 1500s."

"You sure know a lot of about the history, geography, and culture. How'd you learn all this?" Lori asked.

Maura laughed. "My landlady stops me in the evening on my way up to my apartment to give me some leftovers because she thinks I'm too skinny. Her husband usually gives me a history book on the area, so I occasionally read them at night."

"Wow," Trish exhaled. "The books are in German aren't they? You understand German well enough to read history books in German?"

Feeling a bit embarrassed, Maura waved her hand dismissively. "Not that big a deal. I have a knack for languages, and now that I've been here for over a year, I get lots of practice and my German has really improved."

Trish rolled her eyes and exclaimed, "Yeah, well, I could live here for decades and still be struggling. I struggle with English!" This comment made all of them laugh and when the laughter died down, Trish asked Maura, "Why do they call this the *Hohen*-whatever-you-call-it, and what else do you know about it?"

Maura replied, "The name is derived from the shape of the mountain, which forms the shape of a chalice or cup, which is a *Stauf*, and *hohen* is, of course, high. This is the highest peak in Kreis Göppingen. The Hohenstaufen is part of the Swabian Alps and actually peaks down the road here at an elevation of over two thousand feet." Maura turned and pointed to two other peaks in the distance. "Together with the Rechberg, which also has a nice little town on the mountain that we might have time to visit, and the Stuifen, they form the three Kaiser Mountains, which are located between here and Schwäbisch Gmünd. Not sure if we'll have time, but if we do, we can go to Lorch tomorrow, where we can get a much better view of the other peaks and visit the castle ruins."

Trish nodded. "Yeah, sounds cool. Do they have beer?"

Maura smiled and nodded. "Actually, there are a number of footpaths around the castle ruins, and there's a rustic mountain bar that serves beer, wine, and some small snacks."

"Sounds good to me," Trish replied. "Can we go there today? I'm getting some great pictures, and I'd just as soon be outside sightseeing as anything else." Trish stopped abruptly as she realized she'd put a lot of pressure on Maura adding, "Sorry, I'm just really enjoying all this. Lori told me you guys had a busy week, so if you're too tired, it's okay. I'm just so excited about being here, I want to do as much as possible."

Maura smiled and gently replied, "I totally understand, Trish, really, no apologies needed. I just worry about overloading you guys." Looking at Lori and Anne, she asked, "You guys up to a full day of walking through the mountains?"

Anne retorted good-naturedly, "Sure *chéri*. I got billy-goat in my blood."

Trish looked at Lori, who was embarrassed by Trish's boldness in adding activities to an already full day. "Uh, sure..." Lori stammered.

Trish smiled at Lori. "You're the best!" Then turning to look at Anne and Maura, she sheepishly said, "Thanks, guys!"

When they got back to the park, they were directed to a booth, where they showed their stamped passbooks and in return, got nicely painted high-quality metal pins that had *Hohenstaufen Waldrungang, 1978* written just above a replica of Hohenstaufen Castle.

Walking back to the cars, Trish and Lori were admiring their pins, impressed at the quality of the artwork, when Trish commented, "Wow, thanks, guys! This is cool."

"Yeah, and a nice souvenir and memory," Lori added.

Maura replied, "Great. Well, I think the easiest thing to do is drive to Rechberg first. We can walk around a bit and have lunch in the small town. I went to a nice little tavern that has cheap but fantastic food and most likely good beer. From there we'll head to Stuifen, walk around, and check out the ruins and take in the view. You'll get some great pictures."

They all piled into Maura's car and spent the remainder of the day having lunch in Rechberg and roaming through the various footpaths surrounding the ruins of Stuifen. When they returned to the parking lot in Hohenstaufen at four that afternoon, Trish and Lori got in Anne's car so she could drop them off at the BOQ and meet Maura and Anne at the O'Club at eight that evening for dinner.

★ ★ ★

BY THE TIME ANNE got to Maura's apartment, Maura had already showered and changed. Anne put her overnight bag in the spare room, which had a futon-like couch that reclined into a bed. After laying out clean clothes on the futon and taking a long, relaxing shower, Anne joined Maura on the small balcony just outside the living room.

Looking up from the letter she'd been writing to her childhood best friend Elise, Maura pointed to the small teapot and pitcher of tea on the table. "Fresh hot tea, if you like. Think there may be just enough in there for another cup, but I also made a pitcher of blackberry iced tea last night and have a small bag of ice in the freezer."

"Thanks *chéri*, I'll take you up on the iced tea."

Returning with a glass filled with ice a few minutes later, Anne sat down and poured some tea into her glass. "I really enjoy coming here to visit. It's so nice to have a real apartment, and this balcony is my favorite part of your apartment. You've got such a nice view of the town, and I love hearing the chimes of the church ring."

Maura put her letter down on the table. "Yeah, it is nice, but being so close to the train tracks took a bit of getting used to. It sorta messes up the view."

Anne swallowed some iced tea, and then added, "I hear ya, but you only have a half-a-mile walk to the train stop and can avoid the horrendous traffic you'd have on the autobahn when you come to visit me."

"Sure. Speaking of which, when Elise comes to visit in August, I was thinking we could meet you at the Stuttgart bahnhof that Saturday morning. Our train doesn't leave until eleven."

"Sure, sounds good; looking forward to the trip to Strasbourg."

Maura paused, and then said, "You know, I really hadn't thought about it much, but because we spend almost every weekend together, most people probably think we're lesbians."

Maura grimaced wryly at this thought, and Anne interjected sarcastically, "Oh, that's a comforting thought. Don't know 'bout you," she drawled, "but a few guys have made it clear they're interested, and I have dinner with some of them at the club during the week, but nothing's really clicked."

"Yeah, Maura responded. I've had a drink or two with some of the lieutenants in the battalion, but they're a bunch of horny toads and really aren't interested in getting to know me; they just wanna get me drunk and see if they can get lucky."

"Yeah, sorta the same in Stuttgart. I guess I stay busy enough with work that most of the time it doesn't bother me, but sometimes I get really lonely and wonder if I'll ever find someone I really care about—and even if I did, not sure they could put up with me."

"Anne, don't be ridiculous. You'll find someone. I've sorta gotta laugh, though. Here we are, surrounded by guys, and can't find even one we really like. How crazy is that?"

Anne smirked and took another sip of iced tea. "'Bout as crazy as the notion that women only join the Army to find a husband."

"Okay, that's it," Maura stood up and went back into the apartment. With a quizzical look on her face, Anne got up and followed her to the kitchen. She started laughing when she saw Maura pull two wine glasses out of the cabinet. Maura reached inside the fridge and pulled out a cold bottle of white wine, walked back to the balcony, opened the bottle and poured half a glass for herself and looked up at Anne questioningly. "Want some?"

Sitting down, Anne held out the second wine glass. When Maura stopped pouring, Anne raised her glass, took a sip, and leaned back in her chair, musing that she and Maura had not even known each other until Anne's college friend, Amelia, who Maura had met at Fort McClellan, had introduced them to each other at the airport when all three were en route to Germany. Now more than a year and a half later, they were as close as Anne and Amelia were.

Maura interrupted Anne's reverie by saying, "Yeah, only in the army could you put a crazy Louisiana Cajun like you, a sweet Alabama belle like our dear Amelia, and yours truly, a born and bred New York city girl together and have them all band together as friends. Speaking of which, have you heard from our steel magnolia lately?"

"Yeah, Anne drawled languidly. She's doin' okay. She's looking forward to our visit and meeting the cadets. Have you told Lori about going to Berlin for the 4th of July weekend?"

"Yeah, I mentioned it and our other travel plans, to her on her first day here. She was so overwhelmed those first few days; she's probably forgotten half of what I told her."

"Yeah, same with Trish," Anne answered. "But they seem pretty energetic and up to whatever we plan for them. But back to the original discussion though, your friend Elise's visit. Did she get back to you on the itinerary you sent her and can she get the time off from work?"

"Yeah, she's excited about coming, but I still get the occasional letter from her griping that I don't write enough and if I hadn't changed our plan, we'd both be in New York City having the time of our life, instead of her having to come all the way to Europe to see me."

Maura continued, "I know we've had this discussion before, but sometimes I really wonder what my life would be like if I'd turned down the ROTC scholarship, taken out a bunch of school loans, and lived and worked in New York, like Elise and I originally talked about."

"Well, from what you've told me, your friend Elise's life is as crazy as ours, and as I recall, even though she moved out on her own and still pals around with some of the old neighborhood group, there's no romance in her life either, so not sure it would be any better."

Taking another sip of wine, Maura sighed resignedly. "Yeah, I know you're right, but it really stinks. I mean, the Army pays us well, we don't have to worry about being laid off or not getting a paycheck, we're living in Europe and doing important stuff ... but every once in a while, I guess I wish I did have a special guy."

"Yeah, well, when you start thinking that way, remind yourself how happy having a *special guy* has made Amelia."

"Thanks, Anne," Maura retorted sarcastically. "Reminding me of how Charles dumped Amelia when she told him she was joining the Army, makes me feel tons better. I mean, what happened to the *they lived happily ever after* part of the story?"

"That's a fairy tale, not real life, Maura," Anne said softly before taking another sip of wine. "C'mon, snap out of it."

"Yeah, you're right. ... Hey, are you still in touch with Derek?"

Anne laughed. "I hear from him once every few months." Anne responded offhandedly in response to Maura's question about a relationship she'd had with one of her officer basic classmates before coming to Germany. "I don't know how he does it, but he manages to call me at the office on a DSN line."

"Well, he obviously still likes you. I don't know many guys who would go through that much trouble to stay in touch with someone they might never see again. What do you guys talk about?"

"He asks me what I'm up to, and I talk a bit about work and our weekends together."

"And what does he talk about?"

"Nothin'," Anne drawled. "Whenever I ask him about work or what he does for fun, he changes the subject." Laughing suddenly, she added, "One time he did tell me he was at Fort Polk for an exercise and he hates it there but mentioned that he and a group of guys were going to go to New Orleans when the exercise was over. He asked for my advice on where they should go to party and find loose women. I told him I could help with hotels and history but he'd have to find another source for the loose women gouge."

"He didn't?" Maura asked, laughing.

"He most certainly did, and in a later conversation, he told me he'd had a great time and said that when I come home on leave, he'll come down and show me the grown-up side of New Orleans."

"He sounds awesome. Too bad he couldn't get assigned to Germany," Maura mused.

Anne replied abruptly, changing the subject. "Derek and I probably weren't meant to be. How're things going with Lori?"

A bit taken aback by Anne's brusque manner, Maura replied, "Good. I had her read a few of the NBC defense manuals and go over the checklist

I have for assistance visits. We did a unit assistance visit Thursday. She catches on pretty quick. What about Trish?"

"Pretty much the same. Gave her some of the logistics manuals, and she's been helping me with a property book review we're doing. My boss told me yesterday that we're going to do an ORT on a unit just after the Fourth of July. That'll be a good experience for her."

"Well, that should give them something to talk about. We're doing an ORT on the CAV troop on Wednesday."

"Really? Didn't you guys just finish one a few months ago?"

"Yeah, but that was on 1-16th Infantry in Böblingen. Our new commanding general has been here almost a year now, and he's frustrated that the evaluations we've done on 1-16th and 1-26th Infantry Battalions have shown some significant readiness issues even though we did assistance visits six months prior to their ORTs in an effort to focus them on what needed to be fixed. The CG's a former CAV guy and he told the G-3 to schedule a no-notice ORT on C Troop, 1st of the 4th CAV. We'll use the ORT results as an example for the Iron Rangers and Blue Spaders to follow. The G-3 tried to tell the CG that it would be prudent to schedule an assistance visit, to assess the true state of readiness of the troop before doing an ORT, and the CG cut him off, saying the CAV polices itself and prides itself on being better than the rest of the units, and they didn't need an assistance visit."

"You sound worried. I thought you liked the new CG."

Maura took another sip of wine. "I do. He's a really smart guy. ... His previous assignment was in the Army Comptroller's office. Nothing like BG Franklin, who was Infantry through and through, stayed with troops most of his career, and never did what he called pansy-ass assignments in the Pentagon. I think the new CG has some really great ideas and is a textbook example of what good leaders do and say, but the staff got used to Franklin, who was a screamer, yeller, and cusser. I actually saw him physically manhandle soldiers and company-grade officers he felt were not meeting the expected standard. BG James is exactly the opposite: quiet, measured, and deliberate. Some of the staff think he's a joke and routinely ignore his suggestions. I guess they figure unless they're told they have to do something a specific way, they aren't obligated to implement the CG's suggestions."

"Wow," Anne whispered incredulously.

"Yeah, this ORT's gonna be really interesting. The others were on the training schedule and pro forma. This one is being directed by the CG as the one that will set the standard for all the units in the brigade to follow. Some of the staff think the CAV troop is totally dorked up and are taking bets on how the CG'll handle them not doing well."

"Does the CG know about this?"

"Nah, don't think the G-3 even knows what's going on with the staff. A lot of these guys really get off on someone getting burned. Unlike the previous commander, this one is not a grad, and in the eyes of the officers, most of whom are grads, this is just another example of 1st IDF standards taking a nosedive. Apparently, this is one of the more sought-after assignments for West Pointers, and having a non-grad CG for the first time that doesn't fit the mold of the fire-eating, slash-and-burn leader that these guys seem to love, has really created a lot of dissatisfaction."

"Well, for better or worse, I haven't run into any West Pointers at Corps."

"Oh, I'm sure there's some there, but they probably don't advertise it, 'cause the guys that get the brigade and division staff assignments consider those guys total losers. If you're a combat-arms company-grade officer, the *only* place to be is in command or in a battalion or the Brigade 3 shop."

"I guess, but if it weren't for us loser loggy-toads, they wouldn't be able to survive and win. Have these Bogarts ever considered that?"

Maura laughed as she drank the last of the wine. "Oh please, let's not go there. The old CG and I had a talk along those lines when I told him that if he had to make a choice between being physically fit and smart, he should want me to be smart because that's what my position needs. I got a real tongue lashing and warning to not make him regret accepting me."

"Holy shit, Maura, for real?"

"Anne, if you only knew half the shit that goes on in this brigade. … C'mon, let's refill our wine glasses and change the subject."

After refilling their wine glasses, Maura picked up a folder from the table and discussed the proposed trip itinerary with Anne, who said, "This is really nice of you Maura. Sounds like a great itinerary."

"Well, luckily the travel agency in Stuttgart is really good. I wish you could do more than the weekend in Strasbourg with us. My French is passable, but you'd be a great help."

"Yeah, I hear ya, but my guess is Elise will want time alone with you, and while I wouldn't mind going to Nice and Marseilles, Cannes and Monaco are not on my list and I really don't want to burn almost two weeks of leave right now. My dad isn't doing real well, and I may have to go home."

"I'm not real keen on burning two weeks, either, but I did invite her and she's using all her vacation time and had to dip into her savings for this trip, so I need to pull out all the stops."

"Well, I think it's great that this is going to work out. I'm actually a bit envious. Amelia and you are my only friends. It must be nice having a friend that you've known for as long as you can remember."

Maura felt badly. Anne had never confided any details, but Amelia had told Maura that Anne's childhood had been terrible, without giving specific details, but had asked Maura to please be patient with Anne if she had seemed a bit standoffish and unfriendly at first. Amelia had explained it was a defense mechanism and that Anne was really a good person and loyal friend but just needed time to feel that she could trust someone. Maura was glad Amelia had confided in her, because there were times in the first few months when Anne's behavior had confused Maura and if Amelia had not warned her, she might not have worked so hard to keep the friendship going. Whenever Anne's behavior frustrated or hurt Maura, she remembered not only Amelia's request but also her first unhappy weekend in Göppingen when Anne had shown up and helped her through a rough time.

Because she was really uncomfortable about Anne's confession of envy, she got up and gave Anne a hug. "Anne, you're a dear friend, and anything I would do for Elise, I would do for you. So even though we haven't been friends all our life, I've got the feeling that this is the beginning of a lifelong friendship."

Embarrassed and uncomfortable with showing emotion, Anne looked at Maura disdainfully, grabbed her wine glass, and announced, "Okay, no more wine for you; you're getting way too mushy. Besides, it's about time we started getting ready to go out for dinner and meet the gals."

Maura stood up and started clearing the table and an hour later, they pulled up to the O'Club and walked into the bar, expecting to meet Trish and Lori.

Not finding the cadets, Anne looked at Maura. "D'ya think they took a nap and overslept?"

Looking around to make sure they hadn't missed them, Maura smiled wryly. "Anything's possible. But I see the lieutenant Lori introduced me to earlier this week. He hit on her, her first night here, and eats dinner with her most work nights. Let's see if he's seen her."

Walking up to the bar, Maura greeted him cheerfully. "Hi, Del, have you seen Lori tonight?"

Turning around on his barstool, Del answered her in a surly tone, "Yeah, she's out on the patio with some girlfriend. They've been out there several hours, yakking nonstop."

"Thanks, Del, see ya 'round."

He waved his hand dismissively and turned back to his beer and conversation with his buddies. Anne and Maura walked out to the patio and found Lori and Trish with half-empty beer glasses, totally engrossed in conversation. As they approached, Anne cleared her throat, "Well, ladies, how's it going? May we join you?"

"Hi. We totally lost track of time. Is it eight already?" Lori asked.

Sitting down at the two additional seats at the square black wrought-iron table covered with a flowered tablecloth and a small vase of flowers, Anne replied, "Yeah, it's easy to lose track of time, especially in the summer when the sun doesn't set 'til almost eleven."

The waitress had seen Maura and Anne come in. She came up to them and said, "Good evening, ladies. Can I get you something to drink?"

Maura ordered her usual white wine, but Anne ordered a beer. After the waitress walked off, Trish said, "Thanks again for a great day. I can't wait to finish off this roll of film and get it developed." Looking at Anne, she added, "You know, I don't have a clue as to where to go to get my film developed."

Anne smiled. "You can drop it off at the PX. They usually take a week to get it back."

Maura pointed to the half-empty beer glasses. "So, I gather you've been here for a bit?"

Lori piped up. "Yeah, we took a shower and Trish mentioned it was a shame we had to stay inside. I told her we could go to the club, sit on the patio, and have a beer, so that's what we did."

The waitress returned with Maura's and Anne's drinks and menus. They ordered and spent the next hour and a half eating, drinking, and discussing their upcoming trip to Bavaria. Around 2130, they went in to the bar, where the DJ was playing. They ordered some more drinks and chair-danced to the Bee Gees, ELO, Abba, and a few other groups. When Linda Ronstadt's "Blue Bayou" came on, all four started singing, which drew snickers from the German girls there with the single officers. The four young women failed to notice this; they were just enjoying the music and camaraderie and were by this time totally wasted and could not have passed a breathalyzer test if their lives had depended on it. When they left at 2300, Lori and Trish staggered back to the BOQ while Maura cautiously drove back to her apartment. Pulling into one of the few parking spaces left open on her street, Maura laid her head back on the driver's seat and exhaled loudly. "Sure am glad we didn't run into any Polizei on the way home." Anne mumbled something unintelligible as she clumsily got out of the car.

Staggering upstairs, Maura needed a few minutes to pull out her keys and unlock the apartment door. She and Anne silently waved good night to each other as they walked into their respective bedrooms, flopped into bed, and immediately fell asleep.

5

GÖPPINGEN, WEDNESDAY 21 JUNE 1978

THE LOUD BANGING ON her door woke Lori from a sound sleep. Maura had warned her that they would have an alert sometime between midnight and 0400 to do a combat readiness inspection on the Cavalry Troop. Lori had left the light on in the foyer so she wouldn't kill herself trying to get to the door in the middle of the night.

Jumping out of bed, Lori opened the door.

"Okay, get dressed and be up at the headquarters in the next thirty minutes," Maura said brusquely, then walked away.

Closing the door, Lori looked at her watch, groaning inwardly as she realized it was only two in the morning. When she got to the brigade headquarters, she was a bit unsure what to do because everyone was moving quickly and yelling at each other. She decided to sit near the red metal entry gate and wait for Maura.

Coming out of her office, Maura walked up to talk to Master Sergeant Smith. Seeing Lori, she said, "Give me a few minutes and I'll meet you in the hall."

A few minutes later, Maura appeared as promised, with a camouflaged canvas map case over her right shoulder and a Styrofoam cup of steaming hot coffee in her left hand. Maura curtly announced, "Okay, our jeep is downstairs. Let's go." As they got into the jeep, Maura took a large gulp of coffee before asking Lori to hold it. As soon as they were on the autobahn, Maura asked for her coffee again and finished it in three long gulps. Tossing the empty cup behind her, Maura asked, "Do you have any questions about what we're going to do this morning?"

"No, ma'am."

"Are you okay?"

Lori grinned as she held up the can of Tab she'd been drinking. "Once this kicks in, I'll be awake. I'm just amazed at how quickly you finished off that cup of coffee. Are you okay?"

Maura chuckled, "Yeah, just needed a quick jolt. I don't think I'll ever get used to this middle-of-the-night stuff." Maura returned to concentrating on driving while Lori finished her soda and wondered what the day would be like.

They joined the queue of jeeps with other members of the brigade staff who were lined up outside the Panzer Kaserne gate, as the German guard checked everyone's IDs.

They spent the next few hours inspecting the Cavalry Troop NBC room, finding protective masks, NBC suits, and other gear in sufficient quantities and ready for load-out, but the supply of nerve-agent antidote injectors was insufficient and the blood agent antidote capsules were expired, with no replacements on order. The NBC NCO explained that the commander had said they didn't have sufficient funds to order those items, so there was nothing he could do about it. Maura told him not to worry, she understood that he was limited to what the commander would support, and she would make note of that in her final report.

After leaving the NBC room, Maura and Lori went to the company dayroom. The pool table and foosball games, along with the TV, couches, and occasional chairs, were pushed up against the wall, making room for the inspection team to conduct their out-brief. Four rows of metal folding chairs and a podium were set up in the game area.

The first sergeant of the Cav Troop was taping white sheets of paper on the front row of chairs, with the ranks and names of the brigade and Cav Troop leadership. Looking up, he asked, "What can I do for you, ma'am?"

Maura put her hand up. "Nothing, First Sergeant. I'm just going to sit in the back here and write up a few notes."

He nodded and resumed what he had been doing.

Maura motioned Lori to sit by her in the back row. "In the next fifteen minutes, the rest of the team should be here and we'll brief the CG on our findings. The unit leadership will show up around half an hour from now, and they'll wait in the hallway until Sergeant Major Atkins opens the door and tells them to come in. Then each inspector will brief, starting with the G-4, who will brief maintenance and supply functions. The G-1 will cover personnel reporting and readiness status, the G-2 will cover security issues, and the G-3 will cover readiness, operations, and NBC. I'll be the last briefer before the CG ends the garrison out-brief and directs the company leaders to deploy to their general defense plan—GDP—positions. We'll follow them to the field and finish our assessment of their readiness posture. Then everyone will return to home station. We'll go back to Goerp and you can go to the BOQ and get some shut-eye while I do my final report and give it to the G-3. The unit will get a hard copy of the final report at the beginning of next week so they can start working on their deficiencies."

Lori nodded. "What happens if they fail?"

Maura was surprised by this question. "Well, in the eighteen months I've been here, we've inspected each battalion and the five separate company-sized units once, and no one has failed outright. They usually have a small number of deficiencies that need to be worked on and when we return for follow-up inspections, we'll check to see that the earlier deficiencies have been fixed and do a modified inspection to see if there are any new deficiencies."

"How often do the units get inspected?" Lori asked.

"We're required to inspect each unit at least once every eighteen months. For the battalions, that means the commander lives or dies by one inspection because his tour of command lasts two years. You're lucky this is just the Cav Troop, which is a company-sized unit. If we'd done a battalion, we'd be in garrison for about three hours, have them deploy to the field, and it would take about another eight hours to finish our inspection of all the companies and the battalion command post at their GDP positions. Those are brutally long days and all of us get back to garrison pretty worn out. When we inspect a battalion, we turn in our vehicles to the motor pool, go home, take a shower, eat, and get some much-needed shut-eye before coming back early the next day to finish our reports."

"How did the Cav Troop do last time, and how long ago was that?"

Maura pulled out a report and handed it to Lori. "The last inspection was done several months before I got here. The current commander has been in command for eleven months now, so this will be his one chance to shine. It really doesn't matter what he's done up to this point. If he doesn't have a good result from this ORT, his career is totally over."

"Wow, that's a lot of pressure."

Maura nodded. "Yeah, but so is combat, and remember, this is their real-world mission. If they can't do it, then nothing else matters."

"How does this inspection measure that?"

Surprised and impressed that Lori would ask this question, Maura answered, "The checklist identifies the specific actions and capabilities that need to be inspected in order to assess their readiness to deploy to their initial combat positions and be prepared to conduct combat operations in a specified amount of time, which is classified. But everyone here knows what those standards are, and based upon the metrics that are inspected, it's pretty cut and dry: You are either able to deploy and fight, or you're not."

"Thanks, ma'am. I know you've got a briefing to prepare, so I'm gonna get a Tab and look at this report. Do you want one?"

Maura smiled. "Yeah, thanks."

Lori got up, walked over to the bank of vending machines, and returned with the sodas. Meanwhile, some of the other staff had arrived and were whispering and furiously writing notes in preparation for the out-brief to the CG and troop leaders.

The CG arrived about fifteen minutes later, and everyone listened carefully as each inspector briefed their findings. Maura was shocked by the findings, especially in the area of vehicle maintenance and false reporting on the Unit Status Report.

About half way through the briefing, Maura whispered to Lori, "This is really bad. I can't see the CG's face, but I'm sure he's furious. These results normally go to Corps headquarters and stop there, but this is so bad, it'll probably have to be reported to USAREUR headquarters and maybe even to the Pentagon as a serious readiness issue. We're the U.S. portion of the covering force for the Corps, and because the Cav Troop is the commander's eyes and ears on what is happening on the front lines, it affects the ability of the entire Corps to remain combat-effective and accomplish the mission. This is going to be a huge black mark on the CG as well as the unit commander. If this were BG Franklin, he'd be screaming and cussing now and would probably physically assault the commander."

At Lori's look of surprise, Maura added, "Yeah, he was a West Point grad, but he was a bit of a crazy, if you ask me. I've seen him push NCOs and officers so hard, they've fallen down. I was always surprised no one reported him or pressed charges, but for some reason, they liked and trusted him. It'll be interesting to see how BG James handles this."

A few minutes later, Maura walked to the podium, briefed her findings and because she was the last briefer, she closed with, "Sir, subject to your questions, that concludes the pre-brief." The CG quietly thanked her and turned to the G-3, whispered a few things to him and motioned Sergeant Major Atkins to let the troop leaders in.

The staff brief to the unit was as painful as the pre-brief to the CG had been. Maura was leaving the podium as the CG stood up and turned to address the Cav Troop leadership. For a few very uncomfortable minutes he stared intently at the company leaders before announcing in a quiet, venomous tone, "Not good, boys. ... As a matter of fact, downright shitty. Go to war with you? I wouldn't go anywhere in the dark with you cretins!"

Maura and Lori watched as several brigade staff officers turned to look at each other in amazement at this uncharacteristic outburst. Maura smiled, recalling Master Sergeant Smith's saying, *The mouse has roared,* last year at Grafenwöhr, when she finally told her fellow officers that she wasn't going to take any more crap from them.

The CG continued in the same intense but quiet voice, "Gentlemen, to call this a colossal failure of leadership would be an understatement. This goes way beyond that and borders on criminal misconduct. You are non-mission capable on a level that quite frankly, I had heretofore thought impossible, given the reporting system we have. It never occurred to me that any officer, let alone one under my command and a Cav Trooper to boot, would deliberately falsify the monthly Unit Status Report by reporting deadline deficiencies as circle X deficiencies."

The captain started to respond, but the CG cut him off. "Not a word. There are no words you can say that will do anything but lower my already low opinion of you and your cadre's integrity and leadership. You will fix this problem, and you will fix it starting now. I don't care if you have to work nonstop for the next six months; you will fix it. What you will *not* do is punish the soldiers for your leadership failures. You created this problem and you will need the help of your soldiers to fix it, but you will not blame or punish them. Relieving all of you on the spot would be letting you off the hook for the problem that you, the leaders, and you alone created. So, while your soldiers will suffer for your transgressions, all of you will be right alongside them, helping them fix what you broke. I've already devised a plan to monitor your activities, and if I find that any of you punish or make the soldiers pay for this colossal screw-up, I will ensure you end up in Leavenworth—and if you doubt that, go ahead and be dumber than I give you credit for being, and plan on a trip to Leavenworth for the long course. My team will conduct random unannounced assistance visits to see how you are progressing and conduct interviews with the soldiers to ensure they are not being mistreated. My staff will confirm that you are in the motor pool and other sections, actively working alongside your soldiers."

With that, the CG walked over to his chair, picked up his helmet, motioned for the G-3 to follow him, and turned to the company commander. Putting his hand on the troop commander's shoulder, he said in that same quiet, venomous tone, "Don't go anywhere in the dark, boys. We'll be back." He then turned on his heel and walked out.

For a few seconds, it seemed like everyone was frozen in time. Sergeant Major Atkins stood up and, breaking the silence, quietly announced, "Let's move out, gentlemen."

Maura stood up and motioned Lori to follow her, as the rest of the staff got up and started talking in hushed tones, indicating a newfound respect for their quiet general.

"Holy shit! Didn't think the old man had it in him."

"Boy, remind me never to get on his bad side."

Maura and Lori walked out to their jeep in stunned silence and it wasn't until Maura pulled out of the parking lot, that she remarked to Lori, "I don't know what you're thinking, but what you just witnessed was leadership at its best. He never raised his voice, and there was no doubt in anyone's mind the CG is serious and will be hell on wheels until this is fixed. I gotta tell ya, if I were that captain, I'd resign my commission right now, because no matter what he does, he's not gonna survive this."

Lori was surprised by this last comment and asked a bit sharply, "You mean you'd leave and not fix this?"

Maura chuckled silently at Lori's accusatory tone. "No, I'd fix it, but I'd submit my resignation papers so I could get out of the Army as soon as possible and start a new career. Having said that, I would never have falsified the documents in the first place. It appears this has been going on for quite some time. If he had just tried to fix things, he could have survived this. But for reasons I'll never understand, he didn't, and he was stupid enough to think he could get away with it indefinitely."

"Shouldn't he be court-martialed for something like this?" Lori asked. "We had a huge cheating scandal at West Point, and there were a number of firsties that were kicked out and sent to the Army to serve their required time as enlisted soldiers. That's not going to jail, but that's pretty bad."

"Sure, he can do whatever he wants, but it's his decision and he's made it. You didn't experience BG Franklin, but I feel the restraint the CG showed today was far more effective than the usual screaming and cursing that the previous CG and some of the staff engaged in. It will be interesting to see if this changes how the staff deals with our subordinate units in the future. Under Franklin, it was a slash-and-burn leadership style. For the first time since I arrived here, I'm hopeful that I'll actually see some leadership traits and actions that I'll want to emulate."

Lori nodded in agreement. "Yeah, it's the same at West Point. We have a lot of out-of-control leaders who yell, and I don't respect them. The best leaders are calm and lead by example. They identify what you did wrong, show you the right way, and help you learn how not to make the same mistake again."

They spent the remainder of the ride back to Göppingen in silent reflection. For the first time since arriving at the 1st IDF, Maura wondered if she might want to be a company commander someday, forgetting for the moment that her original plan was to fulfill her four-year commitment and get on with the rest of her life. The incident also reminded her that when military leaders fail, the result could be that people died, and for the first time, she began to understand the tremendous responsibility she had as an Army officer.

6

MUNICH, SATURDAY 24 JUNE 1978

EARLY SATURDAY MORNING, MAURA and Anne picked up the two cadets at Trish's BOQ and headed for a weekend to nearby Bavaria. They'd been speeding down the autobahn for about twenty minutes when Lori asked, "Uh, Anne, how fast are you driving?"

"One hundred twenty kilometers per hour. Why?"

"Oh, just curious," Lori replied. "It seems so fast to me. Nothing like going fifty-five on the highway back home."

"You got that right!" Anne replied. "I love having no speed limit. But don't worry, One hundred twenty kilometers per hour is only about seventy-five miles per hour, and this car is just getting warmed up at that speed."

Maura interjected, "We're barely keeping pace with the other cars in the right-hand lane. Wait until a Porsche or Ferrari blows our doors off as they come zipping by us in the left lane at speeds in excess of one hundred miles per hour."

"Don't worry, I'm a good driver," Anne added.

"How long 'til we get to Munich?" Trish asked.

"It's about two hundred kilometers to Munich, but we're stopping in Dachau first, so we should get there in under two hours, depending on how fast I drive."

"I thought we were going to Munich," Trish replied, somewhat agitated.

"I thought Maura told you. We're going to Dachau to see the concentration camp first, because it's on the way to Munich."

"No, I don't recall that. ... Um, I'm not too excited about going to see a concentration camp," Trish said hesitantly.

"Well, I know it's going to be a bit depressing, but we thought since we go right by there, we should see it," Maura said. "Sorry if I forgot to mention it to you."

"I'm still not comfortable about going," Trish said a bit more forcefully.

Surprised by Trish's resistance, Maura turned around and asked, "Lori, what do you want to do?"

Uncomfortable with being put in the middle, Lori said, "Well, I really don't care where we go. I'm just happy to have the time off and appreciate you taking us to different places."

Trish responded sullenly, "I'll just take a nap or walk somewhere nearby while you guys go inside the camp."

"Okay," Maura said. "There's probably a park and *Gasthaus* nearby that we can meet at for lunch after the tour."

That seemed to satisfy Trish, who said somewhat petulantly, "Yeah, we can figure it out when we get there. I'm really tired and didn't get much sleep this week, so I may just curl up in the backseat and go to sleep while you guys sightsee."

Relieved that Trish had calmed down a bit, Maura said, "That's fine."

Shortly thereafter, Lori and Trish both fell asleep and didn't wake up until Anne pulled into the concentration camp parking lot.

Trish announced that she was going back to sleep, and the other three got out of the car. Walking down the tree-lined path to the visitors' center, Lori stared intently at the large metal gate with the words "*Arbeit macht Frei*" that she had seen in her high school history book. She was saddened at the thought of all the misery and inhumane treatment that had occurred under the guise of enlightened social responsibility.

Walking through the exhibits in the drab, gray museum building, Lori was not sure what she had expected, but the experience wasn't anything like she could have imagined.

The placards and displays explained that Dachau had opened in 1933 and was the first Nazi concentration camp. Originally billed as a camp designed to hold political prisoners, the camp quickly expanded its population to include criminals, Jews, foreigners, homosexuals, gypsies, and anyone opposing the Nazi agenda. Over 30,000 people were murdered in the camp during the twelve years it was in operation.

Lori was shocked at the graphic photos, information boards, artifacts, and memorials on display in the museum. She had known that Dachau had been an awful place, but seeing the photos of emaciated people and piles of dead bodies made it more horrific than she could imagine.

As Lori, Anne, and Maura exited the main building onto the grounds, the first thing they saw was a large metal sculpture of skeletons twisted in anguish and pain. As they continued down a path in silence, following the signs to the crematorium, Maura suddenly said to Lori, "I could swear we discussed coming here with both of you. Do you have any idea why Trish didn't tell us before today that she didn't want to come here?"

"I was as surprised as you were about Trish's behavior and really can't explain it. She never said anything to me, but I don't remember you mentioning stopping here, either."

"Oh my gosh! There's the crematorium and gas chamber," Anne interrupted in a horrified whisper. The women entered what had been the gas chamber and saw the now rusted shower heads, empty canisters marked *Zyklon B*, and pictures on the walls of naked men and women either waiting to be gassed or in a large heap of naked dead bodies. Especially horrific was a picture of a Nazi storm trooper with a knife in his raised hand, behind a very young girl. The graphic depiction of some of the atrocities committed here was chilling and emotionally draining. After leaving the gas chamber, they spent a few minutes in the crematorium, which held the ovens allowing bodies burned more efficiently.

Leaving the building with heavy hearts, Maura commented mournfully, "It's so hard to comprehend how humans could do this to other humans. I'm almost sick. I'm not sure I can take any more of this. Are you ready to leave?"

Anne and Lori nodded in agreement, and they slowly walked back to Anne's car.

When they opened the car door, Trish woke up and mumbled, "Well, how was it?"

"It's very haunting and hard to put into words," Lori replied. "Makes me appreciate being born in America with all our freedom and protections."

"I'll never forget this visit as long as I live. It was so sad, tragic, and unbelievable. I'm glad I'm in the Army and belong to a country that's dedicated to preventing this sort of thing from ever happening again," Anne said.

The four women were silent as their car sped down the autobahn toward Munich. After checking in, they decided to eat at the hotel restaurant. Having just had her first sip of the local German beer she had ordered, Lori said, "I'm still not used to the half-liter mugs. They're so much bigger than back home."

"I think they're great! If I have two of these, I get dizzy," Trish said. "These beer glasses are much bigger than the third-of-a-liter glasses in Stuttgart."

"Well, good thing you didn't get the one-liter mugs like those," Maura said, pointing to two men drinking beer from huge ceramic beer steins.

"Wow! Now that's a beer mug," said Lori. "How's the wine?"

"Quite good for table wine," Anne replied.

Maura added, "One of the perks of living here—great inexpensive wine."

The food arrived and the women immediately dug into their large schnitzels and fries. "That was fast. I didn't realize how hungry I was until I smelled the food." Trish exclaimed.

"It wasn't the half liter of beer, was it?" asked Lori playfully.

"Nope, just hungry and glad to be here with the three of you. What's the plan for tonight and tomorrow?"

"Well, I thought we'd walk to the town square, see the Glockenspiel and some other local sights, then go to the Hofbräuhaus to chat, drink, and eat with some of the locals," Maura replied. "We'll get up early tomorrow morning, have breakfast, and check out of the hotel. If the weather holds, we'll drive to Neuschwanstein and Hohenschwangau castles. If it rains, we'll check out some of the great museums. We'll drive to our gasthaus in Oberammergau when we're finished, have dinner, and call it a night. Early Monday, we'll do a walking tour of Oberammergau and get on the road just after lunch so we can all get back home and get ready for the rest of the week."

"What kind of castles are they?" Trish asked.

"Neuschwanstein was the model for the Disney castle. Hohenschwangau was built in the nineteenth century and is right down the hill. It was the childhood home of King Ludwig II of Bavaria. Anne and I went there in March and thought you'd enjoy seeing them. It should be much nicer in this warm weather."

"Yeah, I'd love to see them again," Anne added. "I froze in March because there was no heat in the castles, and I left my camera in the car. I'm looking forward to a much nicer experience and getting pictures this time, especially of the small lake with the black swans."

"Sounds like a good plan," Lori said. "Hope the sun comes out. I'm not big on museums. I'd rather hike and stay active than cooped up in a building."

"Me too," Trish added. "Where and when do we meet?"

"How about meeting in the lobby at six and walking over?" Maura asked.

The women went to their rooms to unpack and freshen up, before heading out to the famous Munich Hofbräuhaus.

★ ★ ★

WALKING INTO THE HOFBRÄUHAUS, Lori and Trish were surprised at the huge space filled with jovial drinkers laughing, singing, and talking. Finding some open seats at the end of one long table, they sat down and ordered beers, which came in huge glass mugs. They started to *shunkel*, locking arms while everyone swayed back and forth, and singing, "*In München steht ein Hofbräuhaus; Eins, Zwei…*" along with the rest of the people, totally enjoying themselves.

After a few hours, Maura burst the bubble and said, "Okay, I think we should head on back and get some shut-eye. Tomorrow will be another jam-packed day."

"I guess you're right. I'll sleep like a baby but may not wake up in time for 0700 breakfast if I have one more beer. Are you sure we need to start so early?" Trish asked.

Maura smiled, nodding.

"How long is the drive?" Lori asked while getting up from the table.

Anne replied, "One to two hours, depending on traffic and if we stop to take photos. Bavaria is my favorite part of Germany; so picturesque and colorful. I love the half-timbered *Fachwerk* houses and small towns. I feel like I'm in a storybook when we drive through them."

"Are we finished talking about tomorrow?" Lori slurred. "I had a strange thing happen to me this week that I want to talk to you guys about. A really cute specialist five asked me out on a date. I told him I have a boyfriend and I'm pretty sure I can't date him because he's enlisted. Is that right?"

"Yes, Lori. As a cadet or officer, you can't date enlisted soldiers. It's called fraternization. You also can't date other officers if they're in your chain of command, or a supervisor," Maura replied.

Trish smiled a bit drunkenly and mischievously asked, "Anne, have you gone out with any officers in Stuttgart?"

"Ahh *chéri*, of course, a few here and there."

"Like who?"

"Well, I went out with the Equal Opportunity officer."

Trish asked, "What the heck is an Equal Opportunity officer?"

"His job is to ensure no one in the command is discriminated against. He checks if soldiers are discriminated against at local German establishments."

"Hmm, sounds like a get-over job. What did you guys do?" Trish asked.

"He took me out to dinner and dancing at a disco. I found out later he got reimbursed for our entire night out. Can you believe it?"

"Are you kidding me?" Trish asked. "Why would the government pay for your dinners and drinks?"

"I don't know why *chéri* and I don't have a problem with the government paying for his duty related expenses but I do take exception to him using his government position to pay for a date with me."

"Maura, have you ever gone out with a German guy?" Lori asked.

"Yeah," Maura hesitantly answered.

"How did you deal with the language barrier?" Trish asked.

"I speak German well enough that that isn't a problem and most younger Germans speak some English. The real issue is that I work very late, only have some weekends free, and am only here for a few years, so it's really not worth the effort to try to have a serious relationship with someone from another country and culture."

"Yeah, I guess you're right," Trish commented thoughtfully, adding in a playful tone, "But a week or two with a foreign guy would be beyond cool!"

Anne laughed, as she pointed toward a group of good looking German guys at a nearby table. "You go for it *chéri!* We've got your six if you get in a bit too deep!"

The four women had a fun evening and it was a happy, but tired group of young women that climbed the stairs to their rooms in the gasthaus, after walking back from the Hofbräuhaus. "Don't know about you guys, but I'm fading fast," Maura said. "I'll say a *guten nacht* and see you first thing in the morning."

Trish lightheartedly remarked, "Pleasant dreams, and don't forget your cameras."

★ ★ ★

"HEY, SLEEPYHEADS!" ANNE GREETED Trish and Lori as they came into the breakfast salon the next morning. "I was just about to check on you guys."

"Sorry. I set the alarm for six p.m. instead of a.m.," Trish replied.

"No problem," Anne said. "We've got the whole day to sightsee, hike, and enjoy the German countryside."

"How's the coffee?" Trish asked.

"Great! It'll wake you right up," Maura said.

After breakfast, they checked out of the hotel and headed to Neuschwanstein. Seeing the castle in the distance, Trish said, "You weren't kidding; this castle looks just like the Disneyland castle. Cool. I hope the inside's as neat as the outside."

"Well, it's got all the stuff you'd expect to see inside a castle—lots of gold, mirrors, chandeliers, crystal, marble floors, antique furniture, Oriental rugs, and china. I've heard only a small part of the castle and original furnishings are on display. Too bad we can't check out the basement and closed-off rooms," Maura said as Anne pulled into a space in the parking lot.

"Yeah, it's a great day to sightsee and explore Germany. Glad we have the entire weekend off and were able to get a three-day pass," Anne said.

"Do you work on the weekends often?" Trish asked.

"Not too often, but whenever there's a field exercise or we're getting ready for a big inspection or ARTEP, it's twenty-four/seven balls to the walls," Anne said.

"What's an ARTEP?" Lori asked.

Anne replied, "It's an Army training evaluation exercise that normally happens once a year. Not my idea of a fun way to spend a weekend. We had one in April, and the whole month was full of extra work hours prepping, getting evaluated, and then fixing our problems. The commander liked it because he got a good assessment of the wartime readiness of the unit, but the soldiers and staff worked super hard the whole month."

After walking up the steep hill to the Neuschwanstein castle entrance for 15 minutes, Maura said, "Almost there."

"Wow, now this is a cool-looking castle!" Lori said as she got a closer look at the tall towers and roughhewn stones.

"I've never been in a real castle before. This is neat!" exclaimed Trish.

After a few hours in the castle, they made their way to Swan Lake, where they were lucky enough to get pictures of one black swan. They walked down the steep hill to Hohenschwangau but were disappointed by the sparsely furnished older castle.

ON MONDAY MORNING, THEY spent several hours walking through the village of Oberammergau. They were mesmerized by the beauty and realism of the famous *Lüftlmalerei*, frescoes depicting traditional Bavarian themes: fairy tales, religious scenes, or architectural *trompe-l'œil*—found on almost every home and many of the municipal buildings.

As they drove out of Oberammergau, Lori thanked Anne and Maura for the weekend. "I wish there was time to take the train up to the

Zugspitze, since it's the highest mountain in Germany and I've heard so much about it. It's frustrating to skip it when we're so close, but I know we have the drive home and work tomorrow."

That evening, Lori pulled out her diary and wrote about her trip to Bavaria.

> I'm beat, but had a fun and interesting weekend. Went with Trish, Maura, and Anne to Dachau, Munich, and Neuschwanstein, followed by Oberammergau. Southern Germany is beautiful! The air is crisp, the sky is blue, beers are huge, and the food is fantastic. Dachau was horrific and gruesome...still trying to figure out all the bad feelings I have for that place, and figure out why Trish wouldn't go in the museum and look at the concentration camp.

7

GÖPPINGEN, TUESDAY 27 JUNE 1978

LORI WAS ASSIGNED TO the brigade Training and Plans section for two weeks, working under the guidance of Major Gaslin, a sharp infantry officer who had been the plans officer for the past ten months. On her first day, they had gotten off to a rocky start because Lori had asked so many questions that Major Gaslin was late getting his briefing together. On her second day, Lori was busy reading, researching, and calling the brigade units for the information she needed for her report. Major Gaslin wanted the report done by Friday, and Lori had thought it would be an easy task.

Lori quickly found out the units were not always forthcoming with their training plan input, especially when a female voice requested the information. On her first call to one of the battalions, the plans captain did not believe she was working a project for Major Gaslin, and he called Major Gaslin to verify that she actually was.

Lori's last call for the information she needed was not any better than the previous calls. "Hello, sir. I'm Cadet Nelson. I'm working a tasker for

Major Gaslin and need to know the status of your training funds for the rest of the fiscal year."

"Who are you? Since when do female cadets work for Major Gaslin?" the captain asked.

"Sir, I'm a CTLT cadet, and I'm trying to do my job," replied Lori, slightly frustrated.

"Well I was a CTLT cadet about six years ago, but that was before they let women go to West Point. How'd you luck out and get to come to Germany? They sent me to Fort Knox. What company are you in?"

"Sir, I'm in A4, and I don't know how I came to Germany, but I'm sure glad I'm here."

"Fair enough. When do you need the information?"

"No later than tomorrow afternoon, sir," Lori replied.

"Okay, I'll get it to you tomorrow by noon."

Lori heard the line go dead and sarcastically said, "Thanks, sir."

The phone rang a minute after she hung up. Trish was on the line. "Hi, Lori! Can you talk?"

"How'd you find my number? I just moved to this desk yesterday."

"Maura answered the phone and gave me your number. Why are you moving around so much? I'm glad I'm in one job for the whole six weeks so I can actually learn something."

"Maura thought this would be better for me than staying in one job. I think she's a little bossy, but she means well. The good news is I'm meeting lots of officers and soldiers and getting a little bit of information on many different staff sections. The bad news is, right when I figure out what I'm supposed to do, I move to a new staff location and position. Enough about me, though. Why did you call?"

"I've misplaced my ID card, have no idea where I put it. I've looked all over my BOQ, and I'm stressed out!" Trish exclaimed.

"Okay, calm down. When did you have it last?"

"Yesterday I went to the PX to cash a check, and then I went to Finance and changed some dollars into Deutsch Marks. That was the last time I remember taking out my ID card."

"Okay, what did you do with your ID card after you left the Finance window yesterday?"

"I thought I put it in my wallet like always, but it's not there!"

"Are you wearing the same uniform you wore yesterday?"

"No, I spilled some coffee on my pants, so I had to change this morning. You think the ID card might be in my old pants?" Trish asked.

"That's where I'd look," Lori quietly replied.

"Good idea, Lori! I think I did put something in my pocket. I'll check as soon as I get back to my BOQ during lunch hour. I'll call you back this afternoon if I still can't find my ID card. I sure hope you're right."

"Take care, Trish. Don't worry too much. The worst case is you'll have to fill out some forms and get a new ID card. You might look dumb, but it's not the end of the world."

"Yeah, you're right. Thanks for putting my head on straight. See you on Friday night for our big trip."

"See you Friday, Trish."

8

RHEIN MAIN AIRBASE, WEST GERMANY, FRIDAY 30 JUNE 1978

MAURA AND LORI LEFT Göppingen right after work and drove to Stuttgart to pick up Anne and Trish before driving to the Gateway Inn at Rhein-Main Air base.

The clerk looked up as they approached the counter, and Maura greeted him. "Hi. We're going to sign up for space A slots on the 0800 flight to Berlin in the morning but need two rooms for tonight. Do you have any open?"

"I do, but it's a lot cheaper at the visiting officers' quarters. Sure you don't want to stay there?"

"Yeah," Maura responded. "We've done this before and like staying here because we can leave our car parked here all weekend and catch the shuttle to the terminal."

The clerk nodded and looked in his reservation book. "Okay, I have three rooms with two single beds, but they're all on different floors. I can put you in two of those, or if you prefer, I have a two-bedroom one-bath family suite, but one of the rooms has a full, versus twin, beds."

The ladies decided to go with the family suite so they could stay together. Maura and Anne volunteered to share the full bed. After signing the paperwork and getting four keys, Maura announced, "It's eight o'clock, and we all need showers and supper. Do ya wanna take showers before or after we eat?"

Anne chimed in, "I don't know about anyone else, but I'm starving. I didn't have time to eat lunch today."

"I'm hungry too," Lori said.

Maura nodded. "We can drive to the O'Club, or we can eat at the snack bar here. They've got great made-to-order burgers, fries, and milkshakes."

Trish exclaimed, "That sounds great! I've enjoyed the German food, but I haven't had a good burger in ages and can't even remember the last time I had a milkshake."

"Yeah," Lori agreed. "Are they like the milkshakes we get back home?"

Anne nodded. "Exactly like the fountain drugstore milkshakes back home *chéri*."

They had barely sat down when Trish bit into her huge burger, juice dripping onto her plate. Having inhaled her first bite of burger and fries, she reached for a gulp of the chocolate milkshake. As she reached for her burger to get another bite, she exclaimed, "Oh my God! I haven't had a burger and milkshake this good in years!" As Trish took another large bite of the burger, Lori nodded in agreement.

There was no conversation as the women savored the large, juicy burgers, hot fries, and creamy, rich chocolate milkshakes. Finishing her meal first, Trish leaned back contentedly. "I don't know if I can get up. Gosh, that was great!"

Lori added, "Yeah, thanks for suggesting this. Good thing we don't have a snack bar like this at Cooke Barracks. I'd go back to the academy looking like the Goodyear blimp!"

Anne swallowed the last bite of her burger. "Yeah, Maura and I feel the same way. We discovered this place on our first trip to Berlin."

Finishing off her milkshake, Lori asked Maura, "What's next?"

"We take showers, change into civvies, and go to the O'Club. We'll have a few drinks and return here to catch the shuttle to the terminal around 1130. We might be able to convince them to let us check in a few minutes before midnight so we can catch the midnight shuttle back and get some shut-eye."

Lori yawned sleepily. "Sure hope we can. I could go to sleep right now."

Maura laughed. "Well, we'll do our best. Remember the peanut butter and M&M cookies I made last night and told you I was taking for a snack in case we wanted one in the morning?"

Lori nodded.

"I plan to offer half of them to the airman as a bribe."

"Excellent!" Trish exclaimed.

Maura stood up and grabbed her tray. "Let's head back to the room to get ready."

★ ★ ★

WHEN THEY GOT TO the club, Lori asked Trish, "Hey, I forgot to ask, did you find your ID?"

"Yeah, just as you thought. I left it in my pocket. I felt so stupid, but at least I found it."

Anne picked up her wineglass, got off her barstool and asked. "Anyone want to play pool?"

Everyone agreed that was a good idea, and several beers, glasses of wine, and games of pool later, they headed to the airport terminal.

As they approached the Space A counter, the airman on duty looked up. "Good evening, ladies. What flight are you here to sign up for?"

Maura pointed to the flight board behind him. "The 0800 to Berlin."

Looking at his watch, the airman replied, "Sorry, ma'am, you'll have to wait until midnight to sign up for that flight."

Smiling, Maura pulled out the Whitman's sampler box that she'd put a dozen cookies in. As she opened it and set it on the counter, she said conspiratorially, "We were hoping that, given that it's just the five of us here, you might consider letting us sign up now so we can catch the midnight shuttle back to the Gateway Inn."

"Ma'am, are you trying to bribe a government official?" the clerk replied, his tone artificially stern.

Maura assumed a similarly mocking tone as she closed the box of cookies. "I would never do that, airman, but I'm awfully tired, and if I just happen to forget this box after we all sign in … well, it would be a shame to let fresh homemade cookies go to waste or get thrown away, so I guess you'd just have to eat them yourself."

The clerk laughed. "Gotta hand it to you, ma'am, you're good." He hesitated for a few seconds, then reached under the counter, pulled out a binder, opened it, and put a sign on the counter saying, *Be back in 15 minutes*. "Ladies, you know you have to report for roll call at 0600, in Class B or A uniform, have ID and your leave form to be put on the manifest, correct?"

All four nodded.

"I've got a sudden urge to hit the latrine, and I might forget to put the binder back under the counter. If you show up while I'm gone, are confused about what to do, see the binder, sign up, close the ledger, and leave before I get back, I won't realize you've signed up early. When I pull it out after midnight and see the signatures, I'll realize I shouldn't have left the binder on the counter and figure you didn't realize you had to wait for me to return to sign up." He turned to walk away, saying, "Make sure you forget those cookies when you leave."

The four ladies looked at each other, and as soon as the clerk walked away, they each filled in the required information. Maura closed the book, and they walked out of the terminal, leaving the binder and box of cookies on the counter.

9

BERLIN, SATURDAY MORNING 1 July 1978

HAVING GOTTEN ONLY FOUR hours of sleep, everyone was groggy when the alarm went off at 0500. They got to the terminal in plenty of time for the 0600 roll call and after confirming they had a seat on the plane, they went to the snack bar.

When Lori and Trish got to the table with juice and omelets, Trish sat down and, shaking her head, pointed to Maura and Anne's coffee cups. "That's all you're having?"

Maura took a sip of coffee. "Might have another cup of coffee. We'll see how I feel after this one."

Anne mumbled, "Not a breakfast eater, *chéri*."

"Okay," Trish muttered as she and Lori started eating.

Having finished breakfast, the two cadets in their khaki uniforms and low quarters, along with Maura and Anne in their lime green dresses and pumps, walked to the gate and boarded their plane. When they arrived at Templehof Airport terminal, they saw Amelia waving to them with a huge smile on her face.

Amelia hugged Maura and Anne. "It's so great to see you guys. I've really missed you!" Extending a hand to Lori and then to Trish, she added, "Hi, I'm Amelia. Nice to meet you. I'm so glad this worked out; I've got a wonderful weekend planned."

After brief introductions, Maura said to Amelia, "Being as there are too many of us for one cab, we figured you could ride with Lori and Trish in one cab to get acquainted and we'll take the luggage in the second cab."

Smiling, Amelia announced proudly, "I've got it covered. I was talking to the brigade commander's wife last week about my concern that with the CTLT cadets there would be five of us, and I wasn't sure how I was going to put everyone up, let alone transport us around and asked for her advice. I was surprised when she responded by standing up, walking away, and shouting, 'Be right back.' Fifteen minutes later, she returned and told me her husband had authorized protocol to let us stay in the distinguished visitors' quarters and provide a van to get us around. I have to drive it, but thanks to the commander and his wife, we're good to go."

Anne laughed. "I think you missed your callin' *chéri*. You should have been a logistics officer. Good job!"

Amelia proudly announced, "I'll take that as a compliment. Everyone ready?"

As the five women walked through the terminal, they garnered a number of stares. People took second looks at their small group. It was unusual to see so many uniformed women together.

Arriving at Clay Barracks, they showed their IDs and made their way to the DVQ. Amelia unlocked the door. The other four women entered the cottage and stood in the living room in stunned silence, taking in the luxurious surroundings. Amelia gleefully exclaimed, "Pretty cool, huh?"

Anne gave her a hug. "*Incroyable, chéri.* ... You've outdone yourself!"

"Agreed!" Maura added enthusiastically. Lori and Trish were equally impressed but remained silent.

Amelia motioned to the group of astonished women. "C'mon, let me show you around." She walked through the spacious living/dining room, furnished in Queen Anne-style furniture, and led them to one of the two doors at the far end of the room. Opening the first door, she motioned to Lori and Trish. "This is your bedroom." Looking at Anne and Maura, she continued, "I gave them the room with twin beds, and you guys will have to sleep in the double bed." Walking into the bedroom that Lori and Trish would share, with the four women trailing behind, she continued, "Each bedroom has a full American-style bathroom. You guys get unpacked and meet us in the living room." Looking at Anne and Maura, she headed back out into the living room, saying, "C'mon, let's get you guys settled. I brought linen from my place and will sleep on the couch, but I'll have to share your bathroom and hung a few things in the closet."

As they walked to their bedroom, Amelia announced excitedly. "I've so been looking forward to seeing you guys! So much has happened since the last time we were all together. Did you cover the itinerary with the cadets?"

"Yeah," Maura replied, opening her suitcase. "But just in outline form. We figured you'd go over the details when we got here. We've all been swamped at work, and they probably would've forgotten most of it if we'd given them too many details."

Amelia sat down on the bed while Anne and Maura unpacked. "Cool. I'll go over the details for today and tonight. Do they know I've arranged a tour of Charlottenburg Schloß for them tomorrow?"

"Yeah," Maura answered. "We explained that we didn't want to do it again because it's quite expensive but a really fantastic experience they shouldn't miss."

"Perfect," Amelia responded. "That'll give us time to catch up and for me to tell you my surprise news."

Anne looked up quizzically. "Just tell us now, *chéri*."

Amelia shook her head. "No, I'm saving it for tomorrow because I know you guys are going to have a million questions." Anne and Maura paused, furrowed their eyebrows, and stared at Amelia, who laughed and said, "I picked up some fresh *brötchen*, pastries, fruit, cold cuts, and cheese. I'll go put everything out and fix a large pot of tea. See you in a few."

Stunned, Maura looked at Anne. "Whaddaya make of that?"

Equally mystified, Anne responded, "You got me, but whatever it is, I'm guessing it's gonna be a real doozy!"

After unpacking, Maura and Anne walked over to Lori and Trish's bedroom. Maura announced, "Amelia picked up some stuff for brunch and is fixing tea. I know you guys probably aren't very hungry, but we'll eat a little something before going to Checkpoint Charlie. We'll spend most of the day walking around East Berlin and spend time at the one department store in Alexanderplatz. They actually have some nice things you might want to buy."

The four women walked into the kitchen where Amelia was putting out a second teapot with the large selection of baked goods and fruit she'd bought fresh that morning.

"Holy smokes, Amelia!" Maura exclaimed. "There's enough food here for an army!"

Amelia responded good-naturedly, "Eat what you want. I'll put the rest away and we can have it for breakfast in the morning."

Anne sat down, grabbed a brötchen, and started putting butter on it. "Chill, Maura, nothin'll go to waste. Besides, no self-respecting Southerner would invite people to eat and risk running out of food."

Amelia nodded in agreement. "Maura, have you forgotten how much food my mom put out that one weekend I took you home? In a Southern home, there's no such thing as too much food on the table."

Maura raised her hands in mock surrender and motioned for Lori and Trish to sit as she commented, "Amelia, there's five place settings but only four chairs."

"I know. Sit down and start eating," Amelia said as she walked out of the kitchen. She returned a moment later with a dining room chair and joined them. After a bit more than an hour of eating and Amelia talking with Lori and Trish, Amelia got up. "Okay, it's one o'clock. We need to clean up, and I need to change into my uniform so we can all go to East Berlin today."

Maura got up and said, "You go change. We'll clean up here. Do you think we can squeeze four of us in the back seat for the short taxi ride to the U-Bahn station?"

Amelia gasped. "I forgot to tell you another one of the surprises I have in store for this weekend. I do a lot of protocol support for the Military Liaison Mission commander. When I mentioned your visit, he asked if we were going to go to East Berlin. When I told him yes, he offered to take us over in one of their vehicles and give us a guided tour so we don't have to worry about all the walking, waiting in line, and we'll actually get to drive through Checkpoint Charlie and East Berlin in a diplomatic vehicle."

"Wow," Lori blurted.

Anne chuckled. "I agree. This is totally amazing, *chéri*."

A bit embarrassed by all the praise, Amelia blushed. "Okay, I just want this to be a fantastic experience for everyone. I've learned so much more about Berlin since your first visit, and given that you guys can't get here often, I want to make every minute as special as possible."

"Thanks, ma'am," Lori said quietly.

Amelia smiled. "Okay, you clean up, and I'll be back soon."

★ ★ ★

AT 1330, AN UGLY but roomy olive drab colored vehicle pulled up in front of the DVQ, where all five women were standing, ready to go. As the colonel got out of the vehicle, all of the women came to attention, saluted, and yelled in unison, "Good afternoon, sir!"

Returning the salutes, he smiled and replied softly, "As you were."

Maura was mesmerized. He was tall, bore a striking resemblance to Sean Connery, and had massive shoulders that tapered to a slim lower body. Amelia made introductions and thanked him for making time to give them a private tour. Maura's knees felt like jelly when he laughed and replied in a mellifluous voice, "It is entirely my pleasure, ladies. I don't normally get to spend an entire afternoon with five gorgeous women."

Maura, Anne, Lori, and Trish were spellbound and speechless. Totally unaffected, but realizing that her friends and the cadets were staring at the colonel; Amelia walked to the van and opened the back door. "Alright, ladies, let's get going. We have a lot to see today."

After they'd all gotten in the van, Maura regained her wits first and nervously asked, "Sir, could you tell us a bit about what you do at the mission?"

Looking in the rearview mirror, he smiled and said in an offhand fashion, "I could, but then I'd have to kill you. When he got no response, he added, Ladies, I'm joking! I know there's a big difference between a colonel and cadets and lieutenants, but we're out for a day of fun in an unofficial capacity, and the only reason we're wearing uniforms is because we're required to, so, for today, my name is Eric and we're just out to have a great day. Got it?"

Maura was the first one to respond. "Yes, sir."

He looked at her in the mirror, "It's Eric, Maura." She took a deep gulp and said a bit hesitantly, "Okay ... Eric."

Looking at Amelia, he remarked good-naturedly, "Amelia, can you get your crew to relax?"

Secretly amused by her friends' awestruck behavior, Amelia turned around to face them. "He's not a colonel today, he's just one of the gang."

Lori and Trish nodded in agreement, but Anne and Maura were a bit embarrassed. True enough, their fascination and tongue-tied behavior were partially because of his rank, but mostly because he was so gorgeous. If they'd met him on the street in civvies, they would have guessed he was around thirty, and with the full head of gorgeous hair he had, they would never have guessed he was in the military.

Anne replied jocularly, "Well, uh, Eric, it's gonna take a bit of getting used to, but I think we can manage to start acting normally, versus a bunch of morons who can't put two words together or remember that your first name is Eric."

That eased some of the nervousness, and Trish asked, "So, what can you tell us about the mission without killing us?" That broke any remaining uneasiness between them as they all laughed.

Responding in kind, Eric told them, "Well, when the US Mission was first established in the late forties, right after the war, our initial mission revolved around genuine liaison tasks like repatriation of prisoners of war, location of Allied service personnel graves, looking for Nazi war criminals and witnesses to Nazi atrocities, as well as monitoring the distribution of food and fuel, but as time has evolved, our mission has changed."

A much more relaxed atmosphere ensued, and shortly after they passed through Checkpoint Charlie, Eric pointed out different government buildings and gave some gruesome accounts of various escape attempts, most of which had failed.

As Eric continued to give an excellent history lesson on the construction of the Berlin Wall and not only the plight of those caught behind the wall but also the tragedy of many families being physically separated by the wall, all five women were silent. Maura and Anne had already experienced and discussed the stark difference between the life and color of West Berlin and the lifeless, gray landscape that marked both a physical and psychological schism between the East and the West, but this was Lori and Trish's first trip to Berlin.

Lori felt as if a heavy veil had been dropped over her eyes. It was a bright, pleasant sunny day, with a clear blue sky, but shortly after they passed Checkpoint Charlie, it seemed as if the sky and the landscape went gray, obscuring the warmth and light that the sun exuded just a few miles to the west. It was Saturday, but very few people were on the streets. All of the buildings were slate colored, or dark brown. Many buildings were damaged, and when Lori asked what had caused the damage, Eric told her it was damage from WWII that the Soviets had never bothered to fix.

Trish felt Lori's hand on her shoulder, and when she looked over, Lori silently pointed to the ground floor of a building that had been almost completely destroyed. There were garbage cans lined up outside of the building, and an old woman was bent over, rummaging through them.

A few minutes later, they approached a large square. Eric parked on the street and told everyone to get out. After a short walk into the plaza, Eric continued, "This is Alexanderplatz. The large tower over there is a television tower that the East German government built. Construction began on 4 August 1965. After four years of construction, the Fernsehturm began test broadcasts on 3 October 1969, and the tower was officially inaugurated four days later on the GDR's National Day."

Lori interrupted, "What does GDR mean?"

"Sorry, I tend to forget most people don't know all the acronyms. GDR stands for German Democratic Republic and denotes East Germany. West Germany is called the FRG, Federal Republic of Germany."

Pointing to the sphere at the top of the tower, he continued, "If you watch for a few minutes, you'll see that the sphere is turning slowly. There's an observation deck and restaurant at the top, and it completes a full rotation every thirty minutes. Notice the silver ball at the top. As you know, the GDR is an atheistic state, but whenever the sun shines directly on the stainless steel dome, it is always reflected as a cross. We'll walk over there later and see if we can catch a glimpse of it, but I can't promise that, because it only happens once or twice a day. Needless to say, this was not an effect desired or anticipated by the architects, and West Berliners call this phenomena, *Rache des Papstes*, or the 'Pope's Revenge.'"

As they continued around the square, Eric pointed out a beautiful fountain and a geometric building with a painted mural, which housed a café. After about fifteen minutes of running dialogue, Eric addressed the one large building in the square. "That's the only department store for miles around. I thought you ladies might like to do a bit of browsing."

Amelia spoke up first. "Thanks, Eric. We mentioned shopping here but didn't know any of the details about the TV tower." Looking at her friends and Lori and Trish, she asked, "Ready to do some shopping?"

They all nodded, but Lori asked, "Do they take German Deutsche Marks?"

Eric answered, "The cashiers don't, but there's a money-changing booth the government runs, and they'll exchange dollars or Deutsche Marks for Ost Marks. Any other questions before I head to the café?" When no one spoke up, he added, "Okay, have fun," and walked away.

As the five women walked into the large department store, they found it drab and utilitarian. There also seemed to be no organization, and they had to wait in line to get on the escalator to go upstairs. When they got upstairs, they had to wait in another line for shopping baskets before they could enter the shoe department, and they could not try on any of the shoes without help from one of the too few, surly clerks.

★ ★ ★

WHEN THE FIVE WOMEN finally walked into the Presse Café, Eric waved and motioned them to come over. After the women apologized for shopping so long, Eric waved his hand dismissively. "I knew it would take you a while." Looking at his watch, he asked, "Is anyone interested in *Kuchenzeit*?"

Looking a bit confused, Lori said, "That translates to cake time, but I'm not familiar with that term."

"It's a German custom to have coffee and some sort of dessert every day, as a break from the flurry of life. Most people do it in their homes, but as a special treat, many go to a café with friends to relax."

"Sounds lovely; I'm in." Maura said excitedly. The other women nodded.

"Okay, then," Eric replied. "We could stay here, but we also have the option of going to the Fernsehturm restaurant." Everyone resoundingly agreed that going to the revolving restaurant at the top of the TV tower would be the most interesting option.

Having sat down and ordered, everyone enjoyed the view and leisurely sipped coffee or hot chocolate and ate dessert while Lori and Trish answered Eric's many questions about what it was like to be the first women at West Point.

When they'd finished, they returned to the van and drove back down Unter den Linden Straße, to Brandenburg Gate, surveying the obstacles emplaced on the east side of Brandenburg Gate, in an area called No-Man's Land that was set up to keep East Germans from escaping to the west.

On the drive back to Checkpoint Charlie, everyone was silent. As they passed through the checkpoint and into West Berlin, Eric tried to lighten the mood a bit. "Back in civilization, where life is good and people are free."

Trish replied somberly, "You read about these sorts of things and know it's horrible, but until you've been here, it's abstract."

"Yeah," Lori added, "You could feel the desperation and depression. I've always felt blessed and proud to be an American, but today's experience reminds me that many people don't enjoy those same freedoms. It's really sad."

As they entered Clay Barracks, Eric said, "Well, ladies, I didn't mean to bring everyone's mood so low, but it is a stark reminder of why we're here. Not sure what you ladies have planned, but I'm free tonight, and if you'd like to experience Berlin nightlife, I know a number of clubs that are fairly safe and GI friendly. Talk about it when you get back to the DVQ. Amelia has my number, and if you want to go out, I'll pick everyone up around 2100, and we can go to a great café on the Spree River, have curry wurst and German fries for dinner, and go to the disco afterwards."

"Thanks, sir," Amelia said first. "That's very nice of you. We'll see how everyone is feeling, and I'll get back to you in the next hour or so." Then they all got out of the van and thanked him for a great day.

★ ★ ★

ONCE INSIDE THE DVQ, Amelia announced, "Okay, if we could just sit down and discuss the invite for tonight, I'll feel better. It was a nice offer, but I was really surprised he made it, and because he is a colonel and the commander of the mission, I'm a bit uncomfortable with the thought of going out for a night on the town with him, but I'll defer to what you guys want."

"Is he married?" Maura asked.

"No."

"Well, I know I only get one vote, but colonel or not, he's a hunk!"

Lori and Trish's jaws dropped. They'd never seen this side of Maura and didn't quite know what to make of it. Amelia and Anne managed to hide their surprise but were equally taken aback at Maura's comment.

Realizing she had surprised everyone with her comment, Maura felt a bit embarrassed for a second and then decided, *Aw hell, I'm just gonna go for broke.* "Hey, he offered, and yes, I'm super attracted to him. It's been a long time since I felt this way, and know it's goin' nowhere, but I sure would like to spend some time in *nowhere* dancing with and being near him!"

Anne broke the uncomfortable silence by bursting into laughter. "Okay, *chéri*, you got my vote."

Amelia looked over at Lori and Trish. "Obviously, both of my friends have totally lost their minds, but if you are uncomfortable with a night on the town with the colonel, I'll be the tiebreaker and tell him thanks, but no thanks."

Lori and Trish looked at each other. Neither one of them felt comfortable with a colonel taking them out for a night of dancing, but Lori liked and trusted Maura and was at odds with feeling that she should say no, because of the fraternization rules, while wanting to say yes, because Maura had shared how lonely she was and that it had been a long time since she'd had a boyfriend.

After a few seconds, Lori exhaled, looked at Maura, and hesitantly asked, "You really like him, don't you?"

Maura grinned ruefully, "Yeah, but I don't want anyone to be uncomfortable for the sake of my raging hormones, so I'm cool if you guys can't hang with the colonel taking us out for an evening."

Lori smiled. "Heck, you only live once, and like you said, he offered, so let's do it!"

Trish hadn't expected that response from Lori, but because she wasn't really sure she objected to the idea, she blurted out, "I'm cool with it."

Amelia shook her head and looked at Maura. "Far be it from me to be the only wet blanket in the crowd. Luckily, he isn't in the brigade, so—"

Maura jumped up and screamed excitedly before Amelia could finish. "Whoa baby, it's gonna be a hot time on the old town tonight! Don't know 'bout anyone else, but I'm gonna catch the shuttle to the exchange to see if they have any hot outfits!" Seeing the stupefied looks on her friends' faces, Maura calmed down for a second. "Thanks, gals. Don't worry, I won't embarrass anyone," but she was so excited, she just couldn't contain herself and excitedly exclaimed, "This is beyond *rad*!" as she walked over to grab her purse. "Anyone wanna come along?"

Everyone shook their heads. Grinning from ear to ear, Maura headed to the front door, calling, "See ya later!"

As the door shut behind Maura, not knowing quite what else to do, Amelia told the stunned group of women, "Guess I'd better call the colonel." Looking at Anne, she added, "Could you see if Lori and Trish want something to drink?" and as an afterthought, "You know where the wine is. Please pour me a glass. I think I'm gonna need one." Amelia then walked over to the small desk in the corner of the living room, to look up the colonel's phone number in her address book.

"Beer?" Anne asked Lori and Trish. They nodded, and Anne walked over to the fridge, motioning them to sit at the kitchen table. Anne put an open bottle of Heineken in front of each of the cadets and then poured glasses of wine for Amelia and herself. Sitting down at the table, she looked over at Lori and Trish. With a crooked, goofy smile and droll tone, Anne raised her glass. "Here's to a hot time on the town tonight, ladies. Bet this one ain't in the West Point Program of Instruction."

Lori and Trish lifted their bottles, taking big gulps of beer, still too stunned to say anything, let alone process Maura's rash behavior. Lori thought, *Boy is she acting weird.*

By this time, Amelia had finished talking to the colonel and came over to join them. She sat down and took a big slug of wine. "Well, things just got a bit more interesting. ... The colonel said he hoped we'd say yes and if it was okay, he'd invited two of his captains, who are also single and didn't have any plans, to join us. I guess I could have said it wasn't okay, but figured in for a penny, in for pound, as the saying goes."

Grabbing the bottle of wine, Anne started pouring some more in her half-empty glass. "Oh, I think I'm gonna need a lotta wine tonight."

Amelia took another large gulp of wine and looked at Anne. "Can you believe this? I've never seen her act so impulsively."

"That ain't impulsive," Anne chortled. "It's more like totally outta control!"

Amelia looked over at Lori and Trish, who had finished their beers. "This is so out of character for Maura, please accept our apologies if this situation is making you uncomfortable. What am I saying? Of course you're uncomfortable; we're totally floored!"

Lori and Trish stared at Amelia. Shaking her head, Amelia stood up, walked to the fridge and took out two fresh bottles of beer, opened them, and handed them to the silent cadets. "Maura is usually the levelheaded, cautious one of our small group. I hope you won't let this affect what I hope thus far has been a good impression of Maura." Amelia's voice trailed off. Not sure what else to say, she took another unusually large gulp of wine, emptying her glass, and reached for the bottle to pour another glass full.

Lori tried to reassure Amelia, "You're right, she's great, and I don't know what to say. I would never have expected her to act like this either."

Realizing there was no making sense of Maura's unexpected outburst and behavior, Anne took a last gulp of wine and stood up. "Don't know 'bout anyone else, but I'm gonna take a shower and relax a bit before we head out tonight." Pausing, she turned to look at Amelia. "What time are we leaving?"

"The colonel said they'd get here around nine."

Trish and Lori stood up. "A shower and short nap sounds good to me too," Lori said.

Amelia looked at Anne. "Perfect. You guys go on. I'll clean up here and take a shower after Anne."

10

BERLIN, SATURDAY ATERNOON 1 July 1978

AMELIA WAS ASLEEP ON the couch when Maura burst through the front door. "I'm back, and wait 'til you guys see what I found!" she exclaimed excitedly. When Amelia woke with a start, Maura realized she'd woken Amelia and that no one else was in the living/kitchen area. Giggling, she whispered, "Oops, sorry I woke you. How can you sleep? I'm so buzzed, I can hardly stand it!"

Sitting up and rubbing her eyes, Amelia replied in a mildly cheeky tone, "Well, not all of us are head over heels in lust."

Maura's ebullient demeanor deflated as quickly as a balloon pricked with a pin. She quietly walked over to one of the nearby chairs, dropped her bag, and looked at Amelia as she said disconsolately, "Oh my God, I'm totally out of control. What's happening to me?"

Amelia got up from the couch and went over to hug her. "We don't have a clue, Maura, and I feel so badly that I'm the one that burst your bubble, but really, what's going on here?"

"I don't know, Amelia, I've never felt or acted this way before. I mean, I saw him, and it was all I could do not to totally lose it. My hormones are on overdrive, and I guess I worked so hard all afternoon to stay subdued and keep my emotions in check that when he mentioned he wanted to take us out dancing tonight, I just couldn't hold it in anymore. Oh my God; you guys must think I'm a total fool. And the cadets … I can't believe I acted this way in front of them!"

"Chill, Maura," Amelia said reassuringly. "No one is standing in judgment of you. We were just shocked at your behavior. No harm done and I can't believe I'm saying this, but yes, he is gorgeous. I guess I just block that out because I only look at him and the other men I deal with professionally as colleagues and never think about them as men or prospective dates."

Maura stood up. "Thanks, Amelia. Even though you didn't do it on purpose, I did need a reality check. If I'd continued in this manic fashion, I probably would have embarrassed myself and all of you tonight."

Unbeknownst to Amelia and Maura, Maura's noisy entry had woken Anne up and she had been standing behind the bedroom door, listening to the latter part of the conversation. Walking out, she said, "*Chéri*, we're cool. Glad to see you come back down to earth, just sorry it was a bit of a rough landing. Don't worry about Trish and Lori. Go get a shower and model whatever gorgeous outfit you bought, and enjoy the evening. We promise to let you have the first dance with charming Eric."

Maura smiled weakly, picked up the bag she had dropped, and started walking toward the bedroom she and Anne shared. "You know, now that I think about it, this is a really bad idea. I'm sorry I rooked all of you into this, but I'm going to pass on going tonight. I feel like such a fool and obviously can't trust my emotions when I'm around him, so just give my apologies for backing out, and have a fun night."

Anne grabbed Maura by the shoulders. "Oh no, *chéri*. You don't get off that lightly, and you *will* have a great time tonight, because you *are* going with us." Grabbing the bag, she opened it and pulled out a shoebox and a gorgeous blue halter mini dress with thick silver brocade trim at the neck and hem. Inside the shoebox was a pair of bejeweled silver platformheeled sandals with diamond and sapphire-colored accent stones. "Maura, you're not the one that's gonna be out of control tonight; when he sees you in this outfit, he and every other guy in the joint are gonna be all over you."

Maura took the bag and put the sandals and dress back inside. "No, I'll take these back tomorrow. I have a much nicer pair of dress slacks and silk top that will look just fine. This is a bit over the top."

Amelia came up behind Maura and said, "Maura, it's beautiful and you're going to be beautiful in it. This is lovely, and sexy, but in a very tasteful fashion. We want you to enjoy yourself, so please, don't be self-conscious. I wasn't going to mention it, but you're not the first woman in Berlin to totally lose it around him. I'm apparently immune to his charms, but he does have a reputation for ruining marriages and being quite the playboy. I'm really not sure how he keeps his security clearance, with some of the antics that have been attributed to him, but he definitely has a way about him. If you want to fall into his orbit for fun, go for it; just be careful, because falling for him could be very painful."

"Do you know if he's ever been married?"

"I don't."

"Hi there. What is everyone looking so serious about?"

Maura, Anne, and Amelia looked up at the sound of Lori's voice. Before any of them could respond, Lori walked over, took the blue dress out of Maura's hand, and held it up. "Very nice, Maura!"

Maura took the dress out of Lori's hands, putting it and the sandals back in the bag. "I'm going to return it tomorrow." Out of the corner of her eye, Maura saw Trish come out of her bedroom. "Hi, come on over. Sorry, not sure what got into me, but please accept my apologies for my behavior earlier today. It won't happen again, and I've decided to stay here and cool my jets a bit."

"Okay, that decided it," Amelia said assertively. "I'm calling the colonel and telling him we have to cancel."

"No!" Maura said sharply. "I've made enough of a mess by making a fool of myself, but I'm sure Lori and Trish would love to have this sort of experience, and with Mattias out of town, we don't have any guys to show us around and party with. If my not going, is going to ruin everything, then I'll suck it up and go."

Anne took Maura by the shoulder and started steering her toward the bedroom. "That's the Maura I know. C'mon, you and I are goin' to have a come-to-Jesus talk and get you ready for a fun evening."

Maura glared at Anne but let her push her into the bedroom. As soon as the door closed behind them, Anne took the shopping bag out of Maura's hand, put it on the bed, and put her hands on Maura's shoulders. "Stop sulking, *chéri*. Okay, you went a little crazy, no big deal. He's handsome and has more charm than any ten people should. If you don't act on this, you'll always wonder what might have happened. So, take a shower, put on your amazing outfit, fix your hair, put on some makeup, and have a glass of wine to take the edge off. You're going to have fun. If the opportunity arises to have a one-night stand, *do it*! You may never get the chance again, and if it feels right and will relieve some of the sexual tension that's obviously built up over the past several years of your self-imposed sexual abstinence, for God's sake, woman, get some relief!"

Maura was shocked into total silence for a few seconds, and Anne, who was starting to wonder if she'd had temporary insanity and just made things worse, forced herself to stare at her friend, willing herself to keep her mouth shut, until Maura responded. Maura started giggling uncontrollably and then burst into sidesplitting laughter. She pushed Anne away exclaiming, "Now we have two crazies in the group! Did you really hear what you just said?"

Anne held up her hands as Maura reached out and hugged her. "I know you mean well, you crazy Cajun, but you know neither one of us would ever do something like that, and you're as lonely and sex-starved as I am."

Anne gave Maura a sheepish look.

"What?!" Maura demanded.

Anne laughed. "Do ya think I tell you every time a guy hits on me or I have a little casual sex? We're friends, but you're not my shrink or mother confessor, not that I'd ever talk to a priest or nun about crap like that!"

Maura smiled. "Okay, I deserved that, but if you don't mind, could you bring me up to speed on this secret life you obviously have … of course, if that's not being too nosy."

Anne groaned as she sat down on the bed. She motioned Maura to sit down as well. "Okay, a few months ago, I was at a hail and farewell, and an MP captain that's been after me for the past six months asked if I'd go out to dinner with him one weekend. I told him that you and I get together on Friday and Saturday. Then he said, 'Shit, you're a lesbo? You gotta be shittin' me.' I almost choked from laughing at his faulty deductive reasoning and told him, 'No, we're just good friends and I'm as normal as any other red-blooded American woman when it comes to liking guys.'"

"What'd he say?"

"He asked me if I was free for dinner that Sunday evening."

"And..."

"We went out to dinner that Sunday evening after you left for Goerp."

"So, are you still going out with him?"

"Yeah, we get together on Sunday evenings."

Surprised by this revelation, Maura raised her eyebrows. "So, is it serious? And thus far, no mention of sex. ... What's up on that front?"

Anne gave Maura a mock glare, followed by a lopsided grin. "No, it's not serious. If it were, I would have mentioned something to you. He's good-looking, nice, and fun to be with, but that's it. It's a nice diversion, and sometimes we meet at the O'Club on a Tuesday or Wednesday evening for dinner and chat, but we're both in agreement that while we enjoy each other's company, neither one of us is looking for a serious or long-term relationship."

"Okay, but I'm still not hearing anything about sex."

"Geesh, Maura, can't a girl get a little privacy?"

"Sure, a bit, but I wanna know how the sex happened and if it's still going on!"

Anne exhaled in mock resignation. "Well, if you insist." She continued, "It had been a typical cold, dreary, January day the first time we went out. I was depressed, lonely, and a bit nervous about having my first date, so I guess I drank too much wine."

"And ..." Maura encouraged.

"Well, not really certain what actually happened, but I guess I was a bit unsteady when we got back to my BOQ, and he insisted on unlocking my door and bringing me in. The next thing I know, he gives me a kiss goodbye and then things took off. Before I knew it, we were in bed, naked, exhausted from a long session, and I think I passed out."

Maura was laughing uncontrollably.

"Glad you find this so amusing," Anne said grumpily as she felt her cheeks blush from embarrassment.

Maura held up her hand, stopped laughing, and gently reassured her friend, "No, sweetheart, I'm just flabbergasted and actually a bit envious. Good for you! Did he spend the night?"

Anne blushed again. "Not sure and never asked. I woke up around seven that morning, saw the clock and my naked body. I was trying to remember what had happened the night before when I saw the note with my name on it, on the other pillow."

"What did it say?"

"Oh, something about having a great night and he'd call me at the office around four."

"Did he?"

"Yeah."

"C'mon, Anne. ... You're killin' me."

"He called me around four, told me he really enjoyed my company, loved that I wasn't sexually inhibited, which almost made me spit up the water I'd just taken a sip of, and said he'd pick me up at six for dinner at the O'Club. During dinner, he asked me if I'd enjoyed the sex and I told him I really couldn't tell him if I'd enjoyed the sex because I really couldn't remember anything clearly after he brought me inside my BOQ and kissed me goodnight."

Maura cracked up again and in between laughs managed to ask, "What did he say to that?"

"He grabbed his napkin and quickly brought it up to his face as he choked on the sip of beer he'd just taken. After wiping his mouth, he gaily announced that we'd just have to do it again so I could give him some feedback."

At that, Maura burst into uncontrollable laughter, grabbing her sides and gasping for breath. Realizing the absurdity of the scene she was portraying, Anne started laughing as well.

Wiping tears from her face, Maura managed to gasp, "And what was your response to that?"

"I thought about it for a sec and told him I'd consider that but I didn't normally meet a guy and have sex with him on the first date and wasn't looking for sex or a serious relationship, but if we could have a nice no-strings relationship that allowed for mutual respect and no speaking out of school about any sex we might decide to have, it might work."

By now, Maura was curled up in a ball of pain from the laughter. She was making so much noise that Amelia walked in and with a look of concern asked uncertainly, "Are you okay? What's going on?"

Maura just nodded and continued to howl.

With a bit of irritation evident in her voice, Anne whispered curtly, "Close the door and come in."

Amelia closed the door and asked again, "What in the world is going on here? You should see the looks on Lori and Trish's faces. They're speechless and nervous, and I'm just stunned. Maura, get yourself under control," Amelia hissed.

Maura managed to get her laughter quieted down to a low whimper and, after what seemed an eternity, finally said cheerfully, "Anne's just trying to cheer me up, and she succeeded beyond either of our wildest expectations."

Irritated, Amelia scolded both of them. "Really, ladies, those poor kids out there are probably afraid there's a lunatic in here, and they just don't know what to do! We're supposed to be setting a good example for them." At that, Anne and Maura looked at each other and, despite trying to be serious, gave up after just a few seconds, much to Amelia's dismay, and both burst into sidesplitting laughter.

Maura got up from the bed, still laughing, walked to the door, opened it, and went out into the living room, where Lori and Trish looked like two deer caught in the headlights of a car. Putting herself in their place, Maura realized she had a lot of explaining to do. She motioned for them to follow her, and when she got to the kitchen and opened the fridge, she casually asked them, "You guys want some juice or soda?"

Lori and Trish, who were feeling very out of place, simultaneously shook their heads.

"Okay," Maura said as she got a glass and poured some juice into it. "Have a seat." After putting the juice bottle back in the fridge, she sat down at the table. "I'm really sorry about today. I can't really explain or excuse my behavior, and you're probably wondering if someone needs to call the guys in the white jackets to take me away, but Anne was trying to cheer me up, and she did, but perhaps a bit too much."

Lori and Trish just nodded, unsure what, if anything, they should say or do. Realizing there wasn't anything else she could say, Maura asked, "Are we cool?" Lori and Trish looked at each other first and then nodded at her. Maura finished off her juice and stood up. "Okay, now we all need to change and get ready for a fun evening on the town."

She walked back to her bedroom, where she found Anne and Amelia deep in conversation. Closing the door behind her, Maura announced, "Thanks for loving me just as I am. Let's get ready and have a nice fun weekend. Lori and Trish are a bit shell-shocked, but I think they'll get over it. And if they don't, so be it. I'm headed in for a shower. I told Lori and Trish to get ready, suggest both of you do likewise."

ABOUT AN HOUR LATER, Amelia, Anne, Trish, and Lori were sitting in the living room, waiting for Maura to finish dressing and for their escorts to arrive. When Maura walked out, the sight of her in the dress she'd bought earlier that day took their breath away. Trish exclaimed involuntarily, "Wow, Maura, you're beautiful."

Lori nodded, and then thoughtfully added, "You should have been a model."

Anne laughed, "Have you arranged for a police escort? You're gonna start a riot when you walk into the club tonight."

Embarrassed by the attention, Maura waved her hand. "Thanks, guys. You look great too." Noticing open beer bottles in front of Lori and Trish and wine in front of Anne and Amelia, Maura hesitantly asked, "Am I allowed some if I promise to be good?"

Amelia pushed an empty wine glass toward Maura. "Your glass has been waiting for you." Relieved, Maura smiled and poured half a glass. The women spent the next fifteen minutes complimenting each other on how they looked. All of the women were wearing platform heels, but that's where the similarities ended. Trish looked sleek and athletic in a black halter-top jersey jumpsuit and black sandals. Lori was dressed in a classy blue, green, and cream paisley top with navy slacks. Anne was stunning in a gossamer sleeveless gray, black, and red paisley top and black silk bell-bottom pants, and Amelia was dressed in a violet strapless jumpsuit with a white linen short-sleeved blouse with a gold and violet fan design on the right side of the jacket.

The women had just finished their drinks when the doorbell rang. "You guys head to the door. I'm just going to put everything in the sink in the kitchen and will join you in a sec," Amelia said.

Anne whispered to Maura, "You get the door." Maura hesitated momentarily, then strode to the front door. When she opened the door, Eric, who was wearing tight-fitting white linen slacks, a black silk tee shirt, and a gray-and-white-flecked sport coat, opened his mouth slightly, raised his eyebrows, and exhaled loudly at the sight of Maura. He whispered, "Wow."

Pleased at his reaction, Maura smiled. "Glad you approve. Come in, we're almost ready." Eric motioned for the two good-looking men behind him to come in. Anne and Lori went a bit slack-jawed at the sight of the two guys, who looked like they'd just stepped out of a New York nightclub or a southern California beach. Amelia, who had just come into the living room from the kitchen, and Trish seemed to be the only two not affected by the three strikingly good-looking men, who would be their dates that evening.

"Ladies," Eric said as he pointed, "Russ and Alan." Pointing to each of the women in turn, he announced, "Guys, this is Maura, Anne, Lori, Trish, and of course you both know Amelia." After the brief introductions, he added, "We have three taxis outside waiting. Each of us will be in a taxi, and you ladies can split up as you see fit. We're taking you to one of Berlin's hottest nightspots. It's a rooftop discotheque on Kudamm, with an ass-kicking DJ."

Amelia declared, "Okay, meters are running on those taxis and the night is wasting away. Let's get going. Anne, you and Trish go with Alan, Lori and I'll go with Russ. Maura, are you okay going alone with Eric? He's got quite the reputation."

Maura smiled mischievously at Amelia, thrilled that her friend was giving her the opportunity to be alone with Eric for a while, and responded quietly, "That'll be fine."

★ ★ ★

ERIC OPENED THE BACK door of the taxi for her, closed the door, walked over to the other side of the cab, and got in. The taxi drivers took off, apparently aware of their final destination.

They were barely out the gate of Clay Barracks when Eric said, "Maura, tell me a bit about yourself."

Not sure she could talk at length calmly, she replied, "Sure, but how about you telling me a bit about yourself first."

"Okay. I'm an Army brat, so technically, I'm from nowhere specific. I was born at Fort Devens, Mass. When I was five, my dad was posted to West Berlin. From there, he got selected to attend the junior class at the Navy War College in Newport, Rhode Island. He did a few years at the Pentagon and we lived in Arlington. His first assignment as a colonel was the embassy in Vienna, followed by another tour in the Pentagon. By that time, I'd graduated from high school and got accepted to Georgetown. To keep from getting drafted, I joined ROTC and was commissioned as a Field Artillery second lieutenant in 1960. What about you?"

"Lived in Manhattan my whole life, went to college there, and the first time I left home, I went to ROTC advanced camp at Fort Bragg. I was commissioned in '76 as a Chemical Corps officer and assigned to Seventh Corps."

"Where in Seventh Corps?"

"1st IDF, in Göppingen."

"You mean like the 1st Infantry Division?"

"Yep, that's the one. No mission too difficult, no sacrifice too great, if you're gonna be one, be a Big Red *One*, duty first!"

Eric threw his head back, laughing. "Wow, not sure what to say to that. You're really into that?"

Maura frowned. "Not really, but they are, and if you're going to be accepted, you just play the game."

"My old man wanted me to go combat arms, so I did, but I told him that someday I'd have to stop being a soldier and do something else. I liked the idea of being a spook of sorts, so when it came time for me to choose an additional specialty, I chose MI, which is how I got considered for this assignment."

"If you don't mind me saying this, you look awfully young to be a full bull."

"Actually, I'm still a lieutenant colonel." Seeing the confused look on Maura's face, he added, "I got picked up for major, lieutenant colonel, and colonel below the zone and then got picked up for this command before my sequence number for promotion to full colonel came up, so they frocked me."

"Below the zone and frocked you? I don't know what that means," Maura said uncertainly.

"Yeah, sorry, I forget you're a lieutenant. When you get considered for field-grade promotion, you get three looks. The first look is at about nine years of active duty, which is your below-the-zone look. Second look is the next year, and if you make it, you are promoted in zone. If you get passed over on your in-the-zone look, you have a third chance, called an above-the-zone look. Most people get promoted during their *in-the-zone* look, but a few get promoted below or above the zone."

"So you're what they call *high speed?*" Maura asked.

"Yeah, guess so. Think I just got a bit lucky to have some really great jobs and did well in them."

"Did you see combat in Vietnam?"

Maura could see him visibly tense up as he replied quietly, "Yeah. ..."

"Sorry if that question made you uncomfortable. I know it wasn't a popular war and you probably took a lot of heat from friends."

Eric didn't respond for a second, turning to look out the window. After a short but uncomfortable silence, he turned back to her and said quietly, tersely, "Not something I talk about or like thinking about. Okay, let's change the subject. ..."

Shit! Maura thought. *Good job, Maura. How do you dig yourself out of this hole?*

Realizing he'd made her feel uncomfortable, Eric forced a smile and said, "I'm surprised they sent you to an infantry unit. You mentioned the 1st IDF. I thought the 1st Infantry Division was at Fort Riley in Kansas."

Relieved at the change in subject, Maura quickly replied, "The headquarters and two of the three brigades are in Kansas, but I'm in the brigade that is forward-deployed to Seventh Corps. So far as I know, it is the only forward-deployed reinforced infantry brigade in the Army. The CG and other staff make a big deal about being assigned there."

"Hmm, I didn't know women were being assigned to combat units, let alone a brigade. Surely there aren't a lot of you. ..." He trailed off as he realized his remarks could be construed as disparaging.

Maura interjected quickly, relieved that she was not the only one that evening who had made an uncomfortable remark, "All I know is I'm there and guess I'm an experiment."

"Are there any other women assigned there?"

"Yes. A few months after I arrived, a female JAG and MI officer were assigned to the brigade, but I was the first female to be assigned there, and to say that I was not welcome would be akin to calling an earthquake a naturally occurring environmental phenomenon."

Eric laughed heartily. "Somehow I get the feeling that you dealt with it pretty well."

Maura smiled wryly. "Well, not sure anyone could deal with what I encountered well, but I had a little bit of support and they got my dander up from the start, and the Irish in me just wouldn't allow me to accept that."

Eric chuckled loudly. "Okay, I gotta hear this one."

Maura told him what the CG had said to her, adding that when the CG had seen her outrun all of the staff and help the two other females, he had reluctantly accepted her as a trooper and life had gotten a lot easier after that. Maura was pleased to see the look of admiration on Eric's face as she finished her story.

"I'm impressed, Maura." Hesitating, he added, "I've gotta share with you that I'm of the opinion that women don't belong in combat units, but you've got my respect. I knew there were changes to what women were allowed to do but had no idea it had progressed this far. I realize that I'm totally out of touch with what's going on in the mainstream Army. Do you like being there? Do you want to be there?"

Maura thought for a second before answering, "I never really thought about it. I mean, they sent me there and I had to make the best of it. Now that I think about it, I would have preferred not to be assigned there, but I was, and because I know there are women who will want to be assigned to combat units, I feel a responsibility to ensure I do well enough so they have that option."

Eric shook his head. "That's a lot to put on the shoulders of a young lieutenant."

"Okay," Maura interjected a bit stridently, "Now it's my turn to feel a bit uncomfortable and ask if we can change the subject. I'm just like any other woman, nothing special."

Eric grinned as he shook his head. "No, Maura, you are special, and for the first time, I'm reminded of how young you really are. Sorry you got stuck with the old guy, but you are absolutely stunning, and I've no doubt Russ and Alan are going to fight over who gets to dance with you first."

Maura couldn't believe what she said next. "What if I don't want them to fight over me and prefer to spend the evening dancing with and getting to know you?" she asked hesitantly.

Eric exhaled loudly and beamed. "Then I'd say it's my lucky night and I'll gladly pull rank!"

Maura smiled. "Lovely. I'm looking forward to a fun night on the town."

Their cab arrived at the night club as Maura said this. Eric paid the cab driver, got out, went around and opened the door, and helped Maura out of the cab as the other two cabs arrived and everyone got out.

11

BERLIN, SATURDAY EVENING 1 July 1978

AS THEY WALKED IN the club, it was apparent to the women that the three guys were regulars and were well-liked. The owner had reserved a private curtained side room for their party, and a number of amazing-looking German women came up occasionally to flirt with the three guys, who were so busy trying to ensure that everyone got to dance that they didn't have time to say more than hi to the German women as they took another of their five escorts to the dance floor.

Eric had taken Trish to dance and Russ and Alan were dancing with Anne and Lori as Amelia and Maura sat at the table, sipping wine and taking a break. This was the first time all night that it was just the two of them at the table, and Amelia asked, "How's it going? Having fun?"

"Yeah," Maura replied dreamily. "He's amazing."

Amelia frowned. "It has not escaped my notice that you've only danced with him and are ignoring Russ and Alan. Just remember, from all accounts, he's not the settling-down type."

"Nothing to worry about, Amelia. I'll probably never see him again. I mean Göppingen is a long way from Berlin. I'm a big girl, no illusions, just enjoying it." They spent the next few minutes watching the others dance to "Boogie Fever."

At the end of the dance, everyone sat down to enjoy their drinks. All night, whenever a slow dance came up, everyone sat at the table, taking a short break, and enjoying their drinks until the next fast dance selection came on.

Barry White's "You're My First, My Last, My Everything" was playing. Eric sat next to Maura and whispered, "Wanna dance?" She nodded silently. He took her hand, and without a word, they walked out on to the dance floor. As he took her in his arms, she buried her face between one of his hard, massive shoulders and strong neck. She could feel his warm breath just above her ear, as he softly caressed her back. She closed her eyes and succumbed to the pleasant tingling that being next to his body evoked.

After a few moments, she smiled in a mixture of surprise and satisfaction as she felt his erection. He gently moaned and nibbled her ear. Maura ceased to hear the music or to be aware of anyone or anything except his warm, hard body close to hers. When the song ended, they kept moving rhythmically together, not wanting the dance to be over, but after a few seconds, Eric pulled away, looking down at her ruefully and smiling.

They went back to the table, and Amelia told Eric, it was her turn to dance with him. He nodded and took her to the dance floor. Alan and Lori followed them.

When Russ asked Anne to dance, she demurred. "I'm gonna sit this one out, cowboy. Trish, take this crazy boy and wear his butt out on the dance floor for a bit."

Shortly after Trish and Russ had left the table, Anne moved over to sit next to Maura and sternly admonished her, "Okay, *chéri*, that dance out there was a bit steamy. What the hell were you thinking?"

Maura raised her hand, refusing to look at Anne or respond to her comment. She knew Anne was right, but a jumble of conflicting thoughts and emotions were swirling through her head. The only reality she'd had during that dance had been of her and Eric; the rest of the world had ceased to exist. When the music had stopped, it had jarred her back into reality, but she hadn't wanted to break off the physical contact they'd made. When Eric had reluctantly pushed her away, he'd whispered, "I know this is wrong, but I don't care."

Maura was still embarrassed by her wanton behavior but felt anger at Anne's admonishment. Knowing Anne was right, and with a great deal of difficulty, she pushed the anger away and turned to look at Anne, who was glaring at her. Maura glared back and tersely replied, "You don't get the right to take me to task or judge me."

Anne was surprised by Maura's sharp reply and took a second before responding. "I'm not judging you. I'm trying to get you to focus and do a reality check. He's a colonel, for God's sake! I hear you wanna get laid, and if he's the one, that's okay, but be discreet about it."

Still angry, Maura snapped, "I'm a big girl; I can take care of myself."

Anne sighed and replied in a resigned tone, "Look, I'm just trying to be the friend I'd want you to be to me if the situation was reversed. I don't know about you, but I haven't had a lot of experience with guys, and if I were in your situation, I'd be scared as hell. You do realize that you'll probably never see him again?"

That admission was more than Maura could handle, and she blurted, "Well, at least you've had sex before!"

Anne's eyes grew wide, and she exclaimed, "Oh my God, Maura, you aren't—"

Maura cut her off angrily. "Don't say it!"

Anne took a large gulp of wine and quietly asked, "You've never done it?"

Maura silently shook her head and a few seconds later burst into hysterical laughter. "I know, bizarre isn't it?! I mean, how many twenty-three-year-old virgins do you think still exist in this crazy world?!" Seeing the look of consternation on Anne's face, Maura reached out and hugged her friend. "I don't expect an answer, goofball!"

Anne replied in a mortified tone, "Maura, I had no idea. I'm so sorry!"

With a mischievous grin, Maura asked, "What are you sorry about? That I'm a virgin or that you forced that admission out of me?"

Anne flopped back in her chair and stared wide-eyed at Maura, who gave her another hug and said, "It's okay. Yeah, I've kept that a secret because I'm just not comfortable talking about it."

Anne asked quietly, "You mean no one's ever tried?"

That sent Maura into a paroxysm of laughter. "Sure, a couple of guys tried during college, but I don't take birth control, and I guess all my years at parochial school and constant admonishment from my mom about boys not marrying girls that give it away, along with the church's stance on birth control and sexual abstinence …" Maura's voice trailed off as she struggled for words to explain further.

Anne took her off the hook by saying, "Well, *chéri*, he ain't no sweet college boy, and after a certain point, there won't be any stopping it."

"I know," Maura said seriously as she took another sip of wine. "But for the first time in my life, I don't care about the church, my mother's ideas, or the Army's rules. If he asked me, I'd do it in a heartbeat and love every minute of it."

Anne shook her head. "Well, luckily, there's no way it'll happen tonight, so I'll just hope that you can dodge this bullet. But the group is coming back, so we'll have to leave things as they are."

For the rest of the evening, the three guys took turns dancing with the five women. Eric surprised Maura by asking Anne to dance with him for the next dance. Maura danced with both Russ and Alan a few times before Eric asked her to dance again. Maura decided to just try to enjoy dancing with him; he never said another personal word to her and didn't ask her to dance the final two slow dances that evening.

It was around 0200 when Amelia announced that it had been fun but they really should call it a night. Eric got two taxis to take the women home. As they got into the taxis, the women thanked the guys for such a great time. All were quiet on the short ride back to their quarters.

BACK AT THE DVQ, Lori and Trish thanked Amelia, Maura, and Anne for a really fun day and immediately went to sleep.

Maura looked at Anne and Amelia. "You guys go to sleep. I'm still a bit wound up." Looking at Anne, she added, "I'll get ready for bed now so when I do come to bed, I won't wake you up."

"Are you sure?" Anne asked. "I can stay up with you if you want company."

Before Maura could say no, Amelia announced, "I'll make some tea and we can sit and chat for a bit," and headed toward the kitchen. Maura and

Anne followed, and a few minutes later, they were all sitting down with hot cups of tea. There was a bit of an awkward silence. In an effort to fill it, Maura pointed out that she had never seen an electric tea kettle and was surprised at how much quicker it was at heating water than a metal kettle on the stove.

Amelia agreed. "I know, it's ingenious."

Maura abruptly said, "You guys don't need to worry about me; I'm fine."

"Anything you want to talk about?" Amelia asked cautiously.

Maura took another sip of tea and looked directly at Amelia. "No. Anne already read me the riot act about the slow dance with the colonel, and I can only imagine what you probably want to—but won't say to me, so if you've got something you want to get off your chest, let's get it over with so we can all get back to being comfortable with each other and have a fun weekend together."

Amelia hesitated before responding, "Aside from the fraternization issue, I'm just concerned about you, Maura. He has a horrible reputation for sleeping with every and any woman he can and has left a string of broken hearts all over Berlin. I just don't want you to get hurt or do something you'll regret."

Maura laughed. "Yes, Mother, I know."

A look of irritation briefly crossed Amelia's face, and Maura remarked, "Nothing to worry about. After that dance, he pretty much ignored me the rest of the night and only danced with me two more times and didn't say a word to me during those two dances."

Amelia exhaled loudly. "You can blame me for that."

Maura gave Amelia a startled look as she asked, "Why would you say that?"

"Because, if you recall, he didn't ask me to dance. I told him to take me out to the dance floor. I was furious with him for that display and told him you were off limits."

Startled by Anne bursting into uproarious laughter at Amelia's admission, Maura first looked at Anne and then turned to address Amelia. "What in the world did you say to him, Amelia, and for God's sake, *why* did you feel it was your place to tell him I was off limits?"

Amelia replied defensively, "I just don't want you to do something stupid or get hurt."

Maura inhaled sharply before responding. "Well that just beats all, Amelia! I know you meant well, but you've really pissed me off! All I did was support you when you confided in me that you still wanted things to work out with you and Charles, even though I feel like Anne does, that you deserve far better. Then you meet Mattias and I take Anne to task for berating you for continuing to defend Charles—" Maura stopped midsentence, realizing Amelia was about to burst into tears.

Walking over to Amelia, Maura gave her a gentle whack on the shoulder. "That's for pissing me off, Amelia. Now stop with the quivering lip, and no waterworks tonight." She paused, then added more gently, "I know you meant well—and aw, hell, nothing was going to come of this anyway, so we're good. Just don't ever do anything like this again! Okay?"

Amelia nodded.

"Okay," Anne interjected, "how 'bout we call it a night and get some shut-eye?"

Amelia motioned to Anne and Maura to stay seated, and then she said, "I was going to wait until tomorrow when the cadets were at the castle to tell you this, but this is as good a time as any to tell you my news."

Maura and Anne raised their eyebrows but said nothing.

Amelia spent the next few minutes telling them about Charles calling at Christmas, her decision to take him back, and his upcoming visit the next month. When she finished, Maura and Anne sat speechless.

A few seconds later, Anne got up.

"Where are you going?" Amelia asked.

"To sleep," Anne said resignedly.

"That's it?" Amelia asked.

"Not sure what you expected, Amelia. You just told us that you made a major life decision over six months ago and are just now informing us of that decision. You didn't call us when all this happened, you didn't ask for our advice. You've made up your mind and let us know your decision. Congratulations! I'm going to sleep." Anne walked off.

Amelia was furious and vented to Maura, "Can you believe that?"

"Believe what, Amelia?" Maura asked tersely. "That Anne is hurt because in your weekly phone calls with her, you never mentioned Charles called, let alone that he wanted to get together, and you agreed to that, and he'll be here next month for a visit? While I'm a bit hurt too, I haven't been your best friend for the past six years, so I can be less emotional about it, but friends confide in friends on the important stuff, and quite frankly, you screwed the pooch on this one, Amelia."

Amelia was tempted to tell Maura she had no right to talk to her that way, but she realized Maura was right. Anne and Maura had always been there for her, and she should have talked to them. Amelia reached for the open bottle of wine and acknowledged that. "You're right, of course. I never really thought of it as keeping things from you and Anne. I just wasn't ready to talk about it because I'm still a mess over all this. I finally gave up on Charles and was happy with Mattias. If Charles had not been so obstinate, we could have spared ourselves and others a lot of hurt and sleepless nights."

Maura gasped. "Oh my God, Amelia, I totally forgot how this would affect Mattias. Please tell me you told him!"

Amelia took another sip of wine before replying. "I did. ... It was one of the hardest, saddest moments in my life. Even harder than accepting that Charles and I were over."

Maura reached for the wine bottle and filled her own glass. "How did he take it?"

Amelia spent the next fifteen minutes telling Maura every detail of that horrible day and ended by saying, "I told him it wouldn't be fair for him to fight for me, because, while I care deeply for him, I'm not sure that I love him, with the 'til-death-do-us-part type of love that he deserves."

Maura reached out to take Amelia's hand. "I can't tell you I agree with your decision, but I don't have the right to tell you that you made a bad decision, either. I know you'll figure out a way to make it right with Anne."

Amelia nodded.

Maura got up and started clearing the table she noticed the clock on the wall said four o'clock. "We need some sleep. What time do Lori and Trish need to be at the palace?"

"Their tour starts at noon."

Maura asked, "How 'bout I take them on the U-Bahn? It'll take me about an hour to drop them off and get back. You can talk to Anne while I'm gone."

"Sounds good," Amelia said.

"See you in the morning." Maura said, walking away.

12

BERLIN, SUNDAY 2 JULY 1978

MAURA WOKE TO THE smell of freshly brewed coffee and sound of laughter coming from the kitchen. Languidly getting out of bed, she walked into the kitchen to see the other women setting the table. Walking up to the counter, she poured a cup of coffee. Turning to look at the table that had been set with bacon, a steaming bowl of scrambled eggs, fruit salad, fresh pastries, brötchen, butter, several jars of jam, and a large stick of butter. She said, "Mornin', ladies. You sure we have enough food?"

Anne replied, "Don't know about you, but we're starving, so while you and Amelia slept in, we found the goodies Amelia bought at the bakery yesterday, raided the fridge, and found OJ, a dozen eggs, bacon, and lots of fresh fruit. You arrived just in time to join us."

Maura took a gulp of coffee and looked over toward the empty couch. "Where's Amelia?"

"In Lori and Trish's bathroom. She didn't want to wake you up," Anne replied.

"Okay," Maura mumbled. As she turned to go into Lori and Trish's room to find Amelia, Amelia walked out.

"Good mornin'," Amelia said, a lot more gaily than she felt. She was feeling nervous about how Anne was going to deal with her today. She poured a cup of coffee as she said, "I see you ladies found the breakfast goodies."

"Thanks for getting such a great selection of yummy food!" Trish exclaimed. We're always in such a rush during the week that breakfast in Stuttgart is usually a Carnation breakfast shake or Pop-Tart. We're used to large hot breakfasts every morning at West Point, and until today, I didn't realize how much of a treat that really is."

Lori added, "And we have all the time in the world to eat as slowly as we want."

"Absolutely," Amelia said. "We don't have to leave until eleven. Eat as much as you want."

Lori and Trish nodded. Their mouths were full.

The five women sat eating for the next twenty minutes without saying a word. Trish and Lori, oblivious to the tension between Maura, Anne, and Amelia, happily devoured their breakfast. As Lori reached for a second glass of juice, she noticed the bottle was almost empty. "Amelia, I feel bad. We've just about killed this entire quart of OJ. Is this all you have?"

Amelia smiled. "Yes, but I can pick more up tomorrow. I obviously didn't know how much juice you all drink, but I do have some German apple juice for breakfast tomorrow.

Lori asked, "Do you have any of the sparkling mineral water?"

Amelia, surprised by this request, responded, "Sure."

Maura interjected, "I've hooked her on *Apfelsaft* shorlies."

Trish mumbled, trying to swallow her last bit of brötchen, "Apfel what?"

Lori answered excitedly, "Oh, Trish, I thought you knew about them. It's a combination of sparkling mineral water and apple juice. It's so refreshing, sort of like ginger ale, but it's apple ale. You'll love it!"

Amelia got up and pulled out a small note pad from the writing desk in the DVQ living room. "Okay, I have two quarts of OJ, and from the looks of it, we'll need more brötchen, pastries, bacon, and fruit. Anything else?"

"Would you mind getting some Tab?" Lori quietly asked.

Amelia added Tab to her list. "Okay, how about you guys get ready while I clean up. Maura will take you to the palace."

Lori and Trish nodded happily and headed to their room. Amelia started clearing the table as Maura got up to pour a cup of coffee and Anne walked into the bedroom.

Amelia walked over to Maura. "Obviously, this is a bit more serious than I thought, and I hate to put you in the middle, but I'd appreciate it if you'd let me take Trish and Lori to the palace and you talk to Anne, while I'm gone. Please ask her to figure out a way to get over this. We haven't seen each other since last Thanksgiving, and I'm not sure when we'll get together again, so when I return, I'd just like her to get whatever is on her chest off, so we can move on and have a nice weekend together. Lori and Trish have not caught on that there's a problem yet, but if Anne keeps up this foolishness, they will."

Almost as if on cue, Lori and Trish came out of the bedroom. "Little change in plans," Maura announced. "Amelia's going to take you guys to the palace."

In a few minutes, they were gone and Maura headed into the bedroom to find Anne sitting on the bed, reading a paperback. "Wanna take a walk?" she asked.

Looking up from her book, Anne responded disdainfully, "Not particularly."

"Okay, sourpuss, enough of the silent treatment. My mission between now and when Amelia returns is to get you to figure out what you want to say to Amelia so the two of you can kiss and make up."

Anne closed her book and put it on the nightstand as she stood up and faced Maura. "I don't want to talk about it."

"Okay, I know you're angry and I'm guessing hurt by Amelia not confiding in you, but she's your best friend. We both agree Charles is a butthole, but she loves him. She loves us too, and you'll only alienate Amelia if you keep this up. She's truly sorry and is ready to take whatever you decide to dish out, but if you don't work this out now, she'll leave the Army, marry butthole, and you'll never hear from her again. Is that how you want this to play out?"

Anne shook her head. "I get it, Maura. Not sure there's anything I can or should say, but I'll let her know we're good." Anne picked up her book and walked out to the living room.

When Amelia walked through the door about an hour later, she found Anne and Maura sitting in the living room reading. "Hey, you two, it's a bit after noon, and given that none of us ate much—" Looking directly at Maura, she added, "or for that matter, ate anything—I thought it might be nice to head to the Tiergarten, have a nice lunch, then all of us can go pick the girls up from the palace."

Maura looked over at Anne questioningly.

"Sounds good," Anne said as she got up from her chair and headed to the bedroom. "I'll be ready in a few."

Amelia looked over at Maura and silently mouthed, *Are we good?* Maura responded by wiping the back of her hand across her forehead and smiling.

Half an hour later, they were all seated at an open-air café between the U-Bahn station and the entrance to the Tiergarten, Berlin's famed urban park, not far from the Brandenburg Gate separating East and West Berlin. They'd each just ordered bratwurst, fries, and wine.

This was one of Amelia's favorite spots. The sound of birds gaily singing mixed seamlessly with the dull rumble of nearby trains pulling into and leaving from the nearby U-Bahn station.

Feeling relaxed for the first time that day, Amelia quietly murmured, "Thank you Anne. I'm so sorry I've made you angry. I just didn't know how to bring all this up in our weekly telephone conversations and figured I'd just tell both of you whenever we got together again. If I can do anything to make this up to you, just let me know."

Anne smiled mischievously. "You could write Charles a Dear Dickhead letter and tell him you had temporary insanity but are over it now and tell him to get a life."

Amelia didn't know how to respond to this sort of sarcasm and just looked at Anne, dumfounded and silent.

Anne laughed. "Close your mouth, Amelia. Obviously, my attempt at humor fell flat. You didn't make me angry. ... I'm really not sure what you made me, and now that I've had some time to think things over, I understand your reluctance to tell me about this over the phone. I'm not happy, because I just think Charles is going to disappoint and hurt you, and you deserve better than that." Seeing a look of momentary irritation cross Amelia's face, Anne added, "I know, we're never goin' to see this the same way, but I want you to know that I will always have your back and will always be your friend, and I hope you feel the same way."

Amelia felt the momentary anger she'd felt at Anne's disparaging remarks melt away. She knew Anne was trying to make up with her and to accept her decision, and she also knew that while she loved Charles, there would be bumpy times ahead, and it helped her to know that Anne would always be there. In an effort to lighten the mood, she replied sardonically, "It's so comforting to know that if I do need a shoulder to cry on, you'll provide one, after you tell me *I told you so.* Thank you, Anne."

Now it was Anne and Maura's turn to stare at Amelia with mouths wide open in shock. "Wow," Maura exclaimed. "That was real conciliatory, Amelia! Geesh, I can't believe you two. Enough of this Southern witch routine; you two need to get over this!"

Amelia smirked as she reached over to hug Anne. "Sorry. The devil made me do it. I do love you, and you will always be my very best friend, and I do need and want you in my life."

Anne grinned. "We're good, and I can take as good as I give."

They spent the next hour eating, laughing, and relaxing, relieved that they had managed to put their disagreement aside and had returned to their normal friendly banter.

They met Trish and Lori outside the gate of Charlottenburg Palace after lunch and listened to the happy voices of the two young women describing how much they'd learned about the palace. After arriving back at the apartment, Amelia announced, "Okay, we're supposed to be at the brigade commander's house for a cookout at 1800, so if anyone needs a shower and change of clothing, this would be a good time."

★ ★ ★

LORI AND TRISH MET the brigade commander and his wife, along with other staff members and their families. They had a relaxing evening eating pork ribs, corn on the cob, and coleslaw, and took turns crowded around the large grill, making s'mores for dessert. After thanking their hosts for a fun evening, they decided it was too early to go home, so they went to the O'Club annex and sang along to the songs playing on the jukebox while drinking beer and wine. The base shuttle bus dropped them off about a block from the DVQ, and as they walked home, they sang the Paul Simon hit "Fifty Ways to Leave Your Lover."

13

BERLIN, TUESDAY 4 JULY 1978

IT WAS A BUSY morning for everyone. Amelia took her four guests to the Templehof terminal to sign up for their flight back to Rhein-Main, and then they ate breakfast when they returned to the DVQ. Lori and Trish thanked the officers for the weekend, which had included a tour of the famous Berlin Zoo and lunch at an outdoor café the previous day, followed by a walk along 17 Juni Straße to Victory Circle, coming back into the Tiergarten.

Amelia cleaned up from breakfast while the other women finished packing. While Anne checked on Lori and Trish, Maura asked Amelia, "What time do you want to head out for the parade?"

"The parade starts at noon, but there'll be a huge crowd and I'd like to get a decent place along the parade route so you can take a few pictures." Amelia mused, "It's about a fifteen-minute walk to headquarters, so we should leave around eleven fifteen."

A little before noon, the five women stood at the curb just across from the headquarters, which gave them a great view of the reviewing stand as well as the street the formation would march down. Standing on the edge of the sidewalk, Amelia pointed down the street, where they could see the Army band, and unit formations lined up. "In a few minutes, they'll march down this street and in front of the headquarters building onto the 4 Ring to do a pass in review. Then we'll walk over to the Harnack House for lunch and relax, until it's time for you guys to go to the airfield."

Trish asked quietly, her voice critical, "They let local Germans come on post?"

"Yes," Amelia replied. "This is a big deal for the local community, so we open the kaserne to the general public for the parade, along with a number of local dignitaries and allied power commanders, who sit on the reviewing stand."

"Do they stay for food and Fourth-of-July fireworks?"

"The majority of the Germans will have to leave at the end of the parade, but the dignitaries on the reviewing stand will attend the picnic at Harnack House," Amelia replied.

Just then, the wind carried the sound of a single drumbeat. "Here they come," Trish announced.

It was an impressive sight as the drum major with his long staff held out high came marching toward them. All they could hear was the sound of a single drum beating in time to the marching cadence and the sound of boots rhythmically hitting the pavement in unison. Then the band starting playing. As the color guard and first units passed by, they heard the rumble of the tanks and artillery pieces that followed the marching units. As the color guard approached, the Americans came to attention and saluted the flag.

The five women gazed at the spectacle in awe and pride. The soldiers were in their dress uniforms, with shiny metal helmets painted black, infantry blue ascots around their necks, and pants tucked and bloused outside shiny black Corcoran jump boots. The tanks and other military vehicles and equipment that passed before them were so clean and shiny they looked like they'd just come off the assembly line.

"Gosh, this is great. I've always been proud to be an American soldier, but this takes it to a new level," Trish said reverentially.

"I felt exactly the same way the first time I saw it," Amelia said. "I still respect how much time and effort is put into this and all the parades we do, but I envy you the feelings you are experiencing now, seeing all of this for the first time. It is truly an honor to be assigned here."

The five women watched the entire parade and, along with all the other spectators lining the sidewalk, clapped as the units came by. When the parade concluded, Amelia silently motioned for the other four women to follow her.

They walked behind the headquarters to the Harnack House. It was already crowded with the VIPs, who were lining up for food and drinks. They went through the buffet line, which had cheeseburgers and hamburgers, hot dogs, grilled chicken, potato salad, coleslaw, corn on the cob, and hush puppies. Tables were also set up with nonalcoholic beverages and various desserts, including an ice cream bar with cones and small bowls, to accommodate different tastes. Everything was included in one price, with the exception of beer and wine, which could be purchased at one of several bars set up at various locations around the Harnack House terrace.

After filling their plates and getting something to drink, the small group of women found an open six-person picnic table on the edge of the lawn and sat down. Surveying the picnic tables that had white, red, or blue tablecloths set with cloth napkins and real silverware, Lori remarked, "This is the fanciest picnic I've ever attended."

They had just finished eating and were debating whether they wanted more beer and wine or if they were going to make ice cream sundaes when they heard a familiar male voice ask, "Is this seat open?"

Glancing over, they saw Eric, looking impossibly gorgeous in tan linen slacks and a seafoam green shirt, opened to his chest, where a bit of hair was visible. Amelia looked questioningly at Maura, who indicated she was okay with Eric joining them. Eric sat down in the open seat next to Maura and asked Lori and Trish if they'd enjoyed the weekend. They told him they had and talked almost nonstop for ten minutes.

As an awkward silence set in, Amelia said, "Well I don't know about you guys, but there's an ice cream sundae calling my name. Anyone else?" With that, Amelia, Lori, and Trish headed to the ice cream bar.

Looking at Eric and Maura, Anne announced, "I'm gonna head to the bar for another beer. Can I get you something?"

"I'd like a beer," Eric said. "Would you like another wine, Maura?" he asked as he reached for his wallet. Maura nodded yes, and Anne motioned Eric to put his wallet away. "I've got this round. You paid for all the drinks the other night; let us treat you today."

When Anne left, Eric turned to look at Maura, pushing away a stray strand of hair that a sudden breeze had pushed over the front of her forehead. "I'm sorry I didn't say a proper goodnight to you the other night. I started to come over several times yesterday, but Amelia read me the riot act on the dance floor, so I stayed away. But when I saw you today, I just decided the hell with it, I'm going to tell you that you're exciting and I really can't put into words what I'm feeling, I just know that I want to see you again."

Giving a huge sigh of relief at the realization that she had not inadvertently done something to turn Eric off, Maura looked at him longingly, trying to etch the memory of his face in her mind. "I was so afraid I'd done something to upset you when you turned a cold shoulder to me the rest of the evening. I didn't say anything because I was embarrassed by my behavior on the dance floor and figured it had been some sort of test that I'd failed miserably." Then with a bit of irritation in her voice, she added, "It never occurred to me that Amelia would threaten you."

Laughing, Eric admitted, "Yeah, me neither. I've never seen that side of her before, but she was like a momma bear, and quite frankly, I was a bit afraid of what she might do."

Maura chuckled. "Yeah, a lot of people underestimate our sweet Amelia, but she's a lot tougher than most people give her credit for."

"Well, I expect I'll get a phone call from her tomorrow morning at the office demanding to know what we talked about."

"No you won't. I'm going to tell her that you and I had a talk and we both agreed that while there is certainly a mutual attraction, we're stationed too far apart for anything to come of it, and agreed that it was wonderful to meet, but nothing further would happen."

"Boy, you're about as tough as she is. ... The truth is, I was going to ask you if it would be okay for me to come visit you in … now where is it you're stationed?"

"Göppingen," Maura replied. "Eric, there's a part of me that wants to say yes, but I'm just not sure it's a good idea. You're a colonel and I'm a lieutenant. That can get both of us in a world of trouble, with the fraternization commies."

"I have a conference in Heidelberg every other month. The next one is in August. How 'bout you coming to Heidelberg for Labor Day weekend so we can spend some time together and get to know each other. I'll make a reservation at the gasthaus I normally stay at, for two rooms, and you just show up and let me show you around Heidelberg."

Maura knew she should say no, but she didn't want to, and the idea of being in neutral territory for both of them, where no one would know or recognize them, was too good to resist. She smiled and nodded, and that was apparently all the encouragement Eric needed. He grabbed her and kissed her right on the lips. The kiss probably would have lasted longer had it not been interrupted by Anne's return from the bar. "Yo! Cut it with the PDA!"

Eric drew back from Maura slowly, smiling at her. Maura was blushing and gave Anne a look of exasperation as she announced, "You could have taken longer and never been missed."

Anne chortled loudly as she put the three drinks on the table. "Hey, just count yourself lucky that it was me who came first and not Amelia." Looking at Eric, Anne admonished, "You better watch it, bud; you're gonna be in a big heap o' dung with Amelia if you keep this up."

Eric's laughter was cut short as he heard Amelia's voice from behind ask, "Why is the colonel going to be in trouble with me?" That sent Maura and Anne into paroxysms of laughter as Eric became uncomfortable, at a loss for words.

Maura took him off the hook. "Take a look at those sundaes you ladies made."

Lori and Trish immediately dove into their sundaes, but Maura motioned Amelia to move closer to her and whispered, "We'll talk about this in detail later next week, but leave Eric alone. I appreciate the well-meaning concern, but I'm a big girl and can take care of myself." Then in an effort to take the sting out of her admonition, she squeezed Amelia's shoulder and asked, "Okay? We good?" Amelia nodded and turned to the business of eating the hot fudge sundae she'd made.

Russ and Alan showed up shortly thereafter and joined the group. After a few more rounds, Amelia announced, "Okay, it's time to get you ladies into uniform, and get to the terminal."

Russ moaned, "You guys are going to miss the best part. The fireworks are so cool."

"Yes, that's true, but it's better than them missing their flight and being AWOL," Amelia admonished mockingly.

After saying a quick good-bye to the guys, the women left and an hour later were getting out of their taxis and heading into the terminal. Amelia stayed for roll call to ensure they all got on the flight, and after all their bags had been checked and boarding passes validated, she hugged each of them, giving each a personal good-bye. She'd left Maura for last and as she hugged her good-bye, Amelia whispered, "I'll support whatever you want, but please be careful. He's the flame and you're the moth right now, and you know how that usually ends."

Maura chuckled quietly. "I'll proceed with caution."

Amelia waved one final good-bye as she walked away.

14

GÖPPINGEN, WEDNESDAY 5 JULY 1978

THE PHONE RINGING IN the hall woke Maura from a deep sleep. Stumbling out of bed in the dark, she lifted the receiver. "Hello?" she asked querulously.

The male voice on the other end of the line crisply barked, "Lariat Advance."

That got Maura's attention, and as she responded authoritatively, "WILCO."

She hung up the phone and got out of bed. Turning on the bathroom light, she threw cold water on her face, looked at her watch, and groaned as she realized it was only 0200. *Shit, it's gonna be a long day,* she thought. Coming out of the bathroom, she went back to the phone and dialed Lori's BOQ, as it was her responsibility to notify Lori in the event that the phone tree was activated.

After about five rings, Lori's sleepy voice mumbled, "Hello?"

"Lori, it's Maura. We've got a recall. Get dressed and bring in your TA-50. Not sure if this is a garrison accountability test or actual rollout, but need to be prepared for rollout, just in case."

"Okay," Lori mumbled and hung up.

Maura walked into the brigade operations shop about thirty minutes later and was told to report to the command conference room. After waiting for Lori to get to the office, Maura and Lori walked into the large conference room. It was jam-packed with inspectors from Corps headquarters and most of the brigade staff. A moment after entering the conference room, Maura did a double take, seeing that Anne and Trish were part of the inspection party. With Lori in tow, she made her way to the back of the conference room, where Anne and Trish were seated.

Greeting Trish and Anne, Lori waved, and Maura asked, "What's goin' on?"

Anne grimaced. "We got notified around midnight we're doing an ORT on you guys."

Maura grumbled, "Man, sure wish this could have waited another month or so."

"I'm with ya. Once the G-3 does his out-brief, Trish and I have to deploy with the S&T battalion and do a full-up inspection."

Maura handed her hot cup of coffee to Anne. "I've got another mug. You take this; we're all gonna need it." Looking at Lori and Trish, Maura asked, "You guys want a soda?"

"Sure," both cadets answered.

Walking down the hall, Maura couldn't help but marvel at the sucky timing of this inspection. Their flight from Berlin had gotten into Rhein-Main around 2000, but by the time they'd collected their bags and driven back to Göppingen, it was almost 2300. Because she still had to prepare for the next morning, Maura hadn't gotten to bed until almost midnight. She tried to console herself with the thought that she'd gotten more sleep than Anne and Trish, who had probably just barely gotten into bed when they were alerted.

Back in the conference room, Maura and Anne listened intently as the Seventh Corps Assistant G-3 introduced the inspection team members and timeline. The inspection was focused on both the ability of the brigade headquarters to command and control their assigned units and on the ability of the subordinate units to deploy and conduct or support combat operations.

Maura leaned over and whispered in Anne's ear. "I bet you dollars to donuts this is all about the report the CG had to send to Corps headquarters when the Cav Troop failed the ORT."

Anne nodded in agreement. "Yeah, I'd forgotten about that." Anne never finished her sentence, because the in-brief had just ended. Anne motioned Trish to follow her, thanked Maura for the coffee, and walked off. Lori stood up and followed Maura back to her office.

Maura pointed to the field gear that they'd left on her desk when they'd headed to the conference room to attend the in-brief. "Okay, let's get this stuff on, and you follow me into the ops area. Master Sergeant Smith will be back with the operations track in about fifteen minutes, and we'll help load out the NRAS and other classified materials."

Lori immediately grabbed her LBE and helmet and enthusiastically said, "Sure, ma'am, just tell me what I need to do to help."

Maura smiled. "Lori, there's really no nice way to say this. The best thing you can do right now is observe what we're doing and stay out of everyone's way. Just stay with me. Once we've got the command track loaded, we'll strap in to one of the jump seats in the back with all the classified material and head out to our GDP."

Lori had a million questions she wanted to ask but she knew this was not the time, so she did exactly as Maura directed. Thirty minutes later, with Master Sergeant Smith in the driver's seat, they hunkered down in one of the pull-down jump seats in the back of the M577 tracked vehicle that was their command post, with the G-3 and sergeant major.

It took them about an hour to get to their GDP. The vehicle had not even come to a complete stop before the G-3 started unlocking the back doors and jumped out.

To the untrained observer, it appeared that total pandemonium reigned, but in fact, everyone knew what to do and they did it quickly, and it usually involved a lot of yelling, swearing, pushing, and grunting.

As Maura jumped out of the tracked vehicle and yelled for Lori to follow her, she noticed the two inspectors responsible for inspecting G-3 Ops standing to the side with notebooks. "We need to help Master Sergeant Smith with the tent extensions so we can get the brigade Tactical Operations Center up and running," Maura told Lori. They spent the next few minutes helping set up the canvas tent areas between the Ops and Intel tracked vehicles. In 30 minutes, MSG Smith was conducting radio checks with all the subordinate units and asking for status updates.

The sergeant major, Maura, and Lori set up the G-3 and CG's desks and briefing area before Maura motioned Lori to follow her to a dark corner in the tented area. "Okay, this is my little NBC cell." Maura pulled out her small wooden field desk and folding chair, along with a beat-up wooden OD green footlocker.

Before Maura could do or say anything, the G-3 bellowed, "LT! Get your ass in gear and account for all NRAS materials. Give me your written report in the next thirty minutes!"

Maura immediately headed toward the ops area to inventory the NRAS materials, leaving Lori unsure as to what she should do next, so Lori set up the field desk and sat there for the next half hour, observing the controlled chaos.

Having finished the NRAS inventory, Maura brought the required report to the G-3. He looked up from the report he was reading and motioned Maura to sit down. After a few minutes, he handed the report back to her. "Thanks, LT, looks good. Give it to Sergeant Major Atkins."

Maura walked over to the back of the M577 that housed the radios, documents, and safe.

Maura held out the NRAS inventory report to him. "NRAS inventory, Sergeant Major. Boss said to give it to you."

Sergeant Major Atkins took the report and handed it to Master Sergeant Smith, who silently took it and walked over to the safe. "What's botherin' you, ma'am?" the sergeant major asked before Maura could walk away.

"What makes you think something's wrong, Sergeant Major?"

"I know that look, ma'am," he said quietly, so no one else would hear. Maura's piercing gaze made him chuckle. "That look scares everyone but me, ma'am. I guess it's unprofessional, but you remind me of my daughter, and I can't help being protective of you. Your expressions are subtle, but when your mouth gets tight and downturned, I know you're upset, so fess up, what's wrong?"

Relieved that her expressions weren't as transparent as she'd feared a few seconds ago, Maura sat down next to Sergeant Major Atkins and quietly responded, "I can't figure out what I've done to piss the colonel off. He's never yelled at me like that before, and I don't know what I did to upset him."

"You didn't, ma'am. You shouldn't be hearing this from me, so just keep it to yourself. He's worried this is a witch hunt and the team is here to gather evidence that will support the corps commander relieving the CG and perhaps his primary staff along with him."

Stunned by this revelation, Maura instantly understood the abrupt change in the G-3's demeanor. Maura shook her head in disbelief. "But he hasn't been here that long, and what happened with the Cav Troop started way before he took command. They can't blame him for that."

"You've got a lot to learn, ma'am. If the old guy leaves and no one uncovers his mistakes, then the new guy takes the fall. Whatever happens on your watch, you're responsible for. End of discussion."

"Well, I guess it is what it is, and I guess I do have a lot to learn, but that just seems so unfair—" Maura stopped midsentence as she saw the look of amusement on the sergeant major's face. "Yeah," she sighed, repeating, "I've got a lot to learn."

The sergeant major chuckled. "We got some fresh coffee back here. Want some?"

"Nah, me on too much caffeine is not pretty, and I'm already over my quota." Standing up, she added, "I just realized I left Cadet Nelson to fend for herself. I need to get back to her." Hesitating, she turned back to him. "Do you think they'll really relieve him?"

The sergeant major shook his head. "It's possible, but I hope not. If we get through this week without anyone being relieved, we'll be fine."

Maura nodded as she left to see how Lori was doing.

Around 0800, the brigade commander came in and told the staff that the best thing they could do would be to go to the battalion positions and see if they could get any information on how things were going and report back to the brigade TOC at noon. Lori and Maura visited two of the battalion positions and returned to the TOC at 1130. The staff gave the CG an update on what they'd discovered, and a few minutes later, the Assistant Corps G-3 walked in. He and the CG walked out.

About twenty minutes later, the G-3's field phone rang. As Lieutenant Colonel Connolly hung up, he cheerfully announced that the CG had called ENDEX and had given the order to break down the TOC and return to garrison. Connolly gave each of the staff section heads specific assignments for their subordinate units to get back to garrison safely and to confirm with the brigade ops center that all units had completed necessary actions prior to dismissing the troops for the day. Maura and Lori were assigned to check out one of the Artillery batteries, which meant driving all the way to Neu-Ulm and back.

Maura dropped off Lori at her BOQ around 1600 that afternoon and drove the ten minutes back to her apartment. As she walked into the hallway that led to her apartment, she encountered her landlord, who remarked that he'd heard her get up early that morning. Maura explained that they'd had an unannounced inspection and that it had been a long but interesting day, but if he would excuse her abruptness, she was tired and just wanted to get ready for bed.

He nodded understandingly, and Maura proceeded up the stairs to her apartment. The hot shower felt great, and she had just gotten into her PJs when there was a knock on the door. Because her entryway door was frosted glass, she could see by the outline of the landlord's daughter. Grabbing her robe, she opened the door. Hannelore held out a dinner plate with a large slice of *Zwiebelrostbraten* and homemade *Spätzle*, pot roast and noodles with gravy. The dinner was warm and smelled great. Maura thanked Hannelore and her mother for their kindness.

Maura had planned to go to sleep without eating because she was just too tired to cook anything, but the smell of the wonderful meal made her realize how hungry she was, so she put the plate on the coffee table in the living room, went to the kitchen to get some orange Fanta, and wolfed down the wonderful homemade meal. When she had finished eating, she put the dirty dishes in the sink, walked the short distance to her bedroom, and was asleep seconds after her head hit the pillow.

15

HEIDELBERG, SATURDAY 8 JULY 1978

EARLY SATURDAY MORNING, MAURA and Lori picked up a grumpy Anne and Trish at their BOQ for the two hour drive to Heidelberg."

"I hope you don't mind if we sleep, Maura. We're all beat from the surprise lariat advance Wednesday morning. I didn't see that coming," Anne said.

"No problem. I'd be sleeping now too if I wasn't driving. I managed to get about seven hours of sleep last night, so I'm good. I also had two cups of coffee."

Within five minutes, Anne, Lori, and Trish were asleep. Maura enjoyed the quiet and focused on her driving. As she pulled into an Esso filling station near Heidelberg to get fuel, everyone woke up.

"Are we in Heidelberg?" Lori asked.

"No, not yet, but we're close. Should be there in fifteen minutes or so," Maura replied. "Anne, can you hand me my coupon booklet in the glove compartment?"

As Anne got the coupons out, Trish asked, "What are the coupons for?"

"You can buy the coupons at the PX and offset the high cost of German gas when you're off post," Maura said.

Curious, Lori asked, "How much of a discount do you get?"

"I'd say about half price. Whadda you think, Anne?" Maura asked.

"Yep, at least half off. The gas prices here are ridiculous! Many Germans don't have a car because they are so expensive to own, insure, and tank up. Plus, if you live in a big city, there are very few parking spots and the mass transit is cheap and convenient," Anne added.

Lori was impressed with how clean and orderly Heidelberg was as Maura drove into the city.

"Okay, should we eat first or go straight to the castle?" Maura asked.

"I'd love to go sightseeing first," Lori said.

When no one else answered, Maura announced, "Castle it is."

As they approached the castle, Maura said, "Check out the statues on the bridge. As soon as I find a place to park, we can walk over and take a few photos."

She found a parking spot, and then the four of them walked up to the old-town Heidelberg Bridge. Lori and Trish were impressed and immediately started taking pictures. "This must have been an old moat," Lori said as they came to the huge wooden door and entrance of the castle.

"Yes, way back when," Anne said.

"Very cool," Trish said as they walked inside and headed toward the courtyard.

"I suggest we go see the huge wine barrel first," Maura said.

The women followed the signs to the cellar. When they arrived, Lori was stunned by the size and guessed the barrel was twenty feet high. They climbed the steps and stood on top of the keg. "This is unbelievable," Lori said while taking photos.

Anne pointed to the photos on the wall. "They've actually had dances up here. Cool!"

Maura announced, "If you guys are ready, the view of the river from the outside terrace on the other side of the castle is amazing."

"Sure," Trish said.

At the terrace, Lori leaned over the stone wall. "Wow, the view is fantastic!"

"Sorta reminds me of home and the Hudson River," Trish said.

"Oh, so school's home now?" Lori kidded Trish.

"Not really, but you know what I mean."

"There's so much to do that I really don't appreciate the beauty of West Point. I see all the visiting tourists, but since I live there, I don't think of school as a sightseeing opportunity."

"Me too. Hey, what are those guys doing on the river?" Trish suddenly asked.

Maura replied, "I think they're getting the fireworks display set up for tonight. After lunch, I thought we'd check into our pension, the hotel, and come back tonight for a great view of the castle on fire."

"Sounds good," Lori said nodding. "I think we'll get the best view from the other side of the river. Can we go over there tonight?"

"Sure," Maura replied. "It'll be super crowded, so we need to get there early. We can stop at an Aldi store later to pack a picnic dinner while we relax and enjoy the fireworks."

After checking into their pension, the women went to a nice café. As they were finishing their lunches, their waitress smiled and asked, "Dessert?"

Lori, an avid ice cream lover, answered, "Yes, I'd like to try the spaghetti ice cream."

"Me too!" Anne and Maura said in unison.

Trish chuckled, "Make that four."

"It sounds really good on the menu, but have either of you had spaghetti ice cream before?" Lori asked while looking at Anne and Maura.

Anne replied, "Yep, it's great. They strain vanilla ice cream through a spätzle maker to make it look like thin spaghetti, then add a strawberry sauce that looks like the tomato sauce, and top it with grated almonds that looks like parmesan cheese. It's my all-time favorite!"

Ten minutes later, the waitress brought out their spaghetti *eis*. As Lori took her first bite she exclaimed, "I've died and gone to heaven! It tastes especially good in this hot weather." Dipping her spoon in for another bite, she cried, "Oh, what's this inside the spaghetti? Whoa, it's whipped cream! I love German whipped cream. It tastes so much better than Cool Whip."

After paying their bill, the women walked back to their pension to take a short nap before leaving for the castle lighting celebration.

A few hours later, the women were seated on the north bank of the Neckar River. The Heidelberg castle was aflame in red light to simulate the burning of the castle.

Lori said, "This castle illumination is so cool! I can't believe there's so many people here. You were right to have us come early, Maura."

"Yeah, I heard it got crowded about an hour before dark. The symbolism of the red flames is to replicate when Louis XIV, the French Sun King, torched the town and the castle was left in ruins."

Anne added, "I read in a visitor brochure that this is the 365th year since the first fireworks display in 1613. Frederick, the king of Bohemia, brought his English bride to Heidelberg and gave her the first fireworks display. The people of Heidelberg have continued on with the tradition each year. Cool, huh?"

"Impressive! Glad we're here instead of on the boats on the river. I'd hate to be that close to water at night," Trish said.

"Are you kidding me? It'd be cool to be on the river! You afraid of water?" Lori asked.

"Yeah, a little. I barely passed survival swimming with a D. I hate being in the water. That's why I joined the Army instead of the Navy!"

Lori shouted, "Good move, Trish. Look at that!" as she pointed to a huge red, white, and blue explosion in the sky.

"These fireworks are terrific! So glad we're here," Anne said as she took another sip of wine. The other women nodded and watched the rest of the fireworks display in stunned silence.

16

GÖPPINGEN, SATURDAY 15 JULY 1978

THE NEXT SATURDAY, LORI and Maura spent the day shopping for souvenirs for Lori's family and eating in the local Göppingen *Gaststube* near the front gate of the kaserne. "I think the nutcrackers we bought are great gifts for my family. Joe and Christa will love them, and even Mom and Dad will think they're authentic German gifts. I'm also buying a soldier nutcracker for my best friend, Reggie. She plays on our basketball team and is a year younger than Trish and I. She will love this gift. Great idea, Maura!" Lori said.

"I wish I could take credit for the idea, but Anne thought of it."

"You both are the best sponsors!" Lori gushed. "Trish and I wouldn't have gotten half as much out of this real-life Army experience without your guidance and opinions."

"We've had a blast sharing our experiences and travelling with you too," Maura said.

"On a more serious note," Lori continued, "last week my dad sent me a newspaper clipping from the *St Paul Dispatch* dated June 27, 1978. The title of the article is 'Report shows bias against women in the Army.' Basically, Army teams studied the performance of women soldiers in European field exercises and found lots of bias and discrimination toward the women. Most of the bias was from vocal male NCOs who didn't want women around."

Interrupting, Maura added, "Well, can't say I'm surprised. I had the same problem with the male officers when I first got assigned to the brigade."

Lori resumed her thoughts. "The main reasons cited in the article were women's lack of upper body strength, risk of women being in combat, and hygiene and billeting factors. The bottom line in the newspaper article was women can perform their field mission at an acceptable level."

Maura interjected, "Of course we can. But it's going to take many years to prove our worth to the soldiers and leaders in the Army."

Lori nodded. "It really gets old after a while. I feel like I continue having to prove myself around the guys. Why are they so hung up on physical prowess? Too bad the guys base my credibility as an officer on making the fast runs and doing as many sit-ups and push-ups as they can. The ability to make good decisions should be much more important than completing a run."

As Maura stopped the car in front of Lori's BOQ, she replied, "Yeah, same thing for me. Good thing we're both good runners. The women who are poor runners or overweight have bigger obstacles to overcome. I hate to cut this short, but I've got commissary shopping and laundry to do. Glad you found some nice souvenirs for your family, Lori. See you tomorrow!"

17

STUTTGART, FRIDAY 21 JULY 1978

LORI AND TRISH'S LAST night of CTLT culminated with a late dinner in Stuttgart at the O'Club with Anne and Maura. Lori asked for a table way in the back of the dining room because some people were loud and rowdy from drinking too much and they wanted a chance to talk.

"I can't believe we've been here six weeks already," Lori told the group.

"I know what you mean," Maura said. "We've gotten to take some really nice short trips and expose you to the Army. It's been intense but fun to show you the sights."

"Thanks both of you. We've gotten to travel to Munich, Austria, East and West Berlin, and Heidelberg. We've experienced Volksmarches, local food, and festivals. We couldn't have done it without your help. Lori and I are basically broke cadets, and you've made our CTLT experience the trip of a lifetime!" Trish commented.

"We're happy to be your sponsors," Anne replied. "I hope we'll stay friends from afar."

"Oh, you can count on it," Trish said. "I'm not good at writing, but I remember who my friends are. You've made our taste of the Army so much better than I imagined. Prior to coming here, I'd never been anywhere except Utah, Fort Knox, and New York. Now I consider myself a world traveler. I love the opportunities that come from being in the Army."

"Same for me," Lori said. "I do write letters, but our studies demand so much of our time. I'll write you periodically, maybe every few months. I hope that's okay."

"No sweat," Maura said. "I hope we get a chance to serve together again. You never know. ... The Army is a small world, and perhaps we'll cross paths again."

"Trish was spot-on when she said you've made our CTLT experience so great. Thank you for all the time you've spent with us, explaining what Army life is like. I've learned so much from the soldiers, NCOs, and officers, but I learned even more from both of you. I'm excited to become a lieutenant like you and lead a platoon."

"Well, I hate to leave, but I need to pack for Paris," Trish said. "Lori, you ready to go back to the Q?"

"Yep! See you both tomorrow! Thanks for the great memories!" Lori said as she and Trish got up from the table to pay their bill and walk back to Trish's BOQ.

"I'm gonna miss those two," Maura said slowly.

"Yeah, it took some extra work, but I sure had fun showing them the ropes and answering their interesting questions," Anne replied.

"Yep. They'll do well if they graduate."

"Whadda you mean, if they graduate?" Anne asked.

"Well, they still have two more years of tough academics and daily stress to put up with. That can take a toll on anyone."

"I guess you're right, but I think they'll do just fine."

EARLY THE NEXT MORNING, Maura and Anne dropped Lori and Trish off at the Stuttgart Hauptbahnhof for their eight-hour train ride to

Paris. After hugs and smiles, Maura said, "We want postcards of Paris and photos of you both in your full dress gray when you get back to school."

"You got it, ma'am!" Lori yelled as she and Trish waved good-bye to Anne and Maura and boarded the train for Paris.

18

STUTTGART AND PARIS, FRANCE, SATURDAY 22 JULY 1978

HAVING FOUND THEIR SEATS, Trish sat down. "I can't believe we're finally on leave! I've been counting the days to get out of my unit and having some fun."

"I'm excited too, but sad about leaving Maura and Anne. They were great."

"Yeah, Anne and Maura were cool, but I'm glad to finally be on our own. You know what I mean?" Trish asked.

"Absolutely! I can't wait to explore Paris together and let our hair down. It's time to party and enjoy our freedom!"

As the train started pulling away, Trish asked, "What time do we arrive in Paris?"

"Our tickets say we're supposed to get in at 1748 hours. That'll give us plenty of time to hop on the Metro and check into our hotel," Lori said. "Glad we mailed most of our equipment and uniforms back to West Point. Having to lug duffle bags on vacation would really suck."

"You got that right. My bag is heavy enough with just my clothes and toothbrush. I'm so glad Anne packed us a great lunch with a bottle of wine. Should be an enjoyable way to see the French countryside," Trish added.

"I also brought a paperback book I'd like to read for fun. Seems like I only read for work now. Have you read this book? *The Sword of Shannara?*"

"Nope, but I heard it was a good book from my roommate, Judy. She doesn't study much. She's smart as a whip, who speed-reads, and remembers almost everything. She's also a smart star-woman and is sort of a nerd. I like her because she's nonjudgmental," Trish remarked.

"Judy Harrison?" Lori asked.

"Yeah, do you know her?"

"She was in my chemistry class last semester. I asked her for help a few times and she showed me what I was doing wrong. She seemed nice but reserved. What do you mean by nonjudgmental?" Lori asked.

"Well, ah, when my girlfriend would come to our barracks room, she never said anything," said Trish.

"Well, why should she?" asked Lori. "My girlfriends come over all the time."

"Well, let's just say she caught us in a bad moment when she came back early from class one day."

Lori was puzzled by this comment but chose not to ask Trish for clarification. Lori held up her paperback. "If you don't mind, I'd like to read for a few hours."

"Sounds good. I didn't get much sleep last night 'cause I was packing. I'm gonna take a nap. Wake me if anything fun happens."

The rest of the train ride was uneventful, and Lori and Trish arrived in the Paris train station on time, hopped on the Metro, and then walked to their hotel on Rue Saint Dominque. "Wow, I had no idea this hotel would be so old," Trish said as they approached the hotel.

"What do you expect for thirty-five dollars a night? The Ritz?" Lori asked.

"No, you're right. I just thought it'd be newer, for some reason. I hope the bathroom is in the room and not down the hall like that gasthaus we stayed at last month."

As Lori and Trish approached the hotel desk, an elderly woman smiled at them. "*Bon jour,*" she said.

"Um, do you speak English?" Lori asked.

"Non," she said while holding up her index finger. "Charla!" shouted the woman.

A teenage girl came to the desk and said in halting English, "Good afternoon. I am Charla. My mother do not speak English. May I help you?"

"Yes. We have a reservation for one room for six nights under the name of Nelson," Lori answered.

Charla pulled out a large lined reservation book while her mother looked over her shoulder. "Here it is, one room, six nights, leaving on Friday. That will be 987 Francs, please."

While counting the money Lori asked, "Are there two beds and a bathroom in the room?"

"There is only one large bed, but your bath quarters are inside your room. I hope that be satisfactory," Charla replied apologetically.

Lori looked over at Trish, who replied, "Um, I'm okay with one bed if you are. At least we don't have to walk down the hall to get to our bathroom."

"Okay," Lori haltingly said.

Charla gave her a relieved smile in return and explained, "Breakfast is served every day from seven to nine thirty a.m. Here is your room key, and please let us know if you have any question. If I am not here, please leave note for my mother and she will get note translated."

"Thank you, Charla," Lori said as she and Trish picked up their suitcases and walked toward the stairs.

"We're in room 204," Lori told Trish.

"Wow, these are steep steps, and lots of them," Trish grumbled as they climbed up two flights of stairs. "I'll never get used to the Europeans counting the ground floor as zero."

Lori opened the old wooden door with a large brass key, and they stepped into the room, dropped their suitcases on the tile floor, and looked around.

"Wow, these are really high ceilings … nothing like the hotel rooms I've been in. I really like these large windows overlooking the street," Trish said as she walked over and looked out.

Lori flopped onto the bed, and the coils creaked. "The furniture looks antique, and this bed has seen better days. Not the most comfortable, but it'll do."

Not interested in the bed, Trish announced, "Hey, I'm hungry. Let's go out for our first French dinner before it gets dark. I saw a neat-looking place around the corner on our way here."

"Sounds good. Let's get unpacked first, and I don't know about you, but I need to use the bathroom," Lori said as she opened her suitcase on the bed. She took her makeup bag into the bathroom to brush her teeth and wash her face.

DINNER AT THE BISTRO around the corner was quite the experience. Neither woman spoke French, so they looked at the menu in the window, and Trish asked, "Lori, what if the waitress doesn't speak English?"

"I guess we take our chances and point to something that looks good."

"Good idea. Should be a hoot," Trish replied as they walked into the bistro for dinner.

A waitress greeted them in French, and Lori and Trish just smiled and nodded their heads. The waitress led them to a small table in the corner and handed them the menu.

Lori asked, "Do you speak English?"

"Non," the waitress replied.

"Bummer," Trish said. She opened her menu and asked, "Coca-Cola?"

"*Oui*," replied the waitress and looked at Lori, holding up her thumb and pointer finger and saying, "*Deux?*"

Lori nodded and opened her menu, looking for something interesting to order.

"I don't have a clue to what all this is," mumbled Trish.

"Yeah, I know whatcha mean. I haven't been this confused since the Juice WPR in May. How 'bout you pick one and I'll pick something else. Hopefully we'll both like what we get."

"Okay ... could be fun," Trish said as the waitress came to the table with their Cokes.

Lori and Trish both pointed to different entrées on the menu and hoped for the best as the waitress nodded and said, "*Oui.*"

"Boy, this Coke tastes good," Lori said after taking a huge swallow.

"Yeah, I'm thirsty and hungry from our long trip. The sandwiches Anne made were good, but that was six hours ago."

"This is really weird," Lori commented. "Here we are in Paris on leave, and we don't speak the language. I assumed most Parisians would speak English in this tourist town."

"Given that tourism is a major industry and lots of Brits travel here, I expected them to speak a little English, or at least have an English menu."

"We'll just have to make the best of it," Lori said.

When their food arrived, Trish and Lori weren't sure what they ordered, but both dishes looked and smelled like fish. Lori tentatively took a bite of hers and said, "Well, it's edible, I guess."

Trish stared at her food. "This sucks. I hate fish!"

"Try the potatoes. The French are known for their great potatoes," Lori suggested.

Picking up a piece of bread, Trish grumbled, "We chose poorly, but the bread is really good, so I'll eat the bread, potatoes, and salad."

"Yup, live and learn. Mine's not too bad. You want to try mine?" Lori asked.

"No, I hate all fish, even if it doesn't taste fishy." Changing the subject, Trish asked, "So what's the game plan for tomorrow?"

"I thought we'd see the Louvre and Notre Dame after breakfast in the hotel. Hopefully, we'll find a good place for lunch."

"Anything would be better than this meal. I thought Paris had good food."

"I think we just need to buy a French phrase book." Grinning, Lori added, "The weather's supposed to be sunny this week; we should get some great pics. I'm glad I got three rolls of film at the PX last week."

"Man, Lori, do you always look at the bright side of things, or what? Our meal sucks, our room is ancient, and you're still excited."

"Yeah, I love adventures and experiencing new things. I think we're lucky to be in Paris at twenty years old. Most Americans never leave the US, and here we are, working in West Germany and on vacation in France. Life is good."

"I wish I thought like you, Lori. I don't see the world the same way you do. Call me a pessimist, but life isn't always so good," Trish said quietly.

"True, but I try to stay positive. Too much negativity out there without me piling on."

"If you say so," Trish said as they counted out their Francs and paid for their meal.

They walked back to their hotel room in silence.

When they arrived back at their room, Lori asked, "Given we only have one bed, what side do you want to sleep on? I don't care and I'm sure I'll sleep like a log until morning."

"Doesn't matter to me," Trish replied offhandedly. "I'll take whatever side you don't. You can use the bathroom first."

★ ★ ★

THE NEXT MORNING, LORI and Trish woke up early and went downstairs to eat the tasty but meager French breakfast provided in their hotel fee. "What should we do first?" Trish asked.

"I say we walk to the Louvre before the tourists arrive and then go to Notre Dame and check that out. Hopefully, we can grab some lunch at a bistro where they speak some English or have an English menu."

"You got that right! I'm not up to ordering a mystery meal again. Let me have one more cup of coffee—this espresso is way too strong, but it tastes good—then I'll be ready to go. How come you don't drink coffee, Lori?"

"I hate the taste. It's too bitter. I normally drink a Tab to get some caffeine."

"I started drinking coffee during Beast Barracks. The mornings in the field were so cold that the coffee warmed me up and tasted okay. Now if I don't have a cup of coffee, I get a headache. Guess I'm addicted, but I don't mind, because I love the kick it gives me."

"Take your time. There's no rush. You got your camera and Francs?"

"Yup, ready and raring to go. Been looking forward to this trip for the past three months. My mom and friends are so envious. I wish they could come too."

"Yeah, I know what you mean. My sister Christa is jealous and wants me to take lots of photos of the buildings and the art masterpieces. I doubt they'll let me take pictures in the Louvre, but I'll try. I'm really hoping to take some pics of the buildings and the churches."

"My mom is going to love the photos."

"What about your dad?" Lori asked.

Trish glared at Lori and gruffly said, "Don't talk about him; ever! He left us when I was five. He's a liar and a womanizer. My mom's the only parent I know. Don't bring him up again."

"Sorry, I didn't know how much he upsets you," Lori quietly said.

LORI AND TRISH WERE dead tired after a long day of walking, queuing up, and sightseeing. It was a lot of data and historical information to comprehend, and they were happy to get back to their hotel room that evening to sit down and relax.

"So what did you like best today?" Trish asked.

"Uh, wow, tough question. I liked Notre Dame and the Louvre. The painting of Napoleon crowning himself emperor was very interesting. I also liked the Venus of Milo statue."

"I was disappointed by the Mona Lisa. I've heard so much about it, but it was so small and I just couldn't get into it." Then, changing the subject, Trish asked, "How far do you think we walked today?"

"At least nine or ten miles, and that doesn't count all the standing in line and slow walking through the museums," Lori replied. "I'd rather run than stand up all day. What would you like to do tomorrow?"

"How about sleeping in and then going to Versailles? I heard it's very cool," Trish said.

"Sounds good, but I think our idea of sleeping in may be 0800 hours," chuckled Lori.

"I'm sure you're right. After getting up at 0530 every day for work or PT, sleeping an extra few hours will be a luxury, but that's what vacation is for."

Lori started writing postcards to her family and friend Willow, while Trish read a book. After an hour, Lori said, "Don't know 'bout you, but I'm taking a shower and going to bed. I'm pooped."

"I'll take my shower after you. I feel dirty from the humid weather and all the walking," Trish replied. "Glad these old rooms are fairly cool without air conditioning."

"Yes, thick walls have their advantages. I'm really glad the bathroom is attached and not down the hall like at school. I didn't bring a bathrobe, and I hate getting dressed and undressed just to use the shower. Life shouldn't be so complicated."

"Yep. It's complex enough as it is," Trish said as she put her book down after marking her page. She closed her eyes as Lori grabbed her PJs and went into the bathroom.

THE NEXT DAY, LORI and Trish boarded the Metro and an hour later arrived at the Versailles palace and grounds. "Wow, this place is huge," Trish said.

"Yeah, I had no idea it would be this big," Lori replied. "Look at this gold fence!"

"Should we see the palace first or check out the park and flowers?" Trish asked.

"Probably the palace. Looks real old and interesting."

"Yep, let's go," Trish said.

After an hour of viewing the antique furniture and artifacts, hall of mirrors, kitchen, ballroom, and bedrooms, they had seen enough. "Let's get some fresh air," Lori said. "I hate being inside on such a nice sunny day."

"I'm with you. Too much inlaid gold, silver, and opulence for us working folk to understand or appreciate."

Lori and Trish headed outside and meandered through the gardens. They ended up in Marie Antoinette's Hamlet at the northeast end of the property where the summer property and farm were located. They sat on the bench and watched the swans swim in the pond. "So Trish, I'm curious. Why didn't you want to go into Dachau with us last month?"

"Um, I just didn't feel like it," Trish replied, unprepared for this topic.

"Your choice, of course, but it did seem strange that you didn't want to go tour the place with Anne, Maura, and I," Lori probed once again.

"Well, it just made me queasy. ... I mean, all those innocent victims killed for no reason, just makes me mad. I wanted no part of it."

"Well, it wasn't a fun thing to do, but I think people must know and remember how cruel and vicious people can be to others. It's a way to document history and make sure these atrocities never happen again."

"Well, how could the German people let millions of Jews, dissidents, gypsies, homosexuals, publishers, and others be murdered for merely not being Aryan or not agreeing with them? It's unbelievable to comprehend."

"You're right, Trish. I don't know ... the Nazi party just got too big for the average German to fight against. They would be killed if they protested, I guess," Lori replied.

"Well, I'd rather not talk about it. The whole thing pisses me off," Trish said. Then she walked down a path to watch the pigs play in the mud.

Lori let Trish cool off before she linked back up with her. "This place sure is something, isn't it?" she asked.

"Yeah, it's beautiful. Sorry I blew up at you, Lori. You had nothing to do with what happened in World War II. I don't know why the whole concentration-camp thing makes me so upset and angry. All those innocent victims murdered really pisses me off! There, I said it. I feel a little better already."

"Wow, I had no idea you were so upset; I thought you were just really tired."

"Like I said, I don't know why I'm so angry; I just am. Does that make any sense?"

"Ya, it does. Sometimes I was so angry at the injustice of our plebe year, I had to find outlets to get rid of my anger," Lori said.

"Yep, I did the same thing. Basketball really helped me cope, along with going off post for some of our away games. Laughing about the silly stuff also helped," Trish said.

Just then, Lori noticed two good-looking young men approaching them.

One man, with shoulder-length brown hair, asked, "Do you speak English?"

"Yes," Lori responded.

"Great! We speak no French, and we were hoping to meet some Americans to talk to on our trip. We're backpacking through Europe this summer before going back to school," he said.

"I'm Lori and this is Trish. We're on leave before we go back to school this summer."

"Leave?" the other man, blond, said. "Are you in the military or something?"

"Yes, we're both in the Army. We go to the military academy at West Point," Lori replied.

"Wow, I heard women started going there, but I never met one, let alone two. How is it?" the blond-haired man asked.

"We're surviving," Trish said curtly.

"We should introduce ourselves. I'm Hugh Fitzpatrick, and this is Randy Jensen," the blond man said, pointing at his brown-haired friend. "We're seniors at Colorado State University."

"Do you live in Denver?" Lori asked.

"No, we're students in Colorado Springs. We've read all about the Air Force Academy women but we've never met one. I guess they don't get out to party much. So we meet two Army cadets at Versailles, halfway around the world. How about that?" Hugh remarked.

"Small world. How did you guess we spoke English?" Lori asked.

"Your tennis shoes and shorts gave you away," Hugh said. "The French and Europeans are more dressed up, even when on vacation."

"I never thought about that," Trish said. "We're always in uniform at school, so wearing civvies is a real treat for us."

"My uncle went to West Point, but he quit his freshman year. Said the hazing was really bad and the wool uniforms made his skin itch all the time," Hugh said. "How's it been for you?"

"Plebe year was really tough due to all the hazing, and I still hate the starched collars in our dress gray and full dress gray uniforms, but like Trish said, we're surviving," Lori replied.

"That's cool. So when do you graduate?" Randy asked.

"Two more years, then we'll be lieutenants in the Army," Lori said.

"Must be a good feeling to have automatic jobs when you graduate. We have to start looking for jobs this year and hopefully land a good one," Randy remarked.

"Yeah, it's nice, but we still have two more tough years. What's your major?" Lori asked.

"I'm a history major; that's why we're here. I love European history," Randy said.

"I'm majoring in mechanical engineering and actually considered going to West Point for their engineering classes, but I didn't like all the discipline," Hugh said. "I also love skiing and hiking in the Rocky Mountains."

"Well, we know all about engineering and science classes. This year, we take mechanical engineering, thermo-fluid dynamics, and physics. It's going to be a bear. I prefer English and the humanities, but most of our classes are prescribed and we don't have a major, only a concentration," Lori said.

"What does that mean?" Hugh asked.

"We graduate with a Bachelor of Science degree. We don't get to pick a major, but we can pick a few electives our senior year for a concentration. Ultimately, we graduate with a general engineering degree," Trish said.

"That doesn't sound too bad," Hugh said.

"It's really tough if you're not good in math," Lori said. "I like math, but I have to study at least three hours every night, or more if I have a test or paper."

"I wouldn't like it," Randy said. "I hate math, barely squeaked out a C in my freshman general math class."

"So what are you going do with your history degree?" Trish asked Randy curiously.

"Well, I don't know. I might go on for my master's degree and teach college. I love reading and talking about history. My parents have asked me the same question. I'm twenty-two, and I have so many different interests, so it's hard to focus on only one."

"Yeah, good point," Lori said. "We're lucky. We have a required five-year stint in the Army when we graduate. I plan on getting out if I don't like it, but I'll give it a good shot."

"Uh, would ya like to grab a Coke at the café?" asked Hugh. "It's getting hot out here."

"Sure. How about we meet you there in a half hour?" Lori asked.

"Okay, see ya then."

After the guys left, Lori looked at Trish. "So what do you think?"

"I guess we're stuck having a Coke with those two."

"I thought you'd like it, and I'm really thirsty," Lori said.

"I'm thirsty too, but I'd rather not make small talk with two Americans."

"Why not? They're kinda cute."

"I dunno, I guess they're not my type," Trish replied.

"Well, who is your type? I've only seen you dance with one cadet in the two years we've been friends."

"Do you really want to know?"

"Yes, of course," Lori replied.

"Can you keep a secret?"

"Sure," Lori replied, thinking Trish was going to tell her she had a crush on a cadet.

"You have to promise me you won't tell anyone. I could get kicked out of school if anyone found out," Trish deliberately said.

"Oh no. You're not dating a married man, are you?"

"No, probably something worse in the eyes of the Army," Trish said.

"No way. Dating a married man is pretty bad and setting yourself up for trouble and heartache."

"Well, I don't know how to say this, so I'll just say it," Trish said haltingly. "I, I… like girls."

Lori digested this unexpected revelation before responding, "Oh, that's not so bad. I thought you might be dating a married man. I mean, I didn't know or have any idea. … I feel a little weird about it but appreciate you trusting me." Looking Trish straight in the eyes, she added, "Your secret is safe with me."

"Thanks, Lori. That means a lot. I really like the Army, but the military doesn't allow homosexuals in the military, even though there are plenty of us serving right now."

"Okay, so now I see why you don't talk about cute guys or go out on dates. Sorry I signed us up for Cokes with Randy and Hugh," Lori apologized.

"That's not a problem. I like guys. I'm just not attracted to them. It's hard to explain. I've been like this since I was a little girl."

"Uh, okay. Let's go get a drink at the café," Lori said as they slowly walked toward the entrance of Versailles.

19

GÖPPINGEN, SATURDAY 29 JULY 1978

MAURA HAD JUST FINISHED changing into jeans and a lavender cashmere pullover when she heard the doorbell to her apartment ring. Opening the door, she waved Anne in and walked back toward the kitchen. "You know where to throw your stuff. I've laid out the linens but haven't made your bed yet."

"No prob, I can do it," Anne said as she headed to Maura's spare bedroom to put her overnight bag on the small coffee table in front of the futon that served as guest bed. She walked into the kitchen as Maura was finishing washing out the percolator and cup she'd used for coffee that morning. Anne asked, "How'd your week go?"

"Pretty well, just the usual stuff. Glad the annual inspection cycle is over. I'm way behind on paperwork and updating the TACSOP."

"What are you doing updating the TACSOP? Isn't that normally done by the combat arms guys?"

"Yeah, but there's a lot going on and G-3 asked me to do it."

"You comfortable with that?" Anne asked.

"Yeah, MSG Smith and Sergeant Major Atkins told me to come to them with any questions. They'll keep me straight."

"Yeah, they saved your butt countless times, haven't they?"

Maura laughed, "Probably more times than I realize. The only thing that really bugs me is that I'm the one who'll get credit for the update and I really couldn't do it without them."

"Did you talk to them about it?"

"Nah, I know them well enough to know that if I did, one of them would bop me up the back of the head and remind me that they don't need the credit and to stop worrying about stupid shit."

Anne opened the bottle of wine Maura had on the counter. "I envy you your relationship with them. First Sergeant is pretty squared away, but he's so formal with me and the other lieutenants, that I'm really not comfortable with him, and I have to supervise my platoon sergeant constantly to make sure he does things correctly, especially paperwork."

Pulling two wine glasses out of the cabinet and handing them to Anne, Maura opened the fridge and put out the fruit and cheese plate she had made earlier. She motioned Anne to follow her outside to the balcony. This was Maura's favorite part of the apartment. The entire back end of the large living/dining room was floor-to-ceiling windows, with a wood-framed glass sliding door. When Maura had first seen the apartment, she had noticed that none of the windows or sliding glass door had screens. The housing agent had told her Germans did not use them because they did not have many flying insects and the few that were stupid enough to enter the house were quickly killed and flushed down the toilet because no self-respecting German would risk someone finding an insect in their house. Maura had started to laugh but immediately stifled it because the look on the faces of the housing office agent and her prospective landlord had indicated they didn't share her amusement.

The balcony had a round wrought-iron table and four chairs with beautiful floral patterned cushions. Maura had set the table with matching damask tablecloth and napkins and a round crystal vase filled with lilacs and yellow roses in the center of the table.

Anne sat down and started pouring wine. She handed a half-full glass to Maura, then raised her own glass in a toast. "To our first weekend in six weeks with no requirements or travel plans."

Grinning wryly, Maura returned the toast. "I'm looking forward to a relaxing weekend, but I forgot to tell you I have to be at our German partnership unit function tomorrow at eleven and my invitation allows me to bring a guest."

Anne took a sip of her wine and groaned, "Geesh, Maura, couldn't you get out of it?"

"Yeah, probably, but in all honesty, I totally forgot about it until today, when the G-3 mentioned he was glad I was coming because the Germans really like the fact that I speak German so well and when there is a communication issue, he and the rest of the brigade staff depend on me to translate. Sorry, I screwed up, but after that, I felt like I couldn't bug out."

"Okay," Anne groused. "But you owe me big time. I enjoyed having the gals for CTLT but was really looking forward to a weekend just sitting on the balcony and heading on post tonight to see whatever movie is playing."

Maura grimaced. "Well, we can have breakfast on the balcony and relax until around 1030 tomorrow, and if you're interested in seeing *The Deer Hunter*, we can go tonight."

Anne shrieked in delight. "I've been dying to see it."

Relieved, Maura added, "Thanks for being such a good sport. Movie and snacks are on me tonight."

Anne laughed, "Isn't it interesting that we get so excited about a movie that's been out since last February in the States? Back home I remember going to see movies the first week they were released. It really frustrates me that it takes our military system so long to get new movie releases here."

Maura swallowed the last bit of cheese and cracker in her mouth and picked up her wine glass. "Yeah, I got a letter from my brother yesterday telling me *Star Wars* just came out and I should go see it. I toyed with the idea of writing back that I'll hope it gets to the post theater by this time next year, but he'd just blow it off, 'cause folks back home don't have any concept of how different things are overseas."

Anne popped a few grapes in her mouth and mumbled, "I hear ya, but there are so many cool things about living overseas that I can live with some of the inconveniences, like the commissary not having fresh seafood and Germans not knowing what crawfish are."

Maura raised her eyebrows, and both of them burst into laughter at the same time, realizing the absurdity of the conversation they were having. Sure, things were different, but wasn't that why they'd asked to go overseas? They sat in silence for bit, sipping wine and enjoying the gorgeous vista of the far mountains and verdant fields in front of them. They were both exhausted from the past six weeks of showing Lori and Trish all the sights they could possibly work into a weekend in addition to the daily demands of their jobs.

Things had settled down for both of them. They were accepted and respected by their peers and had good relationships with their bosses, but taking time off with the cadets and having to take time to train the cadets had meant they did not get everything done at work that they needed to and would be playing catch-up for a while.

Reaching to grab some cheese and crackers, Anne asked, "Are you coming my way next weekend?"

Maura started. "Oh my gosh, I've been so busy, I forgot to talk to you about that."

Responding to Anne's quizzical expression, Maura continued, "Eric has a conference in Heidelberg on August seventh, and he invited me to spend the weekend with him."

Surprised by this revelation, Anne smirked. "Okay, Heidelberg with Eric for the weekend?"

Maura grinned as she reached for her wine glass.

"Okay, do you mind telling me when this was decided and some specifics, so in case you don't return to work on Monday, we know where to look for you?"

Maura replied disdainfully, "Give me a break, I'll be fine. This ain't *Looking for Mr. Goodbar.*"

"Look, Maura, I just want to make sure you've thought through this and don't get yourself into something you can't get out of."

"He actually surprised me by offering to book two rooms," Maura said a bit haughtily.

"Okay, *chéri*, I know you like him. Just go a bit slow, okay?"

"We're good. He told me he wants to get to know me, and I like that. I don't have any plan to have sex next weekend."

"I hear ya, but are you sure he's of the same mind?"

"I think so."

"Just have a plan B, *chéri*, because guys can get pretty worked up when their sexual advances are rebuffed."

"Okay." Changing the subject, Maura asked, "You wanna go to the club before we go to the movie?"

"Nah, if it's okay with you, I just want to chill a bit. How 'bout we just sit here, relax, and drink a few glasses of wine?"

They did exactly that, each lost in thought about various things. Around six, Maura asked Anne if she was hungry. When she said yes, Maura drove to the *Schnellimbiss* for a rotisserie chicken with fries.

After dinner, Maura asked, "What are you doing next weekend?"

Anne said, "I'll let the guy I've been dating know it's his lucky week and plan on going out to dinner and dancing."

20

STUTTGART, FRIDAY 11 AUGUST 1978

ANNE WAS TALKING TO a handsome tall blond officer as Maura walked into the O'Club at Robinson Barracks. Walking up behind them, she greeted Anne, "Hi there."

Startled, Anne turned around quickly but, upon seeing Maura, relaxed and looked at her watch. "Hi back. Wow, you made good time, I wasn't expecting you for another thirty minutes."

"Yeah, got finished at the office a bit early today and didn't run into any traffic." Maura held out her hand to the handsome captain Anne had been talking to. "Sorry if I interrupted your conversation. I'm Maura, and you are…?"

Anne laughed heartily. "I told you she was different," she told the man and then turned back to Maura. "This is my friend Adam. Adam, my friend Maura, I told you about."

Adam reached out to shake hands with Maura. "Nice to meet you," he drawled.

"Oh my gawd," Maura exclaimed. "I thought Anne and Amelia had thick accents. Where do you hail from?"

"Adam smiled. "Hattiesburg, Mississippi, and you?"

"New York City," Maura replied. "Sorry for being so rude, but your speech pattern amazes me. I didn't think it was possible to have that much of a twang and still speak English."

Adam didn't miss a beat as he rejoined, "Welcome to the club. I've always wondered how Northerners keep from swallowin' their tongues and why they don't pronounce t's and r's properly."

Maura laughed heartily and looked at Anne. "I like him," she said. Then without any preamble, she added, "Don't know 'bout you guys, but I could use a nice glass of wine and something to eat. I missed lunch today."

Anne looked at Adam. "See you Sunday afternoon?"

Adam grinned widely. "It's a date; looking forward to it. I'll pick you up at two." Then looking at Maura, he said, "Nice meeting you, Maura," and walked away.

Looking at Anne, Maura commented, "He could have stayed for dinner with us."

"Oh no, *chéri*, you don't get off that easy. I want all of the details of last weekend." With that, Anne motioned Maura to follow her into the dining room. "Okay, *chéri*, how'd it go?"

Maura blushed. "It was magical, but a little nerve-wracking."

"Did you tell him this was your first time?"

Maura nodded.

"And...?"

Maura giggled nervously. "He was pretty freaked out."

Anne leaned forward and said conspiratorially, "Okay, you don't have to, but if you're okay with sharing, I'd love to hear details."

On the drive over, Maura had thought about how she was going to handle this conversation and had come to the conclusion that she wanted to share her experience, because apart from Elise and Amelia, there was no one she trusted more than Anne. "Well, I got to Heidelberg late on Friday and met Eric in the bar of the gasthaus he was staying at. It's in the old city, near the Neckar River and the university. He told me he liked it because there were tons of pubs within walking distance and it was a great place to relax and party. We had a glass of wine, made small talk, and he asked me if I'd ever been to Heidelberg. I told him we'd been twice. He asked me if

I'd seen the annual castle lighting and the inside of the castle. I told him we'd seen it when we'd taken Trish and Lori to the castle lighting, but I didn't mind seeing it again, so we went there on Saturday morning, after we took a morning jog along the Neckar."

"How was it?" Anne asked.

Maura took a sip of wine and continued, "Fantastic! Hardly anyone was out when we took our morning jog. Afterwards, we met downstairs, ordered cappuccinos, and had a leisurely breakfast on the hotel's sidewalk terrace."

Just then, the waiter returned with the mineral water and wine they'd ordered and told Maura and Anne that the buffet was open. They returned with full plates and sat down. Continuing her story, "Our hotel was close enough to walk to the castle, and we learned there was a pharmacy museum in the castle. I was surprised by the collection of apothecary jars and supplies, the apothecary workshops, and alchemy laboratory. I wish we'd taken the cadets on the tour. My favorite part of the castle tour was the royal wine cellar."

When Maura told her the barrel they'd seen earlier was made from 130 oak trees, was seven meters wide, was over eight meters long, and had a capacity of precisely 221,726 liters, Ann laughed and told her that if she couldn't find a job when she got out of the Army, she'd make a great tour guide.

Maura gave Anne a disdainful glare as she ignored the jibe.

"So what did you guys do that evening?" Anne asked.

"We went out to a really nice restaurant that offered a large variety of German, French, and Italian wines, along with a wonderful menu that included fresh fish," Maura said as she wistfully recalled sitting on the terrace of the beautiful restaurant that overlooked the river and castle and being happier than she could ever remember being.

"And ... ?" Anne asked again.

Maura smiled. "Well, we started with a lovely bottle of wine from the Mosel region of Germany that we polished off while eating our snails and salads. Then Eric suggested we order a very light but dry Franken wine he really likes but can only find at that restaurant. About three hours and as many bottles of wine later, we walked back to the gasthaus with Eric protectively wrapping his arm around my shoulders." Maura took a quick sip of her wine before continuing.

Anne sensed Maura's reticence to discuss the details of what happened later and sat in silence, waiting for her friend to continue.

"We got back to the gasthaus, and Eric asked if I wanted to have some more to drink or go upstairs. I was feeling so warm and content being in his arms, I told him I was ready to go upstairs but I didn't want to go to my room."

Anne leaned forward a bit as Maura resumed speaking in a reflective, quiet tone. "He told me he had some sparkling mineral water and nuts in his room and a nice balcony with two chairs we could sit at. I told him that sounded wonderful. We were no sooner in the room when Eric reached over to touch my face and kiss me." Smiling contentedly, Maura whispered, "I just felt like I was floating on a cloud. He picked me up, laid me on the bed." Blushing, Maura paused. "He ran his fingers through my hair, told me how much he wanted me, and asked if I wanted to get undressed myself or have him undress me. That's when it hit me, and I freaked out a bit."

"What happened?" Anne asked a bit tersely.

"Well, I hate to admit it, but I started shaking and couldn't find my voice. He was so sweet and concerned. He asked me what was wrong, and I told him that I wanted him very much but I was really scared."

Anne would realize later that she had bitten her lip in an effort to not scream at Maura for dragging the story out. She managed to stay silent and appear nonchalant as Maura haltingly continued.

"He was so sweet and confused and asked me what he had done to scare me. That's when I burst into tears and told him it was nothing he had done, I was just nervous because this was my first time and I wasn't really sure what to do." Maura giggled quietly at the reminiscence of Eric's reaction to her announcement.

"You're killin' me, Maura! Did you guys do it?" Anne asked bluntly.

"Yes, eventually." Maura giggled again.

Throwing her arms up in mock surrender, Anne said, "Okay, I don't need every detail, but could you please put me out of my misery and finish this story?"

Maura chuckled quietly. "Sorry, I don't remember all the details, but my confession obviously surprised—no, shocked him. He said something like, 'Oh shit, no!' I just nodded yes, and he got up from the bed, walked over to the small cabinet that had the mineral water and a bottle of Scotch, and took a huge gulp of Scotch directly from the bottle."

Anne was leaning forward again, listening intently as Maura quietly continued.

"He turned around and told me he was sorry, he didn't realize I was a virgin, and told me to get off the bed and he'd take me to my room."

"Oh, Maura!" Anne said in a hushed voice.

Maura nodded. "Oh, it gets worse." Now into telling her story, Maura was finally emotionally ready to share details of the highly charged atmosphere that night. "I burst into tears and told him I didn't want to go to my room, that I knew he was a big playboy and I wasn't making any demands on him but had already decided that I wanted him to be the first."

Anne didn't quite know what to say at this point, so she sat quietly until Maura resumed her tale.

Musingly, Maura added, "There I was, a heap of blubbering idiot on the bed, fully clothed, with my face buried in my hands, upset that I'd had cold feet and told him I was a virgin, when I felt him take me by the shoulders, sit me up, and start kissing me gently. The only other thing I'll tell you is that it was the most amazing experience, neither one of us slept much, and when I woke up around nine that morning, he was sitting out on the balcony."

"What did you do then?" Anne asked curtly.

"I walked into the bathroom, wrapped a towel around me, and walked out to the balcony. He turned around when he heard me approach and gently asked how I was feeling. I told him I'd never felt better and reached down to kiss him." Smiling conspiratorially, Maura leaned over the table to get closer to Anne. She whispered, "It was the most amazing weekend of my life. I didn't want it to end. I was in a cloud of joy that nothing could burst and was actually a bit embarrassed when I went to work on Monday and Sergeant Major Atkins said I looked like the cat that ate the canary and asked what had me so happy."

Anne laughed. "How'd you get out of that?"

"I just smiled and walked away."

"Have you heard from him since that weekend?"

"Yes, when we said good-bye on Sunday, he told me he'd call me at the office Tuesday. When he called the office at lunch on Tuesday, he told me he'd managed to get his flight back to Berlin changed from late Thursday night to noon on Friday and needed my apartment address so he could spend Thursday night with me."

"Wow!" Anne exclaimed.

Realizing she didn't want to discuss any more details and had probably said more than she should, Maura stood up. "Don't know about you, but I want some dessert, and the buffet line closes in an hour or so." Not waiting for a response, Maura walked toward the buffet line.

After dessert and some hot tea, they went to Anne's BOQ. Maura took a shower and settled into the makeshift bed Anne had put together on the Army green couch in the other room. After about an hour, she turned out the light and slept a blissfully dreamless deep sleep, not waking up until around seven the next morning.

Maura and Anne went for a run before eating breakfast and had just finished showering and were drinking coffee when the phone rang.

Giving Maura a quizzical look because she was not on duty and no one ever called her on the weekends, Anne picked up the black handset. Shortly after saying "hello" and identifying herself, Anne told whoever was on the other end of the line, "What does it say?" Maura saw the color drain from Anne's face.

A few minutes later, Anne woodenly replaced the handset into the receiver and walked over to the kitchen table, where Maura was still sitting, sipping coffee.

"What's the matter?" Maura asked, concerned. She'd never seen Anne like this before, and when Anne didn't respond, Maura said a bit more forcefully, "Anne, are you okay?"

Anne shook her head and quietly announced, "That was the staff duty officer. I have a Red Cross message. When I told him to read it to me, he told me the message said my father had died and I needed to come home."

Maura immediately got up and went over to hug Anne. "Oh, sweetie, I am so sorry. Come on, we'll go get a bunch of change and make a call home so you can figure out what's happening and what you need to do."

They left the BOQ, got twenty dollars in quarters, and made the long-distance phone call to Anne's oldest brother's house. Because of the time difference, it was four in the morning back in Louisiana, and Anne woke her brother up out of a sound sleep.

He confirmed that he had gone to Fort Polk late the night before to send the message because he'd only been notified of their dad's death earlier that evening. The neighbor they paid to make and deliver supper every day had not gotten an answer to her persistent knocking on the door, so she had walked in and found their dad on the floor. When the ambulance arrived, they pronounced him dead. Anne's brother told Anne that he would not know the autopsy results until Monday or Tuesday but wanted to have the funeral as soon as possible and wanted to know when she could get home. Anne told him she was not sure, but she'd check into how she got put on emergency leave and would try to get out on the first plane Monday morning. Anne asked if he could hold off on the funeral until Friday, in case she ran into a bureaucratic mess. He agreed to do that, and Maura and Anne spent the rest of the day working the details of getting emergency leave and flight reservations for Anne.

Neither of them felt much like eating or talking, so Maura offered to make a salad and pull out some wine. As they sat down to eat, Maura asked, "Would you like to be alone?"

Anne nodded and asked Maura if she minded.

"Of course not."

"Thanks for understanding," Anne said. "I think I'll pack tonight, try to get some sleep, and get up early in the morning to head to Rhein-Main to sign up for a space A flight to Dover or Charleston. My brother will pick me up at the airport."

Maura asked, "Can I do the dishes and clean up?"

"No, I'd prefer to do it. I need to stay busy and not let my mind wander."

Maura reluctantly agreed and after packing up her few belongings said, "I know you have a lot on your mind, but could you send me a short letter letting me know you got home safely and call me when you return?"

"Of course. Thanks for your help today," Anne said as she ushered Maura out of her apartment and closed the door.

Maura knew she could not do anything to help Anne, so she got in her car and drove home, feeling sad and powerless to do anything to help her friend.

21

FRANKFURT INTERNATIONAL AIRPORT, 19 AUGUST 1978

MAURA GOT UP EARLY to take the train to Frankfurt to pick up Elise. There were no direct flights into Stuttgart from JFK. She had gotten to the gate about fifteen minutes before the flight arrived and was there when Elise stepped into the terminal and saw Maura excitedly waving to her. A huge grin spread across Elise's face as she enthusiastically waved back and made a beeline for Maura, who was also walking through the crowd to meet her.

Elise immediately hugged Maura, who returned the hug, exclaiming, "I can't believe you're actually here!" Stepping back, Maura extended the small wrapped box in her hand, saying, "Welcome to Germany. I'm so excited you're here." Elise took the small gold foil-wrapped box adorned with a silver ribbon and small silk daisy.

"It's almost too pretty to open," Elise whispered. Then, grinning, she started to open the package, adding, "I said almost. ..." Having opened the package, she saw it was a box of chocolate truffles. "Thanks. I've heard European chocolates are really tasty."

Taking the wrapping from Elise, Maura remarked, "I know the silk daisy was dorky, but I asked the candy store to add it to the ribbon because the custom here is to give both chocolates and flowers on special occasions, but because we're heading straight to Strasbourg, flowers just weren't practical."

"You've really taken to the lifestyle here, haven't you?" Elise commented.

"Life is a lot simpler and slower here, and Germans love any excuse to give a gift or have a drink, and I happen to like both customs. If you'd come around Christmas, I could have given you a box of my favorite chocolates, but they only make them in the winter. They're *Kirsch liqueur*-filled chocolate-covered cherries called Mon Cheri. You'd love them. Let's go get your luggage and take a taxi to the train station."

"Speaking of which, where's your suitcase and your friend Anne?" Elise asked.

As they walked to baggage claim and customs to get Elise's bag, Maura explained that she'd left her bag at the luggage storage room at the Hauptbahnhof in Frankfurt. She also told Elise that Anne would not be joining them as originally planned because her dad died recently and she was home on emergency leave. Elise expressed sympathy and added that she had a present from Maura's parents in her bag and told her they were healthy and happy and looking forward to Maura getting out of the Army next year and coming back home. Maura just smiled, not wanting to spoil the trip by telling Elise that she was thinking of staying in the Army.

After clearing customs, they went to the Frankfurt Bahnhof. Maura retrieved her bags and told Elise, "Okay, let's head to track twelve and get on the train." Indicating the large cloth bag she had retrieved along with her small suitcase, Maura explained, "I have a small bottle of red wine, fresh fruit, cheese, and crackers in here. With our first-class tickets, we'll get some mineral water and small glasses when we get on the train, so we can use those to put the wine in."

Elise nodded her approval, and ten minutes later, they were seated near the window, with a small tabletop that pulled out from the wall below the large window. Maura set out the snacks she'd carefully wrapped in tinfoil, along with a package of sesame crackers, and they spent the next hour catching up between sipping the wine and munching on the snacks Maura had prepared.

When they were settled on the train in Karlsruhe that would take them to Strasbourg, Maura told Elise to take a nap so she could stay awake until around ten that evening and get over jet lag quicker. They arrived in Strasbourg on schedule, which amazed Elise and amused Maura. "Germans are seriously crazy about being prompt and polite and ensuring everything runs according to plan. If the schedule says the train leaves at one minute past four, the train would be pulling out of the station at exactly that time, with or without you."

After a short streetcar ride, they arrived at the pension where Maura had made reservations, in the *Petite-France* section of Strasbourg. They unpacked and went for a walk along the river.

Around seven that evening, they stopped for dinner at a riverfront café and dined alfresco, marveling at the amazing French-inspired menu and fantastic wines. A sleepy but happy Elise thanked Maura for such a wonderful day as she quickly fell asleep.

22

STRASBOURG, FRANCE, SUNDAY 20 AUGUST 1978

MAURA AND ELISE GOT up early and had a quick breakfast on the terrace of their pension, overlooking the canal. Elise raved about the fantastic cappuccino and warm pastries. After breakfast, they went to the small kiosk that rented bikes. They spent the day riding through the city, starting with the Grand Ile and Parc l'Orangerie, admiring both the English and French gardens, as well as the Parc de la Citadelle, built around the remains of the seventeenth-century fortress erected close to the Rhine River.

After visiting the small zoo, they went to the botanical garden, the Jardin botanique de l'Université de Strasbourg, built in 1881, next to the Observatory of Strasbourg. From there, they biked over to the Parc des Contades, the oldest park of the city, and stopped at an outdoor café for a leisurely lunch. Their waiter was a good-looking German who spoke fluent English and was a graduate student at the university. He asked how long they would be in Strasbourg, and when Maura said they were only there for the day because their train left for Nice at eleven the next day, he gently chastised her for giving Strasbourg so little time. He flirted with her and

Elise for a while, saying that given that they were only there for the day, he would have to be bold and invite them to join him and some friends that evening for a free concert in the garden of the University Palace. Before Maura could politely demur, Elise excitedly said they would love to, and, not wanting to disappoint her best friend, Maura quietly agreed.

After lunch, they biked to Strasbourg Cathedral. Being Jewish, Elise had never been in a cathedral and was awestruck by both its size and beauty. There were no English-speaking tours that day, so they bought a brochure written in English and used it to do a self-guided tour. It contained a wealth of information, explaining, "The cathedral is visible far across the plains of Alsace and can be seen from as far off as the Vosges Mountains or the Black Forest on the other side of the Rhine; it is the sixth-tallest church in the world, and the highest extant structure built entirely in the Middle Ages." The brochure also noted that Victor Hugo referred to the church as a "gigantic and delicate marvel" and Goethe described it as a "sublimely towering, wide-spreading tree of God."

They finished up their day of sightseeing by riding through and around the grounds of the Palais Rohan, stopping to take a few pictures and asking a fellow tourist to take a picture of the two of them with their bikes on the banks of the Ill River.

They returned the bikes just minutes before the kiosk closed and got a bit of a lecture from the owner about cutting it way too close. Maura showed the irate owner the proper amount of remorse while explaining how much they'd fallen in love with his beautiful city and apologizing for losing track of time. He smiled and wished them well, telling them to come back any time, as they gaily headed back to the hotel to shower and change.

They met the waiter at the front of the University Palace. He introduced his friend to Maura and Elise, explaining that in order to get into the concert for free, they either needed a student or faculty ID, or had to be a guest of a student or faculty member, so his friend had graciously agreed to take Maura as a guest and he would take Elise.

After the concert, they went to a bistro on the river, and Elise and Maura entertained numerous questions about America, New York City, and what it was like to be a journalist and an Army officer. They, in turn, asked their companions what it was like to be a student in a large European city and how expensive it was to go to school there. The women were surprised to learn that although the application and acceptance procedures were rigorous and extremely competitive, the French government paid their tuition. Students paid for only books, supplies, and personal expenses.

The group talked, laughed, and drank into the wee hours of the morning. A tired and tipsy Maura and Elise quietly thanked the guys for a wonderful evening, got on tiptoe to kiss their companions' cheeks, and walked up the steps to the hotel entrance to unlock the front door to the lobby.

23

NICE, FRANCE, MONDAY 21 AUGUST 1978

MAURA AND ELISE got on their train in Strasbourg and, after a wonderful lunch of beef bourguignon, lapsed into a comfortable silence as they surveyed the beautiful countryside passing before their eyes. They spent the rest of the afternoon writing in their journals and catching up on some pleasure reading.

Their train arrived in Nice around five p.m. and they headed straight to their hotel. Both had agreed that staying on the shoreline near the beach was worth the splurge, and they were delighted to see that it was actually just a few steps from the strand that led to the beach. The desk clerk was a good-looking young guy named Phillipe. When he found out they were Americans, he complimented them on their ability to speak French and asked if this was their first time in Nice. When they said it was, he offered to show them around town that evening. They enthusiastically replied, "We'd like that very much."

He whispered conspiratorially that because this was the off season they had a nicer room than the one they were supposed to get. They thanked him, went upstairs, unpacked, and rented bikes. After a few hours of biking along the coast, they returned to take showers and meet Phillipe in the lobby, when he got off work at seven that evening.

MAURA AND ELISE GOT quite a few admiring head turns from locals as they walked with Phillipe to the restaurant. Maura, barely five feet six, slender, with pale white skin, (with a smattering of freckles across the bridge of her nose) greenish blue eyes and thick auburn locks that reached almost to her hips, wore a smart, but simple, sleeveless navy jersey mini dress, with a slim gold belt and matching gold evening sandals. Elise, with her equally long, thick jet black hair, azure blue eyes, and pale skin, (minus the freckles) was a striking contrast. Almost six feet tall and model thin, was dressed in a red leather mini skirt, with a black satin, V-neck sleeveless top, and matching black sandals.

They ate dinner at a wonderful but inexpensive outdoor café and insisted on paying for Phillipe's dinner, given that he had been nice enough to give them the beautiful room overlooking the water. Phillipe was a regular at this particular restaurant and recommended fresh mussels in an anise-flavored broth, with freshly baked bread and of course, white wine. From there they went to several clubs, where Phillipe introduced them to his friends. They spent the night dancing and drinking with the group of friends they had met at the first club. When the band took a break, Maura and Elise asked Phillipe and his friends for advice on where to go and what to do for nightlife in Cannes, Monaco, and Marseilles. They were disappointed when the men told them that even though those cities were very close to Nice, they did not party there. They also said most people were friendly and that as long as they stayed in the good parts of town, they could find other young people like themselves who would invite them to join them because everyone liked Americans, especially the guys. Around three in the morning, Phillipe announced that he had to be at work by noon, so if the ladies were ready to leave, he would walk them back to their hotel. It was a happy but tired group that said *au revoir* and left the club.

★ ★ ★

MAURA AWOKE TO SUNLIGHT streaming through the French doors of their hotel room. She was a bit disoriented but after a few minutes remembered they were in Nice. Seeing Elise still sound asleep, she got up, quietly opened the French doors, and stepped out onto a very small balcony. Taking a deep breath, she smelled the sweet, salty air and admired the turquoise waters of the Mediterranean Sea. She still couldn't believe they were actually here. *Cote d'Azur, the stuff of fairy tales*, she thought.

Returning to the bedroom, Maura walked over to Elise's bed, saying, "C'mon, sleepyhead. Up and at 'em." Elise nodded sleepily as Maura announced, "I'm taking a shower. Hopefully you'll be right behind me."

An hour later, they headed downstairs to the small sidewalk café and ordered cappuccinos. When the waiter returned with two steaming cappuccinos, Elise took a small sip, then a larger one. Leaning back in her chair, she let out a long sigh of contentment. "Oh my God, this is incredible. Why can't we make coffee like this back home?"

After two cappuccinos, freshly squeezed orange juice, and homemade yogurt with fresh berries, they picked up the beach bags they had slung across the backs of their chairs, and headed to the beach. Because the exchange rate was so favorable to the dollar, they decided to splurge and rented two wooden lounge chairs with overstuffed cushions for the day. The vendor offered to throw in an umbrella, a small end table, a bottle of sparkling water, and a bottle of wine if they paid him in dollars instead of Francs. A few minutes later, they pulled off their tops, shorts, and sandals, revealing the skimpiest of bikinis.

Lying down, Elise looked out at the ocean, musing, "You know, I could really embrace the dilettante lifestyle if only some amazingly handsome Frenchman would come up and sweep me off my feet."

Maura snorted in mock disapproval as she pulled a paperback out of her beach bag and started to read. They spent the entire day on the beach, reading, swimming, napping, and repeating the sequence before calling it a day.

Phillipe was at the front desk and greeted them as they returned from the beach. Happy to see him, they said they were looking forward to another fun evening on the town with him and his friends.

Meeting up with the group of guys and gals they had met the night before, Maura and Elise spent one final evening dancing, laughing, and drinking into the wee hours of the morning. Phillipe reminded Elise and Maura that checkout time was ten o'clock and he would not be on duty until noon so he could not cut them any slack and if they were not out of the hotel on time, they would automatically be charged another night's tariff.

Maura and Elise nodded understanding, and after a few minutes of kisses on cheeks and pleasantries, they walked back to the hotel with him.

THE NEXT MORNING, THEY checked out, stored their suitcases behind the front desk, and spent the next hour drinking cappuccino, and eating breakfast before catching their train to Cannes.

Because Cannes was even more expensive than Nice, Maura booked only one night. They were a few blocks from the beach and spent the afternoon walking in and out of the fancy shops that lined the beachfront, looking for celebrities and scouting out places to eat dinner and party. They were disappointed because they did not find anyone their age and everything was twice as expensive as in Nice.

In one of the fancy clothing stores, they happened upon an older American couple trying to communicate with the sales girl, who spoke no English. Maura translated for them. The couple thanked them and invited them to have a glass of wine on the beautiful beachside terrace at their fancy hotel. On the terrace, Maura asked the couple to take a picture of Elise and her.

THEY SPENT TWO MAGICAL days in Monaco, in awe of the beautiful people and ecstatic that they glimpsed Princess Grace driving by in her convertible.

From there they spent a week in Marseilles, visiting museums, biking through the city, and dancing the nights away.

Many years later, when things were tense between Maura and Elise, the picture of them on the terrace in Cannes with the turquoise Mediterranean behind them and smiling faces, displayed prominently in each of their homes, would be a reminder of just how much their friendship meant to them.

24

WEST POINT, COW YEAR, FRIDAY 1 SEPTEMBER 1978

LORI AND TRISH HAD finished their first basketball practice since returning from leave and were walking back to their barracks when Lori commented, "We have so much talent to compete with to make the team this year. I think this is going to be our best season yet, especially if some of the taller women make the cut."

"Yeah, Coach Gillis recruited some really good plebes this year. It'll be nice to have some height this season. Some of the teams we played last year dwarfed us," Trish replied.

"How are your knees holding up?" Lori asked.

"They're still sore but the trainer did a good job taping them up. With her help and some Motrin, I'll be fine. I was relieved Coach didn't schedule a session in the weight room today; that might have done me in."

Lori agreed. "Yeah, it was nice to get a break from lifting weights this summer, but I need to get in the weight room on my own so I'm not so sore afterwards."

As they approached one of the sally ports, Trish asked, "When are we supposed to be at Coach's house for the picnic?"

"He said 1600 hours. I'll swing by your room about 1545 if you like."

"Sounds good; see you then," Trish said as she and Lori went their separate ways.

LORI AND TRISH WERE approaching MacArthur's statute on their way to the Coach's annual Labor Day picnic when a group of Japanese tourists asked them to be in one of their photos. Stopping, they stood at attention and smiled into the camera, then resumed their walk to Coach Gillis's quarters. "I'm still not used to posing for the tourists even though it happens pretty regularly," Lori said.

"Yeah, it was nice to get away from all this during the summer," Trish replied. "I wish we could have stayed longer at CTLT. I learned so much in my unit and from my soldiers."

"Me too. My only regret is that I didn't get to be a platoon leader like a lot of our classmates did. I was really disappointed when I found out I would be a staff puke. Having a troop leadership position in Germany would have made that experience so much better."

"I totally agree, but we did get to experience the real Army, which is so much better than the Mickey Mouse stuff we deal with here at Woops."

"No kidding! This place is so idealistic; makes me wanna scream," Lori replied.

"No joke. Hey, I heard we finally got a female colonel on staff."

"Really? What's her position?"

"I heard she's the Chief of Staff of the Corps of Cadets."

Lori slowly nodded her head. "About time we have a senior role model. I didn't even know women colonels existed in the Army. I've never seen one. I bet she's really STRAC or she wouldn't be here. Talk about being under the microscope."

"Yeah, sorta like us plebe year." Abruptly changing the subject, Trish asked, "So what's the deal with you and Scott?"

"Whadda you mean?" Lori asked as they walked on the sidewalk to Coach's house.

"Well, is it serious? You seem to be spending a lot of your weekend time with him rather than with the team."

"Uhhh, yeah, I really like him and he's different than the other guys. I can speak my mind and not worry he'll blab it all over. He's more mature than most of the guys here, and he doesn't care about all the crap that goes along with dating a female cadet. He treats me nice, so yes, I guess it might be getting serious."

"That's great, Lori. You deserve a nice boyfriend. We've had a few classes together, and he's always impressed me. He seems genuinely nice and is always considerate."

"Thanks. We're going to the 500th night dance and ring weekend together."

Trish responded, "I can't wait to get my ring. I ordered an onyx stone with a diamond in the middle; should be a real beaut! That's great that Scott asked you to the dance. Some creepy firstie started talking to me on Saturday and asked me out. I had to tell him sorry, I already have a special friend to get him off my case."

"Cripes," Lori cried, "what's with these guys? Can't they see we're not interested in them?"

"No kidding," Trish said. "I used the word friend so I wouldn't be guilty of an honor code violation, because I didn't know how to gently tell him to bug off. It's the first thing that popped into my head; I hope he doesn't start calling me a homosexual. So many cadets are brainwashed into thinking that all women who go into the military are either lesbos or promiscuous. It really pisses me off."

"Yeah, I've heard the innuendos too, but I ignore them. That reminds me—last spring, one of the guys in my company asked me why the women on the basketball team are so tight. I told him we stick together because most of the male cadets are mean to us or just ignore us and forget to include us in their activities. Don't worry about the stereotypes; it's too hard to change small minds."

By now, Lori and Trish were close enough to the coach's house that they could see the coach and his wife with a bunch of their teammates gathered around the grill and picnic tables set up in the backyard. As she looked the group over, Trish remarked, "Looks like most of the team is already here, but I don't remember the name of the tall black plebe. What's her name again?"

"Her name is Natalie but she goes by Nat," Lori said.

As Lori and Trish walked into the picnic area, Coach greeted them, "Hi, Lori and Trish. Glad you could make it!"

"We wouldn't miss it," Trish said, smiling. "We love our team, and we're hungry, too."

Lori walked over to Nat and said, "Hi, Nat. I'm Lori, the team captain of the *Sugar Smacks* and one of my jobs is to help you during your plebe year. I'm glad you could escape the barracks for a few hours. How's your new company working out?"

"Ma'am, I'm in F1, the zoo, and it's crazy over there," Nat said.

"You don't have to call me ma'am here or on the court or when we're together as a team, only when other cadets and officers are around. What's so crazy about the zoo?" Lori asked.

"Well, my roommate's super strange and she's stressing me out. She thinks she's GI Joe and loves correcting me on my military bearing and plebe poop. I expected that sort of crap from the upperclassmen, but not from a fellow plebe. It's really annoying, and I hope she settles down soon."

"Yeah. Plebe year sucks, but you can do it." Noticing her accent, Lori asked, "Where you from, Nat?"

"I'm from Tyler, Texas," Nat said with a slight drawl.

"I knew you were from the South somewhere. I'm from Minnesota. You might get a little homesick the first semester, so I know you'll really appreciate going home for Christmas leave."

Reggie Howard, a slender yearling and Lori's teammate and best friend, walked over and asked, "What about Christmas leave?"

"I was just telling Nat how great Christmas leave is, and it's less than four months away!"

"Yeah, after taking calculus, physics, chemistry, military science, philosophy, and German, I'll need a vacation," Reggie said.

"Yearling year is notorious for tough academics. I guess they figure you have more free time to study because you don't have plebe duties or plebe poop to learn. I'm sure you'll do fine, Reggie," Lori said while slightly nodding her head.

"Yeah, basketball was a good outlet to work out some of my frustrations and help keep my sanity. If Coach hadn't made sure I went to AI, I might have failed calculus," Reggie said.

"I think I'll need some AI too. I'm not real good in English," Nat said.

Trish joined in on the conversation, "You and half your classmates. Don't worry Nat. If you show up to AI, the professors go out of their way to make sure you understand the concepts. I went twice a week last year, and my grades improved. Just let Coach know where you are so he doesn't worry about you. You can't play ball if you are failing any subjects."

"Great advice; thanks," Nat said.

At that moment, Coach Gillis announced, "The burgers and brats are on the table. Help yourselves, and thanks for bringing the pie and watermelon for dessert."

Lori looked at Reggie and Nat. "Let's eat!" Nodding, Nat and Reggie followed Lori to the picnic table, where some of their teammates were already filling their plates.

25

GÖPPINGEN, GERMANY, FRIDAY 1 SEPTEMBER 1978

MAURA UNLOCKED THE DOOR to her apartment and had barely gotten it open when Elise shoved her out of the way, apologizing as she rushed into the bathroom.

Maura chuckled as she picked up their bags and brought them inside the apartment. It had been a long train ride from Marseilles to Göppingen, requiring several transfers along the way. Their connection in Stuttgart for the train home to Göppingen had been especially tight, and they had barely made the train. Elise was exhausted and Maura had had to wake her up a few minutes before they'd gotten to Göppingen.

A few minutes later Elise walked out of the bathroom, exclaiming, "Wow, I needed that *bad!*"

Laughing, Maura pointed to the bedroom behind Elise. "I put your suitcase in your room. How 'bout we head to Cooke Barracks for a tour and dinner at the O'Club?"

"Sounds good. I'll be ready in just a few," Elise replied.

Maura and Elise spent the next hour driving around Cooke Barracks. Inside the brigade headquarters, Maura punched the code on the door and entered the operations center yelling, "Uncleared personnel."

The NCO on duty looked up and greeted Maura as she came in with Elise following behind. "Sergeant Anderson, this is my friend from the States. I'll sign her in so I can show her my office. We'll just be a few minutes and then get out of your hair."

As they entered Maura's office, Elise looked around at the huge open spaces and desks closely arranged side by side and asked quietly, "How can you work here? It's so drab and crowded. You don't have any privacy."

Feeling a bit irritated at the disdainful tone in Elise's voice, Maura replied a bit curtly, "I guess the same way you work in the crowded office you have in New York, where you actually have to share a desk."

"Sorry, you're right; I guess I just expected you'd have a nicer office, being an officer and all."

Maura relaxed and waved her hand dismissively. "No offense taken. I guess I minimized the physical conditions when I wrote, telling you how interesting my job is and how much I love it here. It did take a bit of adjusting, but I'm only a lieutenant and don't stand a chance of getting a private office until I'm a commander or a field-grade officer."

"Well, given that you'll be a civilian again in less than two years, that's not likely, is it?"

Maura was tempted to tell Elise she was seriously considering making the Army a career, but she decided better of it, knowing that would really piss Elise off. They'd had such a wonderful time together; she didn't want it to end on a sour note. Instead, she just smiled and looked at her watch. "It's almost seven. How 'bout we head over to the club for a nice dinner so we can get back to the apartment and get to bed early?"

Elise was appropriately impressed with the beautiful dining area on the terrace that looked out on the Swabian Alps in the distance. When the waiter returned with their wines, they placed their dinner orders and Elise clinked Maura's wine glass with hers. "I've had the most wonderful time. Thanks so much for planning everything. This trip has been the most amazing experience in my life! I'm so looking forward to your return home. Once you get a job, maybe we can take a trip to Europe together every couple of years."

"I'm glad it worked out, and I've enjoyed exploring France with you," Maura said gaily. "I'd love for us to explore the world together before we both settle down."

"I'm not sure we're the settling-down types, Maura," Elise said jauntily. "There's so much I want to do and see that I'm not sure I'll ever be interested in settling down."

Maura replied musingly, "You never know when Prince Charming will appear and sweep you off your feet, and then it's all over."

Elise asked guardedly, "Is there someone you want to tell me about?"

Maura quickly responded, "No," and subtly changed the subject. They spent the next hour reliving some of their favorite experiences, especially the beaches of Nice and the glitz of Monaco.

They were heading out the front door of the O'Club when Elsie suddenly asked, "What time do we have to get up in the morning?"

"Around six," Maura replied. "It'll take us about three hours to get to the airport, and I'll have to park and get you checked in no later than ten. I don't want to be rushed, so unless there's an accident, we should get to the airport in enough time to have coffee together before you go to the customs clearance area."

"Okay," Elise responded a bit glumly.

Maura was feeling a bit sad at the thought of Elise leaving as well and couldn't find any words to console her friend, so they rode back to the apartment in silence. When they got back, both women started feeling the effects of the long day of travel. When Elise had finished showering and came into the living room to let Maura know the bathroom was all hers, she gave Maura a quick hug and said, "I'll probably be out by the time you're done, so I'll see you in the morning."

26

RHEIN-MAIN AIRPORT, SATURDAY 2 SEPTEMBER 1978

MAURA NERVOUSLY CHECKED HER watch for about the tenth time in the past hour. They had encountered a huge backup on the autobahn just outside of Karlsruhe and had gotten to the airport about half an hour later than she planned. When they got to the terminal, there was a long line of people waiting to check in.

With Elise's luggage and passport checked, Maura motioned for Elise to follow her. She knew her way around the airport and wanted to get to the gate a few minutes before boarding started so they would not feel rushed saying good-bye. Maura pointed and said, "There's your boarding area." A lot of people were already in queue to board, so there were plenty of empty seats. "You can get in line, or we can sit down. What's your preference?"

"Let's sit down. It'll be over a year before we see each other, and I'd like to have a few minutes together before I leave." Maura sat down, with Elise right beside her.

Elise continued, "This has been the most amazing trip of my life. I spent the past six months dreaming about this trip. I was excited at the prospect of seeing Europe for the first time and getting to spend time with you like we did in the old days. The minute I got off the plane, it was like we'd just seen each other the day before, and it was so much fun being together again. But now I know I won't see you for over another year, and I'm depressed. I really do miss having you around." Seeing Maura start to speak, Elise raised her hand. "No, wait, I'm not finished. I'm okay, 'cause I know that when I see you again, it'll be because you've come home to stay. So I won't whine, because I know you hate that sort of thing, but I never realized until you were gone that I don't make friends easily and wanted you to know just how much our friendship means to me."

"You're a goofball. Before you know it, I'll be home, and no matter where in the world I am, we'll always be best friends and support each other."

Elise reached out to hug Maura. "Thanks again for a wonderful time. I'm going to have so much fun bragging about all the cool things we did and showing the great pictures we took. My coworkers were so envious. They couldn't believe I was actually going to spend two weeks in Europe with you."

Maura stood up as she heard the boarding announcement for Elise's plane. "Okay, time for you to get in line. No tears, just smiles, and when you get home, don't forget to give my parents the gift and a big hug from me."

Elise nodded, gave Maura one last hug, picked up her purse and carry-on bag, and walked away. Maura stood there for a bit as an unexpected wave of homesickness enveloped her. She'd thought about flying home for the holidays this year, but if she did that, she'd have to dip into the meager savings she had. She'd also end up using a good portion of her leave, which meant she wouldn't be able to take some trips around Europe that she wanted to take before she went back to the States.

As Elise got in line, Maura gave one final wave good-bye and walked back to the car. On her walk back to the parking garage, she mused over how she was going to break the news to Elise—and more importantly, to her parents—that she'd decided to stay in the Army. She laughed as she told herself, *There's plenty of time to think about this. Just leave it for another day.*

A few minutes later, she was in her car, heading to Stuttgart to see if Anne was back from emergency leave. She had just pulled into a parking space in front of Anne's BOQ when she saw Anne coming out the door. Stepping out of the car, Maura called Anne's name.

Surprised, Anne looked in Maura's direction and started walking toward her. "Hi. I wasn't expecting a visit from you today."

"Yeah, I know. I took Elise to the airport and decided to stop by to see if you were back. How're you doing?" Maura asked.

"Okay. Got back last night. I was gonna call you at work tomorrow," Anne replied. "I'm actually headed to the shoppette to pick up a few things. Had to drink my coffee black this morning. Speaking of which, I brought back a bunch of chicory coffee and have a pound for you."

"Thanks. Not sure I can make café au lait as well as you do, but it'll be fun trying. Have you eaten lunch yet?"

"No, slept in and cupboards are bare, so figured I'd grab a quick bite at the snack bar, then head to the shoppette to pick up a few things until I can get to the commissary next week."

"All I've had is a cup of coffee, and I'm starving, Do you have time for lunch at Langerbruecke Hof?"

"Sure, that actually sounds much better than eating alone at the snack bar. Thanks for stopping by."

"C'mon, I'll drive," Maura said.

Fifteen minutes later, they walked into the small local restaurant they had discovered during their first week in Germany. They were regulars, and the couple who owned the restaurant greeted them as they entered, asking if they'd been on holiday. Maura told them about Elise's visit from the States and their trip to France, leaving them to assume that Anne had joined them. The owners told them to sit at the *Stammtisch* and that their wine would be out in just a minute. Maura thanked them but said Anne and she wanted a bit of privacy and quiet and asked to sit at one of the small tables in the corner. The owner's wife led them to one of the tables in the corner, returning with a bottle of sparkling mineral water and two white wines. She smiled and quickly walked away.

"Do you think we offended them?" Anne asked quietly.

"They're Germans; they respect privacy and realize that sometimes the stammtisch isn't appropriate," Maura replied. "So, how did things go at home?"

Anne took a sip of wine. "It actually wasn't as bad as I thought it would be, just not sure where to start."

Maura asked, "How did you get to the airport?"

"Well, shortly after you left, my boss came by with my leave paperwork. He told me to call him when I got my flight arranged and he'd take me to the airport. I went to the office, called Rhein-Main, told them I was on emergency leave, and asked what flights they had leaving that day. They said there was a flight to Charleston at 2200 that evening and because I was on emergency leave and they didn't have any emergency leave folks signed up for the flight, if I could get there before roll call, I'd go to the top of the list and if there were any open seats on the flight, I could leave that evening."

"Wow, that was lucky. How'd you get home?"

Anne smirked. "Well, that's where it gets interesting. When I got to Charleston, I had just cleared customs and was headed to the travel office to see if I could get a rental car with an open return date when I ran into Derek of all people. He asked if I was still in Germany, and I told him yes but I was home on emergency leave because my dad had just died. He told me he was on leave and had been checking out space A flights to see where he could go for a week or so, but nothing was available, so he offered to drive me home."

"He's the guy you went out in Officer Basic, right?"

Anne smirked. "Yeah, Derek and I had a fling in OB, but I never took him seriously and we agreed to stay friends."

"Sounds like a lot more than just a friend." Maura probed.

"Nah," Anne said dismissively. "He's the sort of guy that has everything and expects everything to go his way. I figure he's attracted to me because I was different and didn't fall all over him like the other women."

"Isn't he the guy who would call you at work from time to time?"

Anne nodded. "Yeah, he went to Airborne and Ranger training and he'd applied to be a Green Beret, and just before we graduated, he gave me his parents' address and told me to write him there when I got settled and let him know my address and telephone number at work. Said he'd get back in touch with me when he finished all his training."

"I vaguely remember you talking about him but didn't realize you were still in touch."

"I took his address, never intending to contact him, but last winter, when I was going through my address book to send Christmas cards, I came across his information and decided what the heck, I'd wish him a Merry Christmas and send my contact information. A few months later there was no one more surprised than me when I got a call from him at the office. He'd gone home for the holidays and his parents gave him my card. He was assigned to 10th Group at Fort Devens, and as part of their training, they travel to Bad Tölz, Germany, for combat ski training. He was wondering if he took leave and got reservations at the Patton Hotel in Garmisch, if I'd spend a few days with him."

"So that's why you went to Garmisch and left me on my own. I always wondered why you did that, and was a bit hurt you didn't invite me, but decided it wasn't any of my business."

Anne gave Maura a sheepish grin. "Sorry."

"We're cool. I'm the one that needs to understand that just because you don't share or seek my advice doesn't mean we're not good friends."

Anne raised her hands in mock surrender. "Guilty as charged. Look, Maura, friends of any kind that I can trust with confidences are a very new thing for me. I had a rough childhood in a town where everyone knows everyone's business and everyone has lived there for generations, some since before the Civil War. I really don't want to go over it in detail, but things were pretty bad at home, and I just learned not to trust or depend on anyone but myself."

Maura felt an overwhelming sympathy for and new insight into Anne's complicated personality. "I know what you mean, and while I'm certainly more open than you, I've been struggling with my friendship with Elise, who has been my very best friend since childhood. We were so symbiotic that we were sure we were meant to be twins but one of God's angels goofed up and sent us to different mothers."

Anne laughed and Maura smiled, acknowledging the childish absurdity of the notion. "But just like you, a lot has happened. Elise and I are on different paths with different life goals, she wants me to buy into the plan that we made when we were little. I wanted to tell her how much I love being in the Army and even though the guys are a pain, I love the challenge and excitement that being in the Army brings. Being in the Army has made me realize that doing the same job for twenty or thirty years isn't what I want. I'm really not sure exactly what I want, but going home, going to grad school, and working at the UN as a translator isn't my dream anymore. The problem is, Elise never changed her dream and expects me to go with the original plan."

"Did you guys get into an argument about that on the trip?" Anne asked solicitously.

Maura frowned. "No, I didn't have the guts to tell her. I just wanted things to be the way they've always been, and we were having so much fun, I didn't want to spoil our time together. Besides, she spent a lot of money and all her vacation to do this. That just wouldn't be fair. But hey, we're supposed to talking about you. Back to this Derek guy... Did he take you home?"

"Yeah, I tried to talk him out of it but finally I said thanks."

Interrupting, Maura asked, "Weren't you surprised that he'd go to such lengths for someone that he'd had a short fling with during OB and hadn't seen much in two years?"

Anne rolled her eyes and admitted that she had been so distraught that she really had not been able to make sense of anything that was happening. "When we stopped for breakfast just outside of Charleston, Derek asked how I was doing, and when I tried to tell him I was fine, I broke down crying hysterically. Derek came over, took me in his arms, and told me he was there for me. Over breakfast, he surprised me again, telling me he'd tried to move on after our weekend in Garmisch but seeing me made him realize that he still had strong feelings, and he asked if it was okay if he stayed for the funeral."

"Did you say yes?"

"No, not at first. But he persisted, and I just couldn't handle fighting him anymore."

"So he went to the funeral?"

"Yeah, he met my brothers and helped me sort through all the legal paperwork."

"What paperwork?" Maura asked. "Couldn't your brothers handle that?"

"Yes, but Dad left the house to me, which was the only thing he actually owned, and my brothers threatened to contest the will."

"Oh, Anne, how horrible!"

"Yeah, so I asked them what that would solve, pointing out that the house could only belong to one person, and they told me they wanted me to sell so we could share the profit. I just couldn't live with that and told them I'd talk to our family lawyer about working something out so we could arrive at a fair market value for the house and if they would agree to a payment plan, I would pay their portion monthly until the debt was satisfied."

"Did they agree to that?"

"Sorta. They agreed but said they wanted five percent interest on the balance until it was paid off."

"Boy, Anne. No wonder you don't trust anyone."

Anne demurred, "You know, without my brothers chipping in to make sure I got a college education, I wouldn't be here. I know they love me. I guess they just felt gypped out of what little affection my dad may have had to give and wanted something in return for all their heartache."

Maura leaned back, totally taken aback by all this. "Can you afford that?"

"I can't, but Derek went into attack-dog mode and told them they should be ashamed of themselves, that I was being more than fair and if they wanted a court battle, he had the money to make sure there was one hell of a court battle coming and he'd make it his singular mission to ensure they didn't get a dime."

"Oh my God," Maura whispered.

"Yeah, so we talked and agreed to a payment plan with no interest that gives them their money over the next five years. So, no vacations or fancy trips for me, *chéri*. You'll have to do them on your own or with enchanting Eric."

"Wow," Maura said quietly. "Am I gonna get to meet this modern-day knight in shining armor?"

"Dunno. He asked me what my plans were after my initial obligation. When I told him I had to stay in the Army to pay off my debt, but wasn't sure of anything beyond that, he told me he was working on an assignment to Fort Bragg and asked me to put Fort Bragg as my first choice on my dream sheet."

"And …" Maura queried.

"I'm thinking about it, but I'll have to go to jump school if I get it, and I'm not so sure I'm up to that."

Maura was speechless. Anne shrugged her shoulders and told Maura that she'd keep her in the loop.

Maura shook her head. "What are you going to do with the house while you're in the Army?"

"I'm paying the lady that took care of Dad to come by the house twice a month to dust, clean, and check things out. Some of the neighbors agreed to keep an eye on the place and let my oldest brother know if anything needs attention. I also told my brothers that if they wanted to bring their families there on vacations to just coordinate with each other. Even though I'm technically the owner, it's our family home and they can stay there any time they want."

The waitress came over to see if they wanted anything else, and they told her no. Then Maura asked Anne if she enjoyed being with Derek. Anne smiled and said yes, a lot more than she liked to admit.

Putting her share of the bill on the small plastic tray, the waitress had left, and Maura decided to go for broke. "Just one more question, and you don't have to answer it if you don't want to. Do you love him?"

Anne furrowed her brow. "I don't really know the answer to that. If you ask me if I'm in love with him right now for being the most amazing guy I've ever met, the answer is an unqualified yes. Whether or not either of us love each other enough to make a go of a marriage should he ask me, I don't have a clue."

The ride back to Anne's BOQ was unusually quiet, but as Anne got out of the car, she thanked Maura for being such a good friend and listener and told her she'd see her in Göppingen the following weekend.

27

WEST POINT, FALL 1978

LORI AND CATE ROOMED together because they were the only two women remaining in Company A4. "Wow, I thought I had tough academics last year, but this term, Juice and Thermo are killing me," Lori said, referring to her electrical engineering and thermofluid dynamics classes.

Cate relied, "Yeah, I'm overloaded too. I should never have signed up for History of the Military Art. My P gives quizzes every day. Last night, I skipped my history readings to study Juice, and I tubed the history quiz this morning."

"That sucks, but I'm sure you did okay. What do you call tubing, a C?" Not waiting for an answer, Lori added, "I'm glad I signed up for the easy half-year history class instead of the in-depth history class for the whole year. So, is history class your toughest class this term?" she asked.

"No. My toughest class this term is bowling."

"Are you kidding me? How hard can bowling be?"

"Well, if you have under a 109 average, you fail the course. I have a 143 average and that is only a B+. Can you believe it? I have to get a 150 average just to earn an A-! This place is incredible. I thought I was a good bowler, but not here. Everything is supercharged," Cate said.

"Yeah, good point. They've figured out how to make every course harder than it needs to be. My favorite class this semester is Cultural and Political Geography. It's interesting and makes a whole lot of sense, and I don't have to study for hours to get a good grade."

"My favorite class is Advanced International Relations," Cate said. "I really like my P. He's a really cool captain from Rutgers who can't believe all the stupid stuff we have to do."

"Yeah. This is definitely not your typical college experience. I miss the freedom I experienced during CTLT. We had Army rules and regulations, but we could actually make decisions on our own. This place is so depressing. It's nothing like the real Army. I guess if we can complete four years here, we can do anything!" Lori said emphatically.

"Well, it's more interesting now that we have plebe women in our company."

"Yep, I'm going to treat them the same as the other plebes, and they'll survive."

"They'll do fine. . .Well, I have five WPRs this week, so I've got to hit the books hard," Cate said as she sat down at her desk and opened her Thermo textbook.

★ ★ ★

IN THE BASKETBALL LOCKER room the next day, Reggie came up to Lori and said, "I've got a problem with someone in my company that's really starting to bug me. I need some advice."

"Sure. What's up?"

"Well, I opened up my green-girl this afternoon for some Z time and I found a condom filled with lotion or something worse on my bed."

"Ish! That's disgusting. Did your roommate see it?" Lori asked.

"No, she was in class. But she did see it in the trash can later. This isn't the first time I've had stuff like this happen to me."

"What else has been happening?" Lori asked, starting to get upset.

"You know, the crude and vulgar jokes like, 'What's it called when female cadets are swimming? The Bay of Pigs,' and 'What's it called when a female yearling and two plebes are together? Pork and beans,' those kind of jokes, but this is getting more personal. What do you think, Lori? You've been here over two years and have more experience," Reggie said.

"A filled condom on your bed is too much to ignore. I think you've got to report it to your Tactical officer. Who is your Tac, by the way?"

"Her name is Captain Dunbar. The cadets call her Bunny behind her back because she wears bright pink lipstick in uniform. I like her and think she'll listen and try to help me."

"Okay, make an appointment to see her tomorrow so these gross and vulgar incidents don't escalate."

Reggie replied, "Thanks, Lori! I needed some advice with this one. I'll ask my roommate to go with me. She saw the condom in the trash can after I told her about it and had a conniption fit."

As Lori turned the corner of one set of lockers, she saw Nat sitting on the bench, putting on her high-top tennis shoes. "Hi, Nat! How's it going?"

"Hi. It's going. I'm glad I can play ball and get some of my frustrations out."

"Plebe year sucks, no doubt about it. What's bugging you the most?"

"I'd say your women classmates are the biggest hazes," Nat said.

Very surprised with Nat's response, Lori said, "What?"

"Yep. In my company, G-1, the women are super tough on the female plebes. For example, we're constantly being told our hair is too long, we're gaining too much weight, and we're total spazzes. Another example was when I was pinging up the steps, I saw men's shoes and I said, 'Good morning, sir.' A woman from your class said, 'Miss, halt! Do I look like a man to you?' I then spent the next fifteen minutes getting blasted by her and reciting my plebe poop."

"Sorry to hear that, Nat. That doesn't happen to our female plebes in A4. I had no idea it was happening in your company," Lori said sadly. "There's not anything I can do about my classmate hazing you. I wish I could change the hazing policies; I hate them."

AFTER DINNER, LORI NOTICED Cate's authorization location card hanging just inside the door was "Unmarked." Lori thought this was unusual because Cate was meticulous about correctly marking her authorization card to show her location. When Cate returned to the room, Lori softly asked, "Hey Cate, I noticed you were unmarked. Was that a mistake?"

"Uh, no. I put my card unmarked for a reason."

"Well, okay. I just don't want you to get into any trouble," Lori said diplomatically.

"I'm trying not to, but I'm really in over my head," Cate replied slowly.

"Can I help?" asked Lori.

"No. I wish you could, but I'm smitten by this officer and I don't know what to do about it," Cate blurted.

"Whoa. Do you mean a cadet officer?"

"Uh, not exactly, he's a captain," Cate said quietly as if someone might hear the discussion.

Lori's eyes widened, "How did that happen?"

"Well, it started out innocently enough, and then our relationship ballooned out of control. He was my math P last year, and we started seeing each other on the weekends at his BOQ. Now I think I love him and he says the same thing to me. I'm going crazy with fear, happiness, and confusion. Lori, I don't know what to do!" Cate said in anguish.

"Wow, it's hard to believe. How long has this been going on?"

"Over six months. We started seeing each other last spring right before term ends. I spent a week on leave with him in Ohio this summer, and now I go to his BOQ almost every weekend. Jim is such a caring, sensitive man," Cate replied. "He's so different than the cadets I've dated."

Lori had a hard time understanding how her smart and squared away roommate was intentionally breaking the rules. *She must be so stressed out covertly dating an officer while being a cadet*, Lori thought to herself.

Cate continued, "You can't imagine how hard it is. I try not to think about him, but he invades my every thought. I'm just crazy about him, and I really don't know what to do about it."

"So... can you tell me why you think you're in love with him?" Lori had to ask.

"Well, Jim's smart, good-looking, has a great sense of humor, and he really cares about me," Cate said. "He makes me feel so special and wanted. I've never felt like this before."

"Now it's starting to make sense. I was wondering why you seemed so distracted. ... Now I know why," Lori said. "Well, last spring you might have been in trouble for fraternizing with your professor, but he's not your P anymore, is he?"

"No. But I know I shouldn't be dating an officer while I'm a cadet," Cate said while rubbing her hands together. "We've been sneaking around on the weekends, hoping no one recognizes us when we go to New York City or the Poconos. I just don't like sneaking around ... makes me feel dishonest or dirty. Can you understand?"

Lori tentatively replied, "Yes. I think so. But, truthfully, I'm not sure I can since I've never thought about this predicament. But, I guess it's sort of natural for a twenty-two-year-old woman to like a young man, even if he is an Army officer. How old is Jim?"

"He's twenty-nine, been an officer for seven years. He's a captain and just got assigned here last year. He's due to rotate in the summer of 1980 when we graduate. Did I mention he's brilliant? He's a math wiz, and so intelligent. I love talking to him about numbers, equations, and exciting theories."

"That's not what gets me excited, but if you both enjoy that, good for you. How does he feel about all of this?"

"He's not happy about the rule breaking, either, but he's dealing with it. He has a lot to lose if we get caught together, but he's told me he loves me and if he loses his career over me he's willing to do it."

"You could get kicked out too. Or more likely walk a few hundred area tours. Do you think you can hide this mutual attraction for another year and a half until you graduate?"

"I hope so. I haven't told anyone about him except for you, Lori. I hope you can keep my secret."

"I'll try Cate. I hope you can figure all of this out. It's hard enough being a cadet here. Adding a secret relationship on top of that ... well if anyone can do it, I think you can."

Cate sighed loudly and gave Lori a hug, "Thanks, Lori. You have no idea how much better I feel confiding in you. Some days I feel like I'm going to burst. I don't know how to describe it. I'm happy, excited, and so forward-thinking, but I'm also terrified we're going to get caught and get in really big trouble."

"I'm happy for you, Cate, but I'm worried too. You both could get in big trouble if you get caught. Let me know what I can do to help, and I'll try to assist."

"You've been a great listener. It's just what I needed," Cate said.

Lori was thoughtful later that night, considering Cate's dilemma as she wrote in her diary:

> Wow, what a revelation Cate told me tonight. She's dating a Captain on the sly. I really hope they don't get caught and into trouble. Now I have 2 huge secrets to keep. I'm worried about both my friends but I'll do my best to help them.

28

WEST POINT, DECEMBER 1978

THE ARMY–NAVY FOOTBALL game was a blowout. Army lost 28-0 to the midshipmen at the Naval Academy, and it was a sad sight for the cadets to behold. The plebes were really upset, knowing they would get the brunt of the anger taken out on them in the form of hazing from the upperclassmen. Once again, Lori's basketball team had to take the early bus back to the academy. After the big loss, Lori was happy to get out of the drinking frenzy that had erupted after the game was over.

On 8 December, the Sugar Smacks basketball team played Catholic University in Central Gym. As was his custom, just before the game, Coach Gillis led the team in a short prayer for a safe and fun game.

When they won, Coach Gillis was ecstatic over the win, and after the game, he praised the entire team for their selfless way of playing. "Great passing today, ladies! I really liked how you kept passing the ball to Nat and Reggie under the basket. They made all those points look easy, but it was because each of you were looking for them that enabled us to attack the basket. Oh, and did I mention defense? Our defense was the best I've seen it this year. That's why we won; our defense prevented their team from scoring."

In the locker room after the game, Lori and Reggie were deep in conversation. "Wow Reggie, you were really on today! I can't believe you scored all those points," Lori said.

"Like Coach said, it was only 'cause you guys kept giving Nat and me all those great passes under the bucket. We're a team, and it doesn't do any good to score a lot of points if we don't win."

"True enough, but you were great today. Hey, what happened with Captain Dunbar and the condom incident?"

"Not much to report. She seemed concerned and discussed the situation with the company commander and his staff. She also discussed the subject of treating all company members with respect at last week's company honor training. So far, I haven't had to deal with off-color jokes or seen anything really gross. I just hope it lasts."

"That's good to know. Sorry you had to deal with a few immature guys. No one should have to put up with some of the crap we deal with."

THE NEXT AFTERNOON, LORI had two of her wisdom teeth pulled. She was given an 800 mg Motrin pill for the pain and put on bed rest for the rest of the day. Scott came over to her room after dinner with a bouquet of flowers. "Hey, Lori! How you feeling?"

"A little sore now that my Novocain is wearing off. I have another pain pill I'm going to take before bed. Have you had your wisdom teeth taken out?" she asked.

"Yeah, had mine taken out last year. Two were fine, but the other two were really impacted and were buggers to get out. The doctor called his buddy in the next office over to look at my mandible. My jaw and head hurt for three days. Anyways, I thought you'd enjoy these flowers," Scott said while presenting Lori with the bouquet of multicolored daisies, carnations, and lilies.

"Aw, thanks, Scott. They're real pretty," Lori said, cracking a faint smile.

"Glad you like them. Well, I'm off to start studying for my Juice class. I know we'll have a quiz tomorrow, and this stuff is getting confusing."

Yawning Lori said, "Yeah, I know what you mean."

"Well, get some sleep. I'll check on you tomorrow," Scott said before he walked out of Lori's barracks room.

A minute after Scott left, Cate walked in the room. "Ooooh! Who're the flowers from, Lori? Your mom?"

"No, Scott brought them over," Lori said softly.

"Nice. He's so thoughtful. You're lucky to be dating Scott; you could do a lot worse."

"Thanks," Lori softly said before she drifted off to sleep.

29

TUSCALOOSA, ALABAMA, 24 DECEMBER 1978

BECAUSE BERLIN WAS SIX hours ahead, it was noon to Amelia's body when she woke up around six a.m. on her first morning home. Amelia wryly considered the fact that about the time she got over jet lag, it would be time to return to Berlin.

Taking a sip of the coffee she'd just made, she headed out to the front porch. It was still dark, but the air was clear, and at a balmy fifty degrees, Amelia felt like it was summer. When she'd left Berlin to catch her flight home, it had been −2 degrees Celsius.

Amelia felt for moisture on one of the rocking chairs and, finding it dry, sat down. Taking another sip of coffee, she wondered what her parents' reaction would be when they discovered she'd taken up drinking coffee.

She'd arrived in Birmingham a bit after two the previous afternoon. Charles and both sets of their parents had been at the gate to greet her. After lots of tearful hugs from both moms, they had set out for Tuscaloosa. Amelia had been surprised when she'd seen the Ford station wagon and asked her dad when he bought it. He'd laughed and told her that their good friend who owned the two car dealerships in Tuscaloosa had lent him the station wagon for the afternoon so everyone could come to the airport. Then she stifled the laugh that had almost burst from her when he told her that the three men would sit up front and the three women could sit in the back and catch up on the way home.

On the way home, her mom asked if she was tired. Amelia's response was that she was so excited to be home, she felt like she could go on for at least another day or two without sleep. That elicited laughs of relief from all the parents, and her mother explained that so many people were just dying to see Amelia that she'd agreed to a dinner party at the country club at seven that evening, so if Amelia felt she needed it, there was time for her to take a nap, shower, and change before they had to show up at the club.

Shortly after they got to the house, Charles's parents left in their car. While her dad took her luggage up to her room, Amelia's mom said she would follow her dad to the dealership to return the station wagon and they would pick up a few things on the way home so Amelia and Charles could have a few moments alone together before they all had to get ready for dinner.

As Amelia's parents drove away, Charles took her in his arms, kissing her urgently and murmuring huskily, "Now for a real welcome home."

Amelia submitted to the long urgent kissing and fondling that ensued, hoping to feel the excitement and overwhelming love she'd once felt for Charles, but try as she might, it just wasn't the same. She'd struggled with this when Charles had visited her the past summer in Berlin, and she'd told herself it would take time for her to get over her anger at him for hurting and deserting her. She'd enjoyed showing him around Berlin, and they'd had a marvelous time, but had steered clear of talking about anything serious or of revisiting his treatment of her when she'd told him she was going into the Army. The first evening of his visit this past summer, they'd had dinner at the same restaurant where she and Maura and Anne had eaten on their first Christmas Eve in Germany. Seeing the look of surprise on Charles's face when she ordered wine and asked him if he wanted a beer, Amelia had smiled and reminded him of their conversation in January, when she'd told him that she was not the same and that the two weeks he was visiting her would be a chance for him to determine if he still felt that they had a future together.

Charles had told her that nothing could change his mind about spending the rest of his life with her, and he had purposed himself to accepting Amelia exactly as she was. He had surprised her by announcing that he had originally planned to wait until after dinner to give her something but that, given their conversation, he had decided to change his original plan.

Bemused, Amelia had looked at him, wondering what he was talking about, but had gasped as he'd pulled the ring box with his grandmother's engagement ring out of his pocket, opened it, and presented it to her once again. She had realized then that she should have expected something like this, but she hadn't really had time to think any of this through. Closing the box, Amelia had pushed it back toward Charles and told him she wanted him to wait until he was sure he could commit to making their life together permanent.

Charles initially objected but, seeing the steely glint in Amelia's eyes, had thought better of it and put the ring back in his pocket. They spent the remainder of his visit having fun together and steering clear of any serious discussions about their future or the differences between them. The night before he returned home, Charles asked if she could come home for the holidays. Amelia hadn't even considered that possibility, and when she had stammered a bit and told him she'd have to see if she could get some advance leave and afford a ticket, he had told her he would buy the ticket if she came home. She had thanked him and agreed to a Christmas visit.

Because she had only one bedroom, she'd let Charles have her bed and she had made up the couch every night like she did when Maura and Anne came for a few days. Long ago, they'd both agreed that they wouldn't have sex until their wedding night. Before the breakup, it had been difficult to break off their heavy petting sessions, and she had sensed that it was even harder for him during their visit, because she suspected but did not want to confirm that he'd had sex with several women since their breakup. What surprised her then was that she didn't feel the same excitement and desire at his touch and kisses that she had felt in the past. Once again, she rationalized it was probably a defense mechanism that would diminish with the passage of time.

After several months of love letters from Charles and his insistence that she come home during the holidays so they could start planning for a wedding for June of 1980, she had started to get excited about the prospect of realizing her dream of raising a family and living in Tuscaloosa for the rest of their lives. It surprised her, when Charles started kissing and fondling her so urgently on her first night home, that she had to fake excitement. She was even more chagrined to discover that she was able to fake sexual excitement so instinctively.

As she sat on the porch in the predawn darkness, Amelia smiled, recalling her mother talking to her about her wifely responsibilities shortly after her and Charles's engagement announcement. Luckily, Charles had not picked up on her lack of excitement, but as she was reviewing her feelings, it bothered her that he had just assumed she would be as ardent in her passion for him as he was for her.

As she continued to sip her coffee, her mind wandered back to the year she had spent with Mattias and the first time he had kissed her. He'd waited almost six months before even trying, and his touch and kiss had elicited a much stronger emotion than she had expected. As they had gotten closer and she had let go of her emotional ties to Charles, she had asked Mattias why he'd taken so long to make any sort of physical advances.

Mattias had told her that although it had been difficult, he had wanted to wait until he felt she was ready to be receptive to the possibility of caring about him. He had laughed uproariously when she timidly asked him if it had been hard for him to refrain from getting physical with her. She smiled recalling that he never actually answered her question, but his laughter had told her what she needed to know. She had been attracted to him from that first night he had taken her and the girls out for the evening, but because she had still considered herself Charles's fiancée, she had resisted acknowledging any feeling of attraction to Mattias as anything other than a brother. From that first kiss until the night Charles had called her and asked her to forgive him and come back to her, however, she had been filled with joy, a sense of trust, and physical longing, which was the equal of what she had felt for Charles. That was one of the reasons she had been so angry with Charles for waiting so long to apologize.

She wondered with not a bit of sadness and longing how Mattias was doing. She recalled her shock the month before at learning about his engagement to one of the women he'd had a long affair with prior to falling in love with her. Just then, Amelia realized her cup was empty and even though she was wearing slacks, a sweater, a jacket, and gloves, the cold morning air was starting to chill her. She got up and walked inside.

As she walked into the kitchen, Amelia saw her father pouring a cup of coffee. Putting his cup down, he walked over to give her a hug. "Mornin', darlin'. I have to admit, having coffee already made is a nice surprise, but either you're having some anxious moments and can't sleep or Army life has changed your sleep habits."

Amelia laughed as she pulled away from him and poured herself another cup of coffee while he put sugar and milk in his. "Probably a bit of both, Daddy, but it's afternoon in Berlin and it'll take about a week or more for my body to adjust to this new time zone."

He nodded knowingly. "Yeah, I forgot about that. They've got a word for that, don't they?"

"It's called jet lag, Daddy." Amelia giggled as she took a sip of coffee.

"Yeah, I sorta—" her father said musingly, abruptly stopping midsentence. "Since when do you drink coffee, girl?"

"Since I discovered German coffee, Daddy. Do you like it?"

He looked at her quizzically and took another sip of coffee. "Well now that you mention it, it does taste sorta different." He took another sip and announced, "Hmm, this is nice. You say it's German coffee?"

"Yes, Daddy. Some of my friends in Germany introduced me to it, and I like it. I can take it or leave it, but it is nice to have a cup first thing in the morning, especially when it's a bit chilly." Pointing to the round kitchen table behind them, Amelia said, "Let's sit down; I have another surprise." Sitting down at the table, she began to unwrap the package on the table. Putting the oval loaf of sweet bread on the serving platter she had taken out of the china cabinet when she'd first come downstairs that morning, she proceeded to cut a slice and put it on a bread plate. "This is called *Stollen*. It's bread with raisins, nuts, and all sorts of other ingredients. The Germans only make it at Christmastime, and it's just lovely."

Taking a small bite, her father murmured approvingly. "It's a bit dense, but it has a very nice taste. … I detect a sort of nutty flavor but can't place it, and it isn't very sweet, which sorta surprises me, but yeah, I could eat this."

Amelia chuckled. "The nutty taste is from the marzipan. It's an almond paste. And you're right, it isn't sweet. That was the hardest thing for me to get used to. When I tasted my first German pastries, I was terribly disappointed. There just wasn't enough sugar to satisfy me, and I longed for some good ole-fashioned pecan pie or coconut cake, but after a while, I guess it grew on me."

As he dipped the piece of stollen into his coffee cup, Mr. Howard musingly asked, "Hmm, I wonder what this'll taste like?" Taking a bite of it, he murmured approvingly, "Very nice, darlin'. Not sure your mama'll like this, but I can see how this might grow on you."

"Daddy, you're a mess!" Amelia exclaimed. Reaching over to give him a long hug, she softly told him, "I love you, Daddy … I've missed you and Mama so very much."

"Well, darlin', that's good to know," he replied jocularly. "Needless to say, we're lookin' forward to you returning home for good. Have you gotten everything out of your system that you needed to?"

Amelia bristled at the remark but hid her irritation by ignoring the comment and going to the percolator to warm up her coffee. "You want a top-off, Daddy?"

"No, sugar, I usually wait and have a cup with your mama, and we talk about stuff over breakfast." Indicating the seat next to him, he said, "Sit down here, and let's talk a bit before your mama gets up and I can't get a word in edgewise."

Amelia kissed him on the top of his head as she smirked knowingly. She loved her mom but knew that even on a good day, she could be a bit overpowering.

Swallowing a bit of his coffee-dipped stollen, her father asked, "How are things with you and Charles?"

"Just fine, Daddy."

"That's good," he said in a patronizing tone that momentarily irritated Amelia. As she tried to appear calm and get over her irritation, she realized for the first time that he had always talked to her that way but that because that was all she'd ever known and had never doubted that he loved her and had her best interests at heart, she'd never taken offense to his behavior. She was beginning to realize that just as Charles had to adjust to the new Amelia, she would have to readjust to life in Tuscaloosa.

Amelia and her dad talked until around nine, when her mom came downstairs to join them. Mrs. Howard approved of the coffee but nixed the stollen as tasting like cardboard. When she reminded Amelia that they had a luncheon at the club with some of her girlfriends and cousins at noon, Amelia excused herself and went upstairs to get ready.

The luncheon lasted three hours, and when Amelia's mom suggested going to the store, Amelia demurred. "Mama, I'm starting to feel jet lag pretty heavily right about now, and if I don't take a nap, I'm not sure I'll be able to hang with the party at the Bannisters' tonight."

"Of course, darlin'. I forgot about that. We can do that and some other stuff after Christmas."

As Amelia lay down on her bed, she wondered if she'd still be able to fit in here in Tuscaloosa. The long, chatty, loud luncheons she used to enjoy bored her to tears now. She had also had to catch herself when the waitress had asked what she wanted to drink and she almost told her she wanted a glass of wine. *Woowee! That would create quite a stir.* Her last conscious thought as she drifted off to sleep was, *Oh my God, the Junior League. I'll not only have to join it but will probably have to be the president in a year or so.*

AMELIA'S MOTHER WAS GENTLY shaking her shoulders. "Wake up, Amelia. It's time to get ready."

Amelia groaned. Looking at the clock, she realized she'd been asleep for three hours, but given that they hadn't gone to bed until after midnight the night before and she'd woken up around five, she struggled to come out of the pleasant, dreamless deep sleep that her mother had roused her out of.

Getting up, she stumbled to the bathroom, hoping a shower might perk her up, but when that didn't work, she walked down to the kitchen in her bathrobe, grabbed a Royal Crown cola, and took a big slug. She missed RC in Germany, and this was her first one in two years. The caffeine and sugar hit her system almost instantly.

Charles was standing at the window as Amelia and her parents pulled into his family's driveway a while later. He walked out to greet them, giving Amelia a possessive hug and a light peck on the cheek. Once they were inside, the housekeeper took their coats, and as they made their way into the parlor, where his parents were fixing cocktails, Charles whispered in Amelia's ear, "You're beautiful."

She looked up at him and instinctively gave him a little kiss, whispering, "Thanks, you're pretty easy on the eyes too."

That pert comment took Charles aback for a second. As he watched his parents hug Amelia and tell her once again how happy they were that she was home and part of the family again, he couldn't help thinking about how much she had changed. Although he had committed to adjusting, he had the sneaking suspicion that the adjustment might be a bit harder than he'd originally thought. The old Amelia would have blushed and hung on his every word, thanking him and asking him again if he really thought she was beautiful. Before Anne and the damned army, Amelia had doted on him and rarely questioned anything he said or did.

His father handed him a whiskey as the ladies were handed cups of wassail punch by his mother. They all sat down in the parlor, and everyone peppered Amelia with questions about Berlin, what was it like, if she knew many Germans, if she had traveled to other cities, as Charles sullenly sipped his whiskey, thinking that in the past, he had been the topic of discussion, not Amelia.

When they went in for dinner, Amelia was surprised to see a bottle of champagne and flutes on the table. Judge Bannister filled everyone's glasses and gave a toast to the future of their two families, followed by a blessing, before the cook brought in the first course of their meal.

After dinner, they went into the parlor again before dessert. Everyone except Charles sat down. Clearing his throat, he announced, "I just want everyone to know just how glad I am that we're all together again." Looking directly at Amelia, he paused before asking her to join him.

Amelia's smile betrayed the knot that had just formed in her stomach as she walked up to join him. She didn't have a clue what Charles was up to, which made her very nervous.

Charles took her gently by the shoulders and stared intently into her eyes. "Amelia, you always have been and always will be the light of my life. I want this Christmas to be a memory of the strength of our love that binds us together eternally." With that, he paused and took the ring box with his grandmother's ring in it, which she had refused to take that summer, out of his pants pocket. Getting down on one knee he said, "Amelia, would you do me the honor of accepting my reaffirmation of my proposal of marriage, by accepting this ring for the second, and last, time?"

Amelia was speechless, and for an awkward second, they both thought she might refuse. Although she was furious with him for not talking to her about this beforehand, her upbringing kicked into overdrive almost immediately. She knew that the consequences of refusing to take the ring in front of their parents, and on Christmas Eve, would be disastrous, so she smiled, extending her hand, as he put the ring on, stood up, took her in his arms, and kissed her.

Her mother was the first to come up and hug her. "Oh, darling, isn't this just too wonderful for words?"

Amelia pasted a smile on her face and pretended to be as happy as everyone else in the room was, resigned to the reality that this was just the way things were done around here.

30

DULUTH, MINNESOTA, 27 DECEMBER 1978

LORI SPENT HER CHRISTMAS leave at home skiing, reading, sleeping in, and enjoying her family time. Her brother Joe was back from college and spending lots of time with his girlfriend, Joyce.

While Lori was listening to Casey Kasem's Top 40 Countdown, Christa, Lori's younger sister, came into the kitchen. "Morning, Lori! How'd you sleep?"

"Not bad. How 'bout you?"

"Good. It really is nice to have you back home for a while. I've really missed having a chance to speak with you. It's not the same talking on the phone. Dad always points to the clock and doesn't want me to talk too long due to the cost. I also hate writing letters. You know I love to talk." Changing the subject Christa asked, "I was wondering, what's your school's mascot?"

"Why do you ask?"

"Just curious, I guess. I just found out the University of Minnesota has a gopher as their mascot. Gross, huh?"

"Yeah, a big rodent doesn't appeal to me. Our mascot is a mule. Our nickname's better; we're the Black Knights."

Christa said, "Uh, that's cool. When do you see your mascot?"

"Primarily at football games. ... Sometimes I think we're the mascots of the academy."

"What does that mean?"

"Well, the tourists are always asking us to pose for photos and have our photos taken with them. We're also on display at all the parades, and I sometimes feel like we're little toy soldiers marching for the public's entertainment."

"Well, you are a novelty. Not many girls go into the Army, let alone go to the military academy..., Ah, if you have time, I really need to talk about my steady boyfriend."

"Sure, but isn't it a little early to talk about serious stuff? It's seven in the morning."

"It's never too early to talk about love. I know I'm in love with Art. He's simply the best boyfriend," Christa said smiling.

"Why do you say that? You're only sixteen; what do you know about love?" Lori quietly asked.

"Yeah, that's the same thing Mom and Dad say. I've been dating Art since last Christmas. He's a senior this year, and I love walking down the hall with him, holding hands. He's super-cute, with his long dark brown hair, brown eyes, and the coolest smile. The best part is, he never interrupts me, and he supports me in all the things I like to do. He likes to go shopping with me and he even plays guitar in a band."

"Wow, that does sound serious," Lori said sarcastically.

"I mean it! He's the coolest boyfriend I've ever had."

"Well, how many boyfriends have you had?"

"Not too many, but Art's the most serious one. We're still at the kissing stage, but it could get much more serious once he goes to college next fall," Christa said.

"I'm glad it's only at the kissing stage, and I'm glad you're really happy. Have you thought about next year when Art graduates? Where's he going to go to school?"

"He's going to the U of M in St. Cloud. I plan on seeing him every other weekend. I got my driver's license a few months ago, and Mom lets me drive her Vega when I ask."

"Sounds like a good plan, Chris. But, have you thought about all the other college freshmen Art will see at college?"

"Yeah, and I wish I were going with him, but if he loves me like I love him, our relationship will survive the two years we'll be apart."

"Oh, does that mean you're going to college in St. Cloud too?"

"Yep! We got it all figured out. I'm not as smart as you Lori, but I always make the honor roll and I've got a good head on my shoulders."

"I know you do, Chris. I'm sure you'll continue to make good decisions. I'm only concerned you might get hurt. Art may be willing to wait for two years but most guys can't."

"We plan on seeing each other every other weekend or more. It's only a three hour drive. We also will call every week and send letters."

"Sounds like you've thought about this quite a lot."

"Yes, Art's the one who explained this all to me. He really wants our relationship to last."

"That does sound promising. I thought you were chasing him."

"Nope, it's the other way around. He's crazy about me. Isn't that cool?"

"Yeah, so when do I get to meet this great guy and do you want me to make you some pancakes?"

"That'd be great. I'm starving for some reason. Art's coming over to go ice skating this afternoon and you'll get to meet him then. I'm so excited! He's heard so much about you."

"I'm looking forward to it. Every letter I've gotten from you is gushing about him. I should be back from my shopping trip with Willow by the time he arrives. By the way, what do Mom and Dad think about Art?"

"They like him. He's polite and quiet and nice to everyone. He also always brings me back on time and walks me up to the door. He's a true gent, and I love that about him too!"

"Okay, I get the picture. Can't wait to meet him. Can you get me the eggs and milk?"

31

WEST POINT, COW YEAR, FEBRUARY 1979

GLOOM PERIOD HIT WEST POINT hard in the new term. The rumor circulating was that ninety-six plebes had failed English and were either separating or taking English at summer school. To alleviate the depressed mood, many of the cadets were drinking in the barracks during the evening. Lori was oblivious to the activity until Trish asked her about it in practice one afternoon. "Hey, Lori," Trish whispered, "have you noticed the firsties and your classmates drinking in the barracks?"

"No, what do you mean? We're not allowed to do that."

"I know, but have you seen all the guys carrying cans of soda during study hours and the weekends?" Trish asked.

"Yeah, but many of them use the pop cans as their snuff spittoons; it's so gross!"

"I know, but this is different. Take a hard look tonight and let me know what you see."

"Okay, I will. How come I don't smell the alcohol on their breath if they're drinking?"

"I think they're mostly drinking, vodka which doesn't smell. I also heard they store it in their Listerine bottles in their medicine cabinets, since most Tacs don't check their rooms with much scrutiny except for our Saturday inspections."

"Interesting, I'll check it out and let you know, Trish."

That evening, Lori noticed about ten cows and firsties hanging out in the hallway with coke cans in their hands before study barracks. Two firsties were spitting into their coke cans, but the other eight were sipping the contents in a relaxed manner. Lori couldn't tell if they were drinking pop or drinking alcohol, so she decided to ask her roommate. "Cate, have you noticed there's a lot of guys drinking pop in the evening?"

"Yeah, but what about it? I drink a Coke once in a while myself."

"Do you think they could be drinking in the barracks?" Lori asked.

"Hmmm. Well, they could be. I've never really thought about it. Why do you ask?"

"A teammate asked me about it today at practice. She said it's happening with the upperclassmen in her company and asked if we had it going on in A4. I told her I'd check it out."

"Well, come to think of it, I did notice some loud and strange comments made last week and during term ends and the cadets were drinking sodas. ... Hmmm, it's not against the honor code to break rules; it's only a violation if we lie, cheat, or steal, or tolerate those behaviors in others."

"Well, I'm not doing an in-depth investigation; I'm just curious. Since plebes can drink at Ike Hall when they're eighteen, I never thought drinking was a big deal. Personally, I don't enjoy drinking unless I'm on vacation. Beer is good, but it makes me sleepy and I need to study every night to pass my courses," Lori said.

"I'm with you. I think drinking's an escape mechanism for lots of people. Sorry to cut you off but I really need to study. I've got eighty pages of military history to read tonight for the big quiz tomorrow."

"Yikes, I thought my forty pages was too much," said Lori as she grabbed her geography textbook and started reading.

Later that night, Lori wrote in her diary:

So tired. The good news is we are 12-3 with less than six weeks left to play. Our season has been another good one so far. I'm really impressed with the recruited plebes and our yearlings are doing well too. The bad news is I feel lots of pressure being the captain of the team, trying to help the plebes survive their classes when we're on the road so much, and trying to keep up with all the classes I'm missing. Thank God I have Cate to help me with my engineering. I'm looking forward to going to the Harry Chapin concert with Scott at the end of the month.

★ ★ ★

IN THE LOCKER ROOM before basketball practice, Lori noticed that Trish's eyes were completely bloodshot. "Man, Trish! What happened to you!?"

"I don't know. I've been on this crash diet because I'm getting hassled about my weight, but I didn't know it would affect my eyes!"

"Who's messing with you about your weight? You're the most physically fit woman in the whole class."

"My Tac," said Trish.

"Are you kidding me? You're not fat; you're all muscle."

"I know that. They don't care, so I'm trying to eat less, and the blood vessels popped in my eyes."

"Have you gone to sick call yet?"

"No, but I think I will. I've lost eight pounds in about five days, so my Tac is off my back for the time being."

"What have you been eating?"

"Not much. Lots of water, coffee, and fruit. I'm so used to hunger pains that my body's getting used to them."

"Trish, I'm really worried about you. Your eyes make you look like a monster, and you really need to eat healthier. Screw the Tac! Anyone with a brain can see you're in great shape and not fat. Muscle weighs more than fat. You need to take better care of yourself and have the doctor call your Tac and explain it to him. What a moron!"

"Yeah, I totally agree. He's a dope. I'll go on sick call tomorrow morning and see what I need to do to fix my eyes and keep the weight off. Let's get to practice, or Coach'll be pissed."

At practice Trish had trouble focusing on the defensive drills they were working on. She was hungry and lacked energy. Trish was thinking about why people were so interested in her body. Yeah, she was heavier than she'd like to be, but she was very muscular and solid. There was not a lot of flab on her body. Trish was happy Julie did not care about her weight. Julie, her girlfriend, loved her for who she was. That thought made Trish smile.

THAT NIGHT, LORI wrote a short letter to her best friend back home:

Dear Willow,

Just a short note to vent a little … I'm really frustrated right now. It's gloom period, and in addition to my heavy academic load with lots of tests and papers to write, I'm getting upset with the officers who think women don't belong in the Army and the cadets who continue to make our lives tough. My friend Trish lost too much weight too fast because of snide comments and counseling she received from her Tac. Her blood vessels burst in her eyes and she looks like a monster! I got her to go to the doctor but this place makes me crazy sometimes. It's stuff like this that makes me wonder if I made the right choice coming here. Sometimes I know for sure it's good for me, but other times I really wonder if it's worth it. But you know I'm not a quitter.

On a positive note, I am getting so excited for your wedding. I can't believe you're tying the knot already, but it seems Jeff's the one! Can't wait to be in your wedding!

Thanks for the Ziggy Valentine's Day card and all the juicy gossip from home. I saw the CBS movie "Women at West Point" starring Linda Purl and thought it was entertaining and about as accurate as the public can handle.

I hope you like this Snoopy card. I really miss you and the gang. See you in three months!

Keep Smiling, Lori

32

WEST POINT, MARCH 1979

SOFTBALL SEASON STARTED ON 1 March. Lori was the pitcher, and fast-pitch was much different than the slow-pitch game Lori was used to playing. Lori's best friend on the softball team was fellow Sugar Smack Reggie Howard, class of 1981. Reggie played left field and was always upbeat and cracking jokes, which made practice a lot of fun. The team was doing extremely well in practice, and Lori knew they would have a good season.

Their coach was Captain Smather from the English department. He loved to talk and explain why he was doing everything. Lori didn't mind some of the strategy explanations, but the daily talks were a bit lengthy. "Last year our record was 11-8 and we had eight monogram winners; this year I think we can do better, have even more letter winners," CPT Smather said.

Reggie whispered, "Can you believe this? He's at it again. I wish he'd just let us play and quit yakking so much."

"Yeah, me too," Lori whispered back.

★ ★ ★

ON SATURDAY EVENING, SCOTT picked Lori up at her room and they walked up the hill to Scott's sponsor's home for dinner. "I'm so happy to wear civvies for a change," Lori said as they passed Most Holy Trinity, the Catholic chapel.

"You know it! The blazer uniform isn't too bad, but my favorite uniform is my gym uniform."

"Me too! It's practically all I wear during study barracks and weekends. At least the shoes are comfy. So tell me about your sponsor."

"Well, LTC Grayson's really smart, teaches history, and he seems nice enough. Has two young daughters, and his wife's a fantastic cook. She also always bakes cookies for us to take back to the barracks when we leave."

"That's nice. Does she work?"

"No, I don't think so. I guess she could. Their girls are both in grade school on post, so she has time to work if she wanted to," Scott said. "I think she said she was a schoolteacher before they got married."

"Thanks for inviting me, Scott. You don't think LTC Grayson will be upset, do you?"

"Upset about what? He invites at least three or four cadets to his home every month. I figured one more wouldn't matter, and his wife was happy to have a female cadet come up for a change when I asked if you could come. I think they're curious to meet you."

"I'll be on my best behavior," said Lori, smiling.

"It'll be fun, just wait and see."

Ten minutes later, Lori and Scott arrived at the Graysons' quarters. Their ten-year-old daughter answered the door. "Mom, they're here!" she yelled, excited.

"Well, take their coats and ask them what they'd like to drink—and shut the door; it's freezing out there," Mrs. Grayson replied as she walked into the living room and greeted Scott and Lori.

"I'm so happy Scott brought you, Lori. The other two cadets have already arrived. Please make yourselves at home. Greg will be down in a few minutes. He's finishing up an article he's been working on for publication. We'll be eating in about thirty minutes and I have a few things left to do," Mrs. Grayson said warmly.

"Can I help you?" Lori eagerly asked.

"No, but thanks for asking. I've only got a few little things to do like bake the rolls and finish the salad. Go into the living room and relax with the other cadets."

When Lori walked into the living room, she said hello to two cadets she had never seen before. They introduced themselves, and Lori found out they were both cows in first regiment. She wondered why Scott had not mentioned them before.

At that moment, LTC Greg Grayson entered the room and bellowed, "Sorry I'm late. I was on a roll and had to finish the conclusion of the history paper I was working on." He saw Lori and added, "You must be Cadet Nelson. Scott's told us a little about you. Glad you could come."

"Thanks for having me, sir. I love getting away from the barracks for a change of pace. You have a beautiful home," Lori said smiling.

"Well, you can thank my wife for that. Work keeps me extremely busy. I just love reading, teaching, and writing about military history."

"Sir, I heard you might be leaving this summer for Fort Bragg. Is that true?" asked one of the cadets.

"Yes, I just got the request for orders last week. I'll miss teaching, but it'll be nice to get back to the Army and lead troops again," LTC Grayson said.

Almost immediately, his wife called out, "Please bring your drinks to the table. We'll be eating in a few minutes."

Dinner was absolutely delicious, and everyone had a good time with pleasant conversation. The Graysons' two daughters kept asking Lori questions about being a cadet. After dinner, as Lori was coming out of the bathroom, she heard the oldest daughter in her bedroom say, "Daddy, I want to be a cadet like Lori."

LTC Grayson replied, "Honey, girls should not be cadets or Army officers."

Shocked, Lori said nothing and walked back into the living room where the cadets were watching TV. With clenched fists she firmly said, "Scott, I need to leave now!"

"Well we can, but I thought we'd stay longer," Scott replied. "What's up?"

"I'll tell you after we leave."

"Okay, well let's thank the Graysons for dinner, and then we can walk back."

Lori and Scott warmly thanked Mrs. Grayson for the delicious dinner she had prepared. Lori did not thank LTC Grayson, merely staring at him, still in disbelief of what she had heard him say about women cadets.

On the walk back to the barracks, Scott said, "Okay. That was weird. Why did we have to leave so early? I was really enjoying the evening. I also noticed you kept glaring at the Colonel."

"I was having a nice time, until I overheard your sponsor telling his daughter that girls shouldn't be cadets or Army officers. After I heard that, I just wanted to get the heck out of there."

"Whoa. I didn't know LTC Grayson was biased toward women … but then again, I've never seen a female cadet in his home and his wife is a stay-at-home mom. Still, I'm surprised he told his daughter that. Sorry you had to hear it, Lori. I'm glad you told me about it. I honestly thought the officers and cadets were accepting women better now since it's the third year, but I might be wrong."

"Yeah, I can't believe a high ranking officer like Grayson would not accept the law and policy changes about women in the military. That just pisses me off!"

"Yeah, the guys still crack jokes about the female cadets all the time. … Sorry you're in the middle of it, Lori. It must be tough to deal with all the time."

"Well, it's much better now that I'm a cow, but plebe year was hell. I was so stressed out from not only the fourth class system but also some of the upperclass jerks we had to put up with purely due to our gender."

"I don't know why so many people think women can't be officers. You certainly are as smart and capable as most of the men I've seen."

"I think it's the way we were raised: Men are supposed to be the breadwinners and aggressors, and women are supposed to take care of the kids and family. Women are just starting to go into leadership roles. It's a huge societal shift, and most people are reluctant or slow to change. Damn, it pisses me off sometimes!" Lori exclaimed.

"Yeah, my sisters have told me the same thing. I get it, but some of my friends and peers don't. The worst guys seem to be the older officers who have never worked with women before. I'm sure they'll come around after they see you in action."

"I'm not holding my breath. I'm so sick of it all. It's a daily struggle for me and the other gals. If it's not the snide comments and vulgar jokes, it's the eye-rolls and derogatory body language. Why can't they just accept reality? We are not going home. We have as much right to be here as the guys! I can't help I was born a female. Just like you can't help you were born a male."

"I get it Lori. I'm sorry so many people don't… Hey, to try to get your mind off of this frustrating stuff, how about going to Ike Hall for a hot fudge sundae?"

"Sure. That's a good idea. You know I'm a chocoholic. … I'd never get through to graduation without my chocolate treats and boodle packages from Grandma Nelson."

33

WEST POINT, APRIL 1979

ON SATURDAY, LORI PULLED a thirteen-hour guard duty. She was exhausted from the standing, walking, and filling out the required report forms. She had just changed out of her uniform into her gray cotton cadet sweatsuit when Scott came to her room to visit. "Hi, Lori! How was your guard duty this time?"

"It sucked as usual, but it's finally over. What should we do tonight?"

"Um, I'd like to take you to Flirtie if you'd like to go," Scott replied.

"Sure, let me brush my teeth and mark my card."

As Lori and Scott walked past MacArthur's statute on their way toward Flirtation Walk, they saw Cate walking back from the PX carrying two bags. "Hi, Cate!" Lori said.

"Hey, Lori, Scott! The weather's great tonight. Have a nice evening!" Cate said, smiling, as they passed each other on the sidewalk.

"I haven't seen Cate in weeks. What's she been up to?" Scott asked.

Lori quickly decided not to confide in Scott and keep the secret Cate had divulged to her six months ago. She trusted Scott to not repeat the news, but she decided to be loyal to her roommate. "Same old stuff, studying, teaching plebes, and staying in shape."

A few minutes later, Lori and Scott arrived at the front entrance of the walkway near the Hudson River. Scott took Lori's hand in his and continued walking. "We've been good friends for over a year now, and I really like you, Lori."

"The feeling's mutual, Scott. You're the nicest guy I've ever known, other than my dad, of course."

"Thanks, Lori. I know the situation here is surreal and it's not a normal college experience in any way besides academics, but I want you to know, I really care about you and want to remain good friends with you after we graduate."

"So you think we're both going to graduate?" Lori teased.

"No doubt about it! We've made it through this far; only another 13 months to go!"

"Yeah, of course you're right. I know I'll enjoy being an Army officer compared to being a cadet. I had so much fun last summer at CTLT. I loved seeing the real Army, and Trish and I had two great officers as our sponsors in Germany."

"I had a good time at Fort Bragg too. I really liked the soldiers in my platoon. Maybe we could be stationed at the same duty assignment," Scott said.

"That would be cool. I'd really like that."

As Lori and Scott walked hand in hand along Flirtie, Lori was enjoying her leisurely walk with Scott. He was easy to talk to, understanding, and nice. It helped that he was attractive and had a huge smile that he flashed often. She savored the moment.

As they rounded the turn on the rocky path, Scott stopped and looked her squarely in the eyes. He gently placed his hands on her shoulders, smiled, and kissed her.

Lori was pleased that Scott had finally made the move and she kissed him back with emotion. She had visualized this moment for the past six months. She had thought about making the first move if he had not initiated the kiss, but was glad she did not need to be assertive.

The first kiss led to many more, and they started to get excited.

"Uh, maybe we should keep walking," Scott finally said, pulling himself away from her.

Lori was surprised at how great it felt to have Scott in her arms, and she was disappointed when their kissing session ended. "Okay sure," she said reluctantly. "Wow, that was nice, Scott. I felt myself melting into you."

"Yeah, me too. How about going to Ike Hall for a drink or sundae?"

"Okay. It won't be as good as kissing you, but it'll be nice, and I never turn down ice cream," Lori said, very happy with the world.

THE NEXT WEEK, THE softball team beat Yale University at Buffalo Soldier's field. Lori was walking back to their barracks with Reggie after the game. "Great game, huh?" Lori asked.

"Yeah. Your pitching was so fast today. What was that all about?"

"Don't know. I felt good and I was in the groove. I only gave up a few hits. You had two great hits, Regg. That helped us finish them off."

"Yeah, thanks, Lori. You had a great double, yourself. Coach should be happy. We started off slow, but we've won our last three games."

"Yeah, I'm pumped and excited for our team. We've got some great plebe recruits this year."

"Very true! I feel so good today for a change. I'm getting excited for our double-header coming up next weekend, and of course the state tournament at Adelphi next month. I love getting out of here and playing other teams."

Lori replied, "Yeah, me too. The worst part of away games is playing catchup with our classes."

"Tell me about it. I'm close to failing differential equations. If it wasn't for AI, I wouldn't be playing ball right now."

"Yeah, people don't realize it's a big sacrifice to play sports here, but I love the escape and friendships that come with it," Lori remarked.

"If it wasn't for basketball and softball, I'd have quit a long time ago. This place is crazy hard!"

"Yeah. I still think about quitting once in a while, but not like I did plebe year. I got a good dose of reality at CTLT last summer, and the Army is a great job and profession. Most of the time I know I'm getting well prepared for leading soldiers; other times, I feel jerked around for no good reason."

"I'm going to the Presidio at Fort Ord for CTLT this summer," Reggie announced.

"Where's that?"

"It's in California, just south of San Francisco. I'm going to a military police company, so I hope I get to be a platoon leader."

"I hope so too. I was disappointed I didn't get a platoon, but I got to spend six weeks in Germany learning how to be a staff officer and seeing how a combat brigade works. Trish and I also had two sponsors who showed us around the German countryside. We had a blast!"

"Very cool. I can't wait to be a platoon leader and see some real soldiers. West Point is okay but everyone thinks they're the boss here. I'm ready for a dose of reality and a real mission. Academics is fine but it's not the Army… Well, this is where I peel off. See you tomorrow," Reggie said as she went into her barracks.

34

WEST POINT, MAY 1979

THE WEEK PRIOR TO the class of 1979's graduation, Lori was very upset. Her best friend from Denfield high school, Willow Schuda, was getting married to Jeff Anderson, one of their mutual friends from high school, and Lori was supposed to be the maid of honor, but Lori's Tac had not approved Lori's three-day-weekend leave request, so instead of being the maid of honor in Duluth, Minnesota, for Willow, Lori spent the Saturday washing clothes. As she waited for her clothes to dry, Lori thought of Willow and her own family enjoying the wedding and prayed Willow and her new husband would have a wonderful life together. She also realized the Army was an impersonal institution that did not value personal friendships and commitments. It was an eye-opening moment for the third-year cadet.

★ ★ ★

ON JUNE 6, 1979, the Honorable Charles Duncan, Deputy Secretary of Defense, was the commencement speaker for the graduation of the 882-member class of 1979. It was a beautiful warm day, and the cadets and family members in Michie Stadium were joyful. The only negative part of the graduation festivities was when a newly commissioned second lieutenant shouted at Lori and Cate, "Class of '79, last class with balls!"

"Thank God they're gone," Cate said, and Lori nodded in agreement. "Good riddance! Now that we're officially firsties, life will be better."

Lori spotted a couple of their friends and replied, "Hey, there's Trish and Julie. Let's say hi to them and congratulate them on their promotion."

As Lori and Cate walked over to the south side of the stadium to see their friends, another new graduate sneered at them as they passed by. Lori and Cate ignored him, and Lori greeted Trish and Julie warmly. "Hey guys! Congrats on being firsties! Isn't it cool?"

"Yeah! We've waited three *long* years for this moment, and we need to savor the experience. How about coming with us to my sponsor's place tonight for dinner and drinks?" Trish asked.

Cate smiled and said, "Thanks for the invite. I'd love to, but I've already got plans."

"That's okay, Cate. I realize it's a last-minute invite. CPT Howell said I could invite a few friends over tonight to celebrate. She's a cool sponsor who teaches military science. She lives on post in the BOQ."

Lori said, "Sure! Sounds great. I'll come to your room after I finish packing. What time?"

"Oh, about six would be good," Trish replied. "Her BOQ is less than a mile away and not worth driving to. I think a few other basketball gals will be there, so it'll be lots of fun. We're all wearing jeans. See ya later!"

Lori looked over at Cate and whispered, "Do your plans involve Jim?"

Cate immediately smiled, "Of course. I can't wait to be with him."

"You've got it bad kiddo. I'm glad you're so happy but I worry about you two getting caught. I really don't want you ruining your career before it starts."

"Thanks Lori. We're always very careful. Don't worry about me."

35

WEST GERMANY, 2 June 1979

ON 1 JUNE, LIEUTENANTS Collins, Deveraux, and Howard were promoted to the rank of captain. After three years of being lieutenants, this was a huge milestone. They wanted to share the joy of this day and agreed that on Friday, 2 June, Anne would be at Maura's office by 1500 and Amelia would call from Berlin so they could all be together and greet each other as captains.

Around 0730, Maura's phone rang. Irritated because a call this early usually meant there was a problem with the duty log that had been forwarded to Corps headquarters at 0600, Maura picked up the phone. "Lieutenant Collins. May I help you, sir?"

Anne howled as she announced, "You owe me a drink, Captain Collins, and the copious amount of free drinks I'll get at your promotion party tonight don't count!"

They had been were told it was an old Army custom for any newly promoted officers to pay a fine—a drink—any time the officers identified themselves with their previous rank.

"Shit!" Maura exclaimed. "I told myself not to do that!" Then regaining her composure, she said, "Oh Anne, that's just plain mean!"

"Gotcha!" chuckled Anne.

"Okay, small things amuse small minds. Just laugh your head off, but do it on your own. I've got better things to do than to listen to your cackling," Maura replied in mock anger as she started laughing at herself, frustrated that Anne had played this joke on her first.

"I'm going to leave around 1330 so I'm sure I'm in your office when Amelia calls."

"Great," Maura replied, then continued wistfully, "I sure wish there had been a way all three of us could have been together today and this entire weekend."

"Yeah," Anne said, subdued at the reminder that Amelia wouldn't be able to join them at the promotion party that Maura's unit expected her to host tonight.

"I hope the congratulations card I sent her got there," Maura said.

"Well, ask for both of us when she calls; I sent her one too."

"Oh good; I know that will help." Looking at her watch, Maura added derisively, "Okay, you've had your fun for the day, I've got three meetings and an NRAS inventory to finish before you get here, so I'm gonna get some work done. See you this afternoon, Captain Devereaux!" Maura hung up the phone, grinning as she heard Anne howling with laughter.

That afternoon, Maura was just finishing up a memo to one of the companies she'd inspected when she heard Master Sergeant Smith yell, "Ma'am, you got a visitor up front."

Maura went out to the operations area and signed Anne in. Picking up the classified document she'd put on the counter, Maura motioned Anne to follow her, saying, "C'mon, I just need to finish this memo and lock up my classified materials." Maura was opening the safe in her office when her phone rang. "That may be Amelia," she told Anne. "Can you get it?"

Walking over to Maura's desk, Anne picked up the receiver and announced, "Lieutenant Devereaux. May I help you, sir?"

"Gotcha!" Maura howled at Anne for making the same mistake she'd made that day.

With both of them laughing uncontrollably, poor Amelia didn't quite know what to say, so putting on her best protocol voice, she said imperiously, "You two! What if this wasn't me? This is a gross violation of proper military phone etiquette." She immediately joined her two friends in uncontrollable laughter.

"Congratulations, Amelia! Did you get our cards?"

"Yes, thanks."

The three friends spent the next thirty minutes talking about how in some ways it seemed like they'd been in Germany forever, and in other ways it was hard to believe they'd been here for three years and were now captains. Amelia asked what they were going to do to celebrate, and Anne and Maura downplayed the fact they were having a big promotion party at the O'Club.

Maura asked, "Did you do anything to celebrate?"

"Yes, I had a nice catered reception at Harnack House after my promotion ceremony."

"Any plans for the weekend?" Maura asked.

"Yes, Eric and the guys are taking me out to celebrate tonight. I couldn't get him to admit that you put him up to it, but I'll thank you anyway; that is very sweet and helped keep me from getting depressed about not being able to be with you guys when you celebrate tonight."

"You guys have a drink for us tonight and we'll do the same," Anne replied gaily.

Amelia announced, "Okay, we don't want to get caught by the phone monitors having a personal conversation on a Class A line that is supposed to be for official business only, so have a lovely weekend, and I'll give Eric a kiss from you, Maura."

When they'd hung up, Anne followed Maura out of the office. Most of the staff was already gone for the day, and Maura reminded Master Sergeant Smith and Sergeant Major Atkins that she expected them at the O'Club no later than 1700.

Maura had an open bar and a table with appetizers at the O'Club. Everyone was joking and relaxing when someone bellowed, "Attention!" Surprised, everyone looked toward the door.

Much to Maura's surprise, she saw and heard the CG say, "As you were!" as he walked toward her. "Congratulations, Captain Collins. You've earned those railroad tracks, and I know this is only the beginning of many promotions that will come your way in the Army."

Maura stammered a bit as she thanked the general and asked him what he wanted to drink. He told her this was her night to relax and have fun and he would get his own drink, then he walked up to the bar to order a beer, and walked around talking to the other officers and noncommissioned officers.

When Maura walked up to get a refill on her wine, the bartender told her, "Ma'am, your open bar closes at 1900. Do you want me to do a last call?" Maura told him thanks, but no, she'd do it.

"At ease!" she bellowed. "Sorry, guys, but that was the quickest way to get your attention. I want to thank everyone for coming tonight, and a special thanks to the Ops sergeant major and Operations sergeant, the G-3, and the chaplain. They're the only ones here tonight that were here the very first day I arrived in this brigade as a scared second lieutenant. I want them to know that I know I would not be here today if it were not for their support and professionalism. Thank you, guys. Now get your butts up here for one more drink on me!"

The G-3 came up to Maura and hugged her. "I'm proud of you, trooper."

Blushing, Maura said, "Thanks, sir."

Looking at her and Anne, he asked, "What are you guys doing after this?"

"Haven't really thought about it, sir," Maura replied.

"My wife popped her head in a moment ago. We're going to have dinner together, and she got a table for four, in the hopes that the two of you would be our guests and join us."

Maura and Anne thanked him and joined the Connollys after Maura paid her bar bill.

A drunk but happy pair of newly minted captains staggered up the stairs to Maura's apartment around ten that evening.

36

WEST POINT, CAMP BUCKNER CADRE, JULY 1979

LORI WAS ASSIGNED TO the Land Navigation Committee for her summer training detail. She was the cadet in charge of the Night Land Navigation Committee. The four-week training detail consisted of teaching all of the class of 1982 training at Camp Buckner night time land-navigation skills. Her Buckner roommate was Julie Norton, her friend on the basketball team.

"Hey, Julie. So glad we'll be working together this summer. How cool is that?" asked Lori.

"Way cool," Julie replied. "I don't know too much about night land nav, but I know we can figure it out together."

"You got that right. I'm so happy you're my bunkmate here at Buckner and it'll be so much more fun than two years ago when we were yuks here for summer training."

"True. Camp Buckner was not the most physically demanding experience of my life, but close. I especially hated Recondo Week and the morning runs."

"Yeah, I barely got my Recondo badge, and the runs really sucked. So glad we aren't doing that again this summer. As the CIC, I'll get to influence our work hours, and I plan on having lots of free time during the days and nights we aren't working."

"That's great! I need a break from all the studying. I barely passed all my courses last year, and I had to study every weekend just to pass," Julie said. "I also really like the fact that we can stay up late working and sleep in every morning."

"Yeah, me too. And we'll have lots of free time to relax and actually enjoy the scenery and lake. Way different from our first Buckner summer as new yearlings." Lori said as she remembered how hard the Army training and morning runs at Camp Buckner had been.

"True. Say, I'm hungry. You ready to go to lunch?" Julie asked.

Lori nodded and both women grabbed their tan garrison caps and headed to the Camp Buckner mess hall down the road.

THE NEXT TUESDAY NIGHT, all of the rehearsals and reconnaissance of the Camp Buckner land-navigation site were put into action. Fourth Company reported for their night land-navigation training. The 140 cadets and their cadre members were trucked in deuce-and-a-half trucks, wearing their green utility uniforms, black combat boots, LBE with two canteens, and soft caps with two small reflectorized tapes called cat eyes sewn on the back of the cap.

Lori stepped forward after the cadets were in formation and the company commander had taken the accountability report. The commander saluted her and said, "Ma'am, Fourth Company, All present and accounted for!"

Lori returned the salute and said loudly said, "Stand at ease!"

The cadets moved to the at-ease position.

Lori continued, "Good evening, cadets. I am Cadet Nelson, the Cadet in Charge of the Night Land Navigation Committee. This is a very important evening training session. All Army leaders and soldiers must be able to map read and navigate over all types of terrain. This includes navigating in periods of darkness. Tonight's timed navigation test will assess your ability to use your lensatic compass and communicate with your partner in total darkness. I expect you to use good judgment, be back here not later than 0100 hours, and be safe in all of your actions. That's not to say you won't walk into trees and scrubs and stumble; that's to be expected. Each platoon will now have specific refresher training at four stations with my cadre members prior to commencing the night land-nav course. Company Commander!"

The commander ran up front, saluted Lori, and took charge of his unit. Two hours later, the cadets in 4th Company began their three-hour training in the darkness. At 0100 hours, eight cadets were unaccounted for, so Lori and her cadre went into the dark woods and found them.

THE FOLLOWING SATURDAY, JULIE and Lori had a free day and headed to Poughkeepsie to see what they could do for a few hours. McDonald's was a treat for both of them, and they enjoyed their cheeseburgers and milkshakes before heading to the movie theater to see the matinee showing of *Animal House*.

Julie commented first as they walked to her car, "What a great movie! I laughed so hard I almost peed my pants."

"Me too. Now I know what everyone is yelling when they yell, 'Toga!' That's one crazy, funny movie. I needed a good laugh, and that was the best comedy I've ever seen."

"Yep, ditto for me. Dean Wormer was so mad, he almost blew a gasket. I think that college is about the opposite of our college experience. They seemed to have maximum fun, and we seem to have maximum pain and discipline," Julie said.

"Yeah, come to think of it, the movie was so different from what we're experiencing here; maybe that's why it was so funny!"

THE NEXT DAY, SCOTT picked up Lori and they had an excellent dinner at Beefsteak Charlie's in New York City. They walked along the crowded streets and saw Radio City Music Hall, the Roosevelt Center, and

Grand Central Station. That evening, Scott started driving back to West Point when a black sedan ran a red light. Scott shouted Lori's name, and she looked up from the road map in time to feel the impact as the sedan sideswiped the right rear of Scott's new blue Camaro, causing the car to spin clockwise. Lori started praying, thinking her life was ending. Fortunately, both cadets had their seat belts on.

The car came to a stop a few seconds later and Scott asked, "Are you all right?"

"Yeah, I think so."

Scott and Lori slowly got out of the car after assessing the inside damage. All of the glass had been busted out of the rear window. Scott's new car looked totaled from the rear end. They were sad to see that the driver of the black car who had hit them had not stopped but instead had fled the accident scene.

"Man, am I glad I have insurance. I'm pissed about my new car, but at least we're not hurt. Let's see if the car still works." The car started right up and was mobile. "I need to flag down a cop to write up a report," he told her. "Then we need to find a telephone so I can call USAA and report the accident. I'm shaken up a bit about the whole thing."

"Yeah, me too. I thought we were going to die when the car hit us," Lori said. "All I have is a bump on my head and a few scratches."

"I'm so glad we both weren't hurt; our careers could have been over before they began."

The following night, Lori once again wrote in her diary:

> I had the most scary experience last night, and this morning clinched it. A yearling on the softball team came up to me in the Buckner mess hall at breakfast and said, "Lori, I'm so glad to see you!" (I had this weird feeling about what she was going to say.) "I had the worst dream. I dreamt you died and everyone sat on the bench and cried. It's so great to see you this morning!" I had chills running up my spine by this time. I looked at her and said, "That's funny because I almost did die last night." I guess God does have a plan for my life and I need to graduate and get on with it!

37

WEST POINT, FIRSTIE YEAR, FALL 1979

REORGY WEEK STARTED EARLY on 14 August 1979 so cadets could take TEEs before Christmas leave. Lori was happy to find out her firstie leadership position in company A4 was a snuffie sergeant with little responsibilities since she wore the rank of a cadet lieutenant as the Sugar Smacks basketball team captain. Being team captain kept her very busy, especially making the plebe recruits feel welcome. She knew she would be either a lieutenant platoon leader or another leadership position next term to fulfill her company leadership assignment requirement prior to graduation. Cate was a cadet lieutenant, and Lori's platoon leader.

As they were getting ready for breakfast formation, Lori told Cate, "This is the first year I have electives I actually like. I really like my business law and counseling classes, and I'm also taking Marriage and the Family. Seems sound like fun classes for a change."

"Those classes do sound interesting. I'm taking three engineering electives plus Military Science, and Chinese. Not to change the subject, but have you heard from our former roommate Roni lately? I really miss her."

"Me too," Lori replied. "She always made me laugh with her ideas on life, fairness, and survival here our plebe and yearling year."

"I loved her devil-may-care attitude. In Roni's last letter she hinted at visiting us one weekend this fall and, quote, 'shoot the shit,' unquote."

"That would be so cool! I'd love to catch up with Roni. She's one of the reasons I survived plebe year. You're another one of the reasons. With your tutoring me in calculus, I made a decent grade. I guess the basketball team also helped keep my sanity. Yes! Let's link up with Roni whenever she can make it up here. I'll write her a letter encouraging her to come!"

THE AMERICA CONCERT COINCIDED with Roni's visit and was held at Ike Auditorium on 13 October 1979. Lori and Cate met Roni at Trophy Point at 1800. They hadn't seen Roni since she had reluctantly left in their yearling year after failing English again. They barely recognized her as she walked up to them in her dark purple blazer and matching flared slacks. "Hi, Lori, Cate!" Roni happily said as she gave each of them a big hug.

"You look great! I love your long hair," Lori said.

"Yep. Started growing it out right when I left, almost two years ago. I really like having choices again. You both look good. How's it going?"

"Well now that we're firsties, it's so much better than when we were plebes together," Cate said. "I don't like this blazer uniform, but it still beats wearing dress gray. I'm envious of your long hair. We still can't let our hair grow beyond our collar, even though women in the Army are allowed to put it up while in uniform."

Chuckling Roni said, "I'll never forget my first new cadet haircut. I started screaming when the barber started shaving my neck. We all looked scalped with men's haircuts for the first six months until they trained the barbers on how to cut women's hair."

Lori added laughing, "Yeah, my hair plebe year looked so bad, I stopped looking in the mirror... Well, school's still a bear—except for star woman Cate and the other top five percenters, but we're surviving."

"It is getting exciting now that we're on the home stretch," Cate added.

"Come on, let me see your rings," Roni said, looking down at their hands.

Cate showed Roni her green-gemmed 14-karat gold Pride and Excellence 1980 class ring, and Lori did the same.

"I really like your blue stone, Lori. What kind is it?"

"It's a fire blue spinel, fake of course. I couldn't afford a real stone. The gold is 14-karat and I love how it looks in the sun."

"Wow, they both look great," Roni said. "I still wish I were here, but I guess my ROTC program is okay. I was so far ahead of all my fellow cadets at SUNY. They didn't even know how to spit-shine their shoes. I'm a company commander this year, and we pick our Army branches next month. I'm getting excited to be commissioned. I'm going to pick quartermaster or military intelligence. How 'bout you guys?"

"Very cool, Roni! I'm a snuffie this term and Cate's a lieutenant. I'm leaning toward military police at Fort Bragg. Cate?"

"I'm thinking about military intelligence, and I'd love to be stationed in Hawaii. Heard it's fabulous there," Cate replied as they slowly walked toward Ike Hall for the concert, enjoying the beautiful sunset and yellow, orange, and red fall foliage along the river.

"Yeah, that's my dream location too. Very few ROTC cadets get their first choice, but we'll see. With my high leadership job, I might have a chance to get my branch and location choice. They keep telling us, 'The needs of the Army come first.' I'm so sick of hearing that. Makes me feel like a pawn and subhuman."

"Yeah, tell me about it. I spent a Saturday afternoon doing laundry instead of being Willow's maid of honor due to the needs of the Army," Lori said.

"That really sucks! How's Willow doing, by the way?" Roni asked. "She was so cool when I met her during plebe-parent weekend."

"She's a newlywed and madly in love with her hubby, Jeff. They met at St. Scholastica in Duluth. They're both going to graduate this year too. I'm really happy for them. So, how's SUNY?"

"Not too bad. I'm dating two guys, and school's going well. I even got a B in my history class last year. I finally learned how to write after I left here. So what's new here?"

Cate replied, "Not much. We still live in a fish bowl. The trash can still has to be in the doorway when males are in the room. We still get bad haircuts, and the plebes still deliver the *New York Times* before breakfast formation. The plebes can still only have seven items on their desk and they get their stereos after Christmas."

"You forgot one big change," Lori added. "All the women cadets got their full dress reissued."

"Why?" asked Roni.

"They decided we needed tails for uniformity after all!" Lori said.

"What a joke, as if no tails on the full dress would make the women's butts smaller," Roni said. "Glad someone made a command decision."

"It was General Goodson, the supe, who made the decision. He's a great guy," Cate said.

Roni said, "That reminds me, remember when he came into our room yearling year when we were all laughing and eating Tony's pizza and calzones?"

"Yeah, he was so nice, he reminded me of my grandfather. I had never seen a three-star up close. He had to tell us twice we could sit down and relax," added Lori.

"I remember it well because I sat halfway on the bed and landed on my ass. I was slightly embarrassed," Roni said.

Cate added, "Oh, that's right! I'd forgotten that part. We laughed so hard after he left the room when you started recounting the conversation. Boy, do we miss you, Roni! We haven't laughed nearly as much without you."

"I missed you guys, too." Looking at the Hudson River, Roni said, "I never realized how beautiful Trophy Point is. Look at this view!"

Lori replied, "You're right, Roni. We're so busy, we really don't get much of a chance to relax and enjoy the beautiful views."

Roni replied, "You need to stop and smell the roses! Life's too short to not have some fun."

"Speaking of fun, let's go in and check this concert out," urged Cate as she ushered the others inside the auditorium.

38

WEST POINT, NOVEMBER 1979

SCHOOL WAS DEPRESSING AND tedious, and Lori was so ready to graduate. The main things keeping her sane were her basketball friends and Cate. Right before Taps one Sunday night, Lori asked Cate, "Excuse my curiosity, but how's it going with Jim?"

"Good, I guess. I hate the sneaking around, but Jim's so fantastic. So mature, and I love being with him. We're hoping to get assigned together. … The Army will not assign us together unless we're married, so that's something we're thinking about."

"Wow! Sounds really serious. When do I get to meet the lucky man?" Lori asked.

"I'll check with Jim. Does Scott know about us?" Cate asked hesitantly.

"No, I promised I would keep your secret. I haven't told him."

"Oh, Lori. Thanks so much for not telling! Your trust means the world to me. Do you think Scott would make a big deal about it?"

"No, he's practical, not into gossip, and doesn't get too involved in the private lives of others. Why do you ask?"

"I thought it'd be fun to double-date one weekend. I think Jim would like it too. What do you think? Are you game?"

"Sure. We could go somewhere remote so no one would see us together. I don't want you getting into trouble. I can tell Scott and swear him to secrecy. I'm ninety-nine percent sure he'd be cool with it."

"That'd be great, Lori. I'll let Jim know and see what we can do."

ON THE WAY TO practice, Lori saw her best friend ahead of her, and she jogged over. "Hey, Reggie! You ready? … What's the matter? You look like you've been crying."

"I, uh, oh shit. I might as well be straight with you, Lori. Last May, I found out I was pregnant. I was so surprised, and I couldn't believe it. I only had sex one time and I didn't think I could get pregnant. I found out the day before graduation, and everyone was so busy packing and getting ready to go on summer leave and their summer training that I didn't really tell anyone."

"Okay, so what did you do? I thought you went to CTLT in California last summer. You said you had a good time minus your sponsor."

"True. I found out I was pregnant when I went on sick call thinking I had the flu. The PA sent me for a follow-up at the hospital for a blood test. Since I was only eight weeks pregnant, they cleared me to attend CTLT and recommended I take care of my situation. I was so upset. I did not want to abort my baby."

"Are you serious? What doctor would tell you to do that?" Lori asked.

"The doctor told me I could not be a cadet and be pregnant and have a baby. It's against the regulations. But my story gets worse. I go to CTLT and I went to the hospital because I was spotting. The chief warrant officer doesn't even give me an exam. He spends forty-five minutes telling me, 'You know, you only have so long to take care of this.' I was so stressed out. In July, I went home on leave and told my parents. My mom was supportive, but at first my dad was mad I had ruined my chance to become an officer. Then he got used to the idea and was supportive too."

"Thank goodness. I don't know what my parents would do. They'd probably be disappointed, but they would still love and support me."

"True; they were really disappointed. Uh, remember when I was in the hospital for a few days in August? I went there and the doctor asked if I had ever heard the heartbeat or felt the baby inside my womb. I said no, and they did a sonogram. That's when I found out I had a molar pregnancy."

"What's that?"

"It's when you are not really pregnant but you have an abnormal growth growing in your uterus. I had morning sickness and my body thought I was pregnant. Next thing I know, that afternoon I had a D&C. I could have gone back to the barracks the next day, but they kept me in the hospital for an extra four days."

"Oh, Reggie, I'm so sorry, I had no idea. I could have helped you."

"You weren't back from leave, or I would've called you. It happened right before school started. Then the real stressful part happened."

"Are you kidding me? You'd already been stressed enough."

"The dean came to visit me the day after my procedure. He asked me to resign while I was in the hospital."

"What? Are you serious?"

"Serious as a heart attack."

"How can a general be so cruel? That's ridiculous. You weren't even pregnant at that time. Why did he want you to resign?"

"He said I broke the regulations."

"Are you kidding me? What about all the guys here who break the rules and become fathers while they are cadets?"

"I don't know, but my dad got really mad about the discrimination. He hired a civil liberties lawyer and got actively involved when I got a letter the next week saying the dean was starting separation procedures against me."

"You've been through hell, Reggie. This place is hard enough without a brigadier general on your back. No wonder why you're not acting normal. What can I do to help?"

"You've been a great friend, Lori. Sorry I didn't tell you sooner. I thought I could just forget about all this since it happened a few months ago, but I'm so worried that any day, I'll be told I'm getting kicked out."

"Don't worry, Regg. They've let you start your cow year, so I think you've got a good chance to overcome this hurdle. You can talk to me any time. I won't tell anyone."

★ ★ ★

TWO DAYS LATER, SCOTT picked Lori up for Sunday mass. As they walked to the Catholic chapel, Lori asked, "Uh, Scott, are you good at keeping secrets?"

"I like to think I am. Why? What's up?"

"Well, I've been keeping a big secret about Cate, but she trusts my judgment and said I could tell you her secret."

Scott stopped walking and looked at Lori. "Okay, let's have it."

"Cate has a boyfriend."

"That's it? That's not much of a secret."

Lori sighed and continued, "Well, the secret part is he's a faculty member in the math department."

"Oh, that's different. Goody two shoes Cate is breaking the rules? Well, what do ya know? Don't worry, I won't tell anyone."

"I don't know his last name, but I call him CPT Jim. Cate thought it might be nice to go out together after we get back from Christmas leave. I told her I'd ask you and see what you thought about it."

"Seems okay to me as long as we go to a remote location. I don't want them to get into trouble, especially during Cate's firstie year."

"I knew you'd be cool with it. Thanks, Scott," Lori said as they climbed the slate steps to the chapel.

After mass, Scott continued the conversation. "Now I've got a secret to tell you."

"Really? I thought I knew quite a bit about you already," teased Lori.

"Well, you don't know this part. Yearling year, I was inducted into a secret USMA society, called the mole society."

Intrigued, Lori frowned and asked, "What does the group do, and who's in it?"

"We're a small group of seven cadets who have access to the bowels of the institution."

"What does that mean? Sounds strange and unearthly."

"Every month or so, we access the steam tunnels under the roads and buildings. It's fun to check out the connecting tunnels and go into hidden areas."

"It does sound exciting. How come I've never heard of the steam tunnels?"

"They're dirty and not glamorous. But they're cool and it's fun to sneak around once in a while. One tunnel entrance leads into the audiovisual room in the basement of Thayer Hall."

"Cool. Thanks for telling me about this secret group. So glad you trust me."

"Are you ready for brunch in the mess hall?"

"You bet! I'm really hungry for some reason."

"Must be all the talk about secrets is revving up your appetite."

Later that week, Lori wrote Willow:

Dear Willow,

Lots of interesting secrets coming to light this week...I'll clue you in when I get home at Christmas next month. I really miss talking to you Willow. I think the cadets here are lonely partially because they don't trust anyone. There are so many ridiculous rules and regulations compared to the Army. I really liked CTLT last summer compared to what I'm dealing with right now...

How's Jeff doing? Joe said he saw him at the football game a few weeks ago. Joe was with his girlfriend Joyce and so they didn't talk much. How's married life? I know you are probably both having fun while studying hard to graduate this spring.

Yesterday I bought my dad a really cool Christmas gift from the cadet store. The USMA cadet sabre with a gold plate inscription and shadow box cost me $135. but I know he'll be touched.

Sorry to cut this short, but I have a 2500 word analysis on the US negotiating position on the SALT II talks and deterrence theory due on Monday and I need to get cranking on it!

Take care! Your friend,

Lori

39

RHEIN-MAIN AIRPORT, FRANKFURT, 6 DECEMBER 1979

AMELIA, MAURA, AND ANNE had all arrived the day before and spent their last night in Germany together at the Gateway Inn reminiscing. Seated in the departure lounge waiting for their flight to JFK, they continued to talk about what the future held for each of them and how ready they were to go back home.

Maura and Anne were going to their respective chemical and quartermaster advanced courses and, after that, Airborne school at Fort Benning, Georgia, because both of them were going to Fort Bragg in North Carolina for their next assignment.

Anne was going straight to her advanced course at Fort Lee and would snowbird for the first few weeks, then take leave starting on the twenty-third, when Derek was flying his plane from Fort Bragg to the executive airport in Petersburg. They would drive to his parents' place on Tangier Island for the holidays.

Maura was going home for three weeks of leave before her advanced course. Eric, who was already assigned to Fort Bragg, was flying in on Christmas Eve and staying through the fourth of January to meet Maura's family and celebrate New Years Eve with Elise and her latest guy. They planned on attending a free concert in Central Park, followed by a party in the Village, that would end with breakfast at Katz's Deli.

Amelia wistfully commented that she envied them their adventures. "All I'm gonna be doing is out-processing out of the Army and spending a quiet Christmas with Charles and our parents, followed by a New Year's Eve celebration at the Country Club. I used to think it was just the best party until I experienced New Years with you guys and Mattias."

They all agreed that their first New Year's Eve in Berlin with Mattias and his friends was one of the most amazing nights they had ever experienced. There was a moment of awkward silence as they all remembered Mattias was no longer a part of their small but tightly knit group of friends. Amelia told them not to feel badly; it was her decision and it was for the best.

In an effort to change the subject, Anne asked, "So, how are the wedding preparations coming along? Are you excited?"

Amelia spent the rest of the time talking about all the planning that needed to be done and asking for reassurance that they would be able to take leave and be the maid of honor and bridesmaid for her wedding. They assured her that nothing would keep them from the wedding and they would send their measurements to Amelia to have their dresses made. They would arrive a week before the wedding to throw a shower for her and get final dress alterations.

Before they knew it, they were boarding their plane. When they landed at JFK, Anne asked, "Do you guys realize we've been talking non-stop for almost twenty-five hours?"

"If I look in the mirror at my bloodshot eyes, yes…" Maura replied, chuckling.

After clearing customs, the three friends gave final hugs and Anne and Amelia caught a shuttle to LaGuardia to catch their connecting flights to Birmingham and Richmond, while Maura headed out to the terminal, where her parents were anxiously awaiting her return home.

40

WEST POINT, DECEMBER 1979

ON 1 DECEMBER 1979, Navy once again trounced Army in football, 31-7. The cadets were extremely disappointed. Lori was not a football fan, but she had really wanted her team to win. Basketball was in full swing, and Lori was once again the captain of the team. Their busy academic and athletic schedule kept Lori very busy.

Lori and most of the cadets were ecstatic that term-end exam week had been moved to before Christmas instead of after Christmas in January. In their barracks room one night during TEE week, Lori and Cate heard cadets yelling out their windows at the top of their lungs, "I'm mad as hell and I'm not going to take it anymore."

Lori said, "My TEEs seem far less stressful than the other three years. I think it's because I like and am doing well in all my classes."

Cate replied, "Yeah, now that we're firsties, I think we have a huge advantage on what TEEs are and how to prepare for them. I love taking them before Christmas leave. I hated bringing my books home and studying during my time at home."

"Same here. I'm thrilled to knock them out now too."

★ ★ ★

LORI FLEW HOME FOR CHRISTMAS vacation looking forward to seeing her family and relaxing. Because General Goodson had changed the timing of the TEEs, Lori was mentally exhausted from taking her mechanical engineering, business law, military leadership, and history of the 20th century society and culture (nicknamed garbage) exams.

Upon arrival at the Minneapolis-St. Paul International airport gate, Lori was surrounded by her immediate family minus her brother Joe, who was finishing up his final exams at college. Christa was now seventeen years old and a junior in high school. "Hi, Lori!" Christa said while giving her a great big hug and a kiss on the cheek. "We missed you!"

"Hi, Chrissy! Have you grown up and out!" Lori said as she noticed Christa was now 5'10" and suddenly had large breasts.

Christa proudly said, "Yes, I am finally a grown-up adult, and I love it."

"Well, let's not get too carried away. Who's paying your car insurance and feeding you?" Mr. Nelson asked.

"Dad, you know what I mean. I'm no longer your little girl and the baby anymore," Christa replied.

"You will always be my little girl, Christa, even if you grow taller than me. Just get used to it."

Mrs. Nelson smiled and added, "Yes, Christa's grown two to three inches in the last six months, and her feet have grown too. She's costing us a fortune in new clothes and shoes."

"Mom, you know that's not true. I buy my own clothes now, from all my babysitting jobs. I even pay for my own gas when I drive your Vega."

"Yes, that's true, I was exaggerating a bit, but you've grown like a weed since Lori was last home." Looking at Lori, Mrs. Nelson asked, "How've you been, honey?"

"Ah, pretty good. I'm so happy finals are over. I think I did fairly well on them. I only have one more term to go, and I'm looking forward to graduating and being an officer at the end of May."

"I can't believe it's been four years already. Seems like just last month when we drove you to the military academy for Beast Barracks in the station wagon," her dad replied.

"Well, it seems like ten years to me. I'm glad to know the end is in sight. It's a very stressful place to go to school. Scott and my friends have made it tolerable."

"If it was easy, everyone would go there. We're so proud of you, Lori. You are doing so well in that tough environment. After graduating from West Point, we know you can do anything!"

"Thanks, Mom. All of your support and Grandma Nelson's letters and boodle packages have helped me so much. More than you will ever know."

Mr. Nelson interjected, "Okay, let's get your suitcase and drive home before the snowstorm comes in. We're supposed to get three to five inches tonight, and I'd like to be home before it comes."

WHEN LORI WOKE UP the next morning, the wall clock said 9:42 a.m. She almost jumped out of bed to start her day, but she remembered where she was and smiled. She was in her bed at home and had two weeks of glorious Christmas leave without having to study. She planned on sleeping in, visiting her friends, skiing, watching Joe play basketball, and enjoying her family.

At that moment, Lori heard the phone downstairs ring. A moment later, her mom faintly called upstairs, "Lori, it's Willow!"

"Okay, Mom, I'll be right down!" Lori jumped out of bed, grabbed her bathrobe, and went downstairs to speak with her best friend from high school.

"Hi, Willow! I slept in, but I was up. … No, you didn't wake me. Yes, lunch at your new apartment sounds great. What's your apartment number again? … See you in a few!" Lori hung up.

"Sounds like you're having lunch with Willow today."

"Yep! Can't wait to see Willow and Jeff. I felt like a real slug when I couldn't attend their wedding last summer. She said she has news for me."

"I'm sure she does. She just told me she's finishing her nursing degree this spring and she might have a job offer. We seem to have a nursing shortage, and she's very marketable."

"That's so cool! I wonder what Jeff will do when he graduates?"

"Willow didn't say, but you can ask him at lunch. I plan on making your favorite meal of hamburgers, mashed potatoes, and corn for supper. We still eat at 5:30, so don't be late."

"Mom, you know I wouldn't miss your hamburgers. Any ice cream for dessert?"

"Of course. We bought some rocky road and strawberry just for your visit. Dad insisted on it."

"Good to know some things haven't changed," Lori said as she went back upstairs to get dressed for her visit with Willow.

Lori drove her mom's red Vega to Willow's apartment. The parking lot had been shoveled and the snowplows had plowed the snow from the side streets that morning. As Lori walked up to the door, Willow opened the door, joyfully screamed, and gave Lori a great big bear hug. "I can't believe you're finally here! I've been waiting months to see you," Willow said.

Jeff met them in the hallway, giving Lori a big hug. "Nice to see you, Lori. We've been waiting to tell you our good news in person."

"Your good news?" Lori asked. "I thought Willow was going to tell me she got a full-time job with great benefits."

"Well, that's part of the news," Willow happily said. "Let's go sit down and catch up. Letters and telephone calls are okay, but I really miss seeing and speaking with you in person."

"Yeah, I know the feeling." Lori sat down on the plaid couch and added, "So first, let me say again how really sorry I am that I couldn't be your maid of honor for your wedding. The Army has no feelings when it comes to friends and family and special life events. I was so mad I couldn't fly home that weekend, but my Tac had no sympathy and said it wasn't his decision. The bottom line was my Tac was not willing to go to bat for me, so that left a bitter taste in my mouth."

Willow smiled, "Don't worry, Lori. We all missed you, but we knew it was not your fault. It's water under the bridge. We had a beautiful wedding last summer and you were definitely missed. Now Jeff and I are focused on graduating this spring, and I already have a good job offer."

"Yes, Willow will be a nurse and I'll be a mechanical engineer. I plan on sending my resume out next month. The job market looks very promising, and I know I'll get a job too. What about you? What will you do when you graduate?"

"Well, I'll be picking my branch and first duty location when I get back to school. My first choice is MP, military police, and my second choice is MI, military intelligence. My other goal is to be stationed at Fort Bragg, North Carolina, where Scott is trying to go. I really want to be a platoon leader and lead real Army soldiers."

Jeff grinned, "You mean West Point isn't the real Army?"

"Heck no! You wouldn't believe all the *macht nichts* junk the administration makes us do to keep us super busy. Plus, I'll have my Bachelor of Science degree and I won't have to study and write papers every night. That'll be wonderful!"

"What kind of stuff do you do that's not like a regular college?" asked Jeff, intrigued.

"Marching three or four times a week in the spring and fall; wearing a wool uniform with an awful starched collar; breakfast, lunch, and dinner formations where we stand at attention; Saturday-morning classes; room inspections; standing at all the mandatory football games; mandatory summer military training. ... I think you get the picture."

"Wow! Willow said you had a tough academic load and played basketball and softball, but I had no idea you had to march, have Saturday classes, and have room inspections."

"Yeah, the room inspections are sometimes white-glove inspections. The inspectors wear white cotton gloves and check above the doorframe and other obscure areas for dust on their gloves. But enough about me. Spill it, Willow, what's your good news?"

Willow smiled and announced, "We're going to have a baby! Jeff and I are so excited."

"Wow! I should have guessed, but it never crossed my mind, perhaps because my reality is so different. That's fantastic! Do you know when?"

"We're not sure, but we think the beginning of June. I'm still a little nauseous. I hope it goes away soon."

"You'll be a great mom, Willow. But wait. What about your job?"

"My mom will watch the baby the first two years, and then we'd like to put him or her in a day-care program to be around other kids."

"You're lucky. If I get married and stay in the Army, I won't have family nearby. That's a drawback about serving in the Army."

"That would be tough," Jeff chimed in. "My parents are super excited, too. They want to be the babysitters every Saturday night so Willow and I can have some alone time."

"Wow, Willow, I'm still trying to wrap my brain around you having a child at twenty-one years old!"

"Almost twenty-two, and Jeff is twenty-three. I don't think age has much to do with it. We're ready to make this big change in our lives, and I'm so happy our families are so supportive. Now if I could just not have this morning sickness, I'd feel so much better."

"When does the morning sickness end?"

"The doctor said it's fairly common the first trimester and then it may subside or go away. I sure hope he's right."

"Well, for three months, I can't even tell you're pregnant. When do you start showing?"

"In a month or two. My pants are already tight, and I'll soon need to start wearing maternity clothes. I've bought a few clothes already."

"I'll go get the sandwiches and pop," Jeff said as Lori and Willow continued their intimate discussion alone.

★ ★ ★

WHEN LORI RETURNED HOME for dinner, her mom gently asked, "Good news?"

"Oh yeah! Not only will they both have jobs upon graduation in May, they're going to have a baby, and if it's a girl, they're going to name the baby after me!" Lori said.

"I suspected they were having a child, but why would they name the baby after you?"

"Since I was Willow's best friend for fifteen years and got her to come out of her shell, helped her in school, and introduced her to Jeff, they felt it was the least they could do to show me how much they love me, I guess."

"Won't their parents be concerned?"

"Knowing Willow's parents, no. They just want a healthy baby. I'm flattered they would think of it, let alone do it. ... Well, if they have a boy, it won't be my namesake."

"True enough, let's go eat our dinner," Mrs. Nelson said while taking in the happy news.

41

WEST POINT, 100th NIGHT, 27 FEBRUARY 1980

"**I THOUGHT RING WEEKEND** last year was a big deal, but tonight's even better," Lori told Scott while eating dinner at the 100th night dinner dance.

"Very true. Have I told you how great you look tonight, Lori?"

"Only twice, but it's nice to hear it again. I even wore a little makeup for the big event. I wasn't going to, but Cate suggested I do it for the photos. Cate said, 'Twenty years from now, you'll be glad you did,' so I thought I'd give the mascara and lipstick a try."

"I'm glad you did, but I think you look great with or without makeup," replied Scott in his starched white dress uniform with crimson sash. "I really like your full dress mess uniform and the long black skirt. It looks so elegant."

Not used to and embarrassed by the praise, Lori pointed to a table near them in the mess hall and said, "Look, there's Trish, Julie, and Henry. Let's go say hi."

Lori and Scott walked over to Trish's table and started chatting with their friends. They were all dressed up and looking good for the formal evening.

"Wow, Lori! You look spiffy," Julie said.

"Thanks, you're wearing the same uniform, so I say the same thing to you and Trish. Henry, you look great too!" replied Lori.

"So what're we having for dinner?" asked Henry, a fellow firstie in Julie's company.

Trish picked up the menu on the plate, opened it, and read, "Shrimp cocktail, Thayer mixed salad, surf and turf, baked potato, asparagus, assorted rolls, and pecan pie for dessert. Sounds yummy."

Scott picked up the wine bottle and started pouring it into the goblets next to the water glasses, "I'm getting hungry, too. Well, let's toast to a hot time tonight!"

The five friends raised their glasses with smiles and toasted to friendship and graduation in 100 days. A male cadet at another table yelled at Scott, "Hey buddy, wait until we start. You got too much estrogen at your table, or what?"

Hearing those derogatory words, Scott put down his wine glass and walked over to the cadet who had yelled and quietly had a few words with him. The cadet quickly turned around and started talking to his buddy.

"I wish they'd get over it," Trish said when Scott walked back to the table. "I'm so sick of sticking out and not being accepted, even by our peers."

"Yeah, it's getting old. I just ignore it now, or if it's an underclassman, I make them talk with me about their prejudices," Julie said.

Changing the subject, Scott walked over to Henry and said, "Hi, Henry! I haven't seen you since the Iranian hostages and their families were bused on post last month."

"What a great day that was. I was standing on Thayer Road when the buses drove by. I've never seen so many yellow ribbons and US flags as I did that day."

"True. It was great to see how many people came out to cheer and honor the hostages," Scott added.

"When they welcomed the freed hostages from the poop deck at dinner that night, they received the loudest and longest applause I've heard in my four years here," Henry said.

"Yeah, that was the best."

The rest of the evening was uneventful, and Lori, Scott, and their friends had a splendid evening dancing to such hits as "YMCA," "Bad Girls," "My Sharona," "The Gambler," and "I Will Survive."

THE FOLLOWING WEEKEND, LORI and Scott went on a double date with Cate and her boyfriend, Captain Jim. The rendezvous point was the parking lot of Delafield pond, where cadets, faculty, and family members could swim during the summer. Very few people walked to this parking lot in the snow, and no one saw Jim's Saab pick up the three firsties.

Once in the car, Cate was the first to speak. "Lori and Scott, this is my boyfriend, Jim Ragsdale. Thanks so much for coming. We're going to have a great time."

Jim added, "Nice meeting you both. Cate's told me so many nice things about you, and it's great to put faces with names. I know it's a little awkward to have to sneak around, but we really care for each other and we're glad you decided to come to the cabin with us."

"We haven't been to the Poconos yet, sir, and we're looking forward to it," Scott said.

"Please call me Jim. We're not on campus, and I'd like to be casual this weekend."

"Okay, sir. I mean Jim," Scott replied. "How long will it take to get to the cabin you rented for the weekend?"

"Less than two hours. I went to the commissary and Class VI store before I picked you up, so we have plenty of food and drinks. I hope you've brought your cameras. The area is beautiful, even in March."

"We brought them," Lori answered. "I've been looking forward to this trip for two months. I know Cate has too."

"You got that right. The cabin we're going to is on a small lake and has a kitchen and huge stone fireplace with two bedrooms. It is a beautiful setting any time of the year. Jim's grilling the steaks and salmon tonight, and I'm making my specialty vegetable casserole and a hearty potato cheese soup. I can't wait to cook again. I love cooking, and there's not many opportunities at school to cook or bake, other than at my sponsor's house."

"Very cool, Cate," Scott said. "I like to BBQ but I'm not a cook; too many sisters at home to even try. Lori, how's your cooking skill?"

"Uh, not too good. I was too busy in high school with sports, and newspaper staff, and other activities, and my mom didn't like me in her kitchen. But Grandma Nelson taught me to bake some mean brownies and cookies," Lori said with a chuckle.

"Cookies are good," Jim said. "Cate made me some great ones last week with walnuts and chocolate chips. Cate's a fantastic cook, and you're in for a real treat."

"We've been roommates for almost four years and I didn't know you could cook. Cate, you're good at everything!"

"I try, but you know I'm uncoordinated and a spaz when it comes to sports. You're such a good athlete, Lori. I would have failed the indoor obstacle course if it wasn't for your help and making me practice the month before the test. I think we make a great team."

"We're lucky. Many of the roommates at school have problems because they are so competitive. Glad we're not like that," said Lori. "You always make the time to help me with my engineering formulas so I do okay in those classes."

"I've got a decent roommate too," Scott said. "Do you know Dave McConnell?"

"I had him in my math class last year. Smart guy," Jim said.

"Yeah, he's a star man like you, Cate. He's always willing to help me when I get stuck on a problem. The only thing I hate is, he never studies. He's so smart and has a photographic memory. He branched engineers, and he'll be a real asset if they use him well," Scott said.

Cate replied, "I'm excited to be going to Hawaii as a new MI lieutenant. Jim has a request for orders to go to the 2nd Infantry Division at Schofield Barracks, and I'll be stationed at Fort Shafter, a few miles away. I can't wait!"

"That'll be great," Lori replied. "Scott and I are both going to Fort Bragg after our officer basic schools, and we're happy it all worked out."

"Yeah, I'm going to Benning for the basic course while Lori's at Fort McClellan for her MP school, and we'll only be ninety minutes apart. We plan on seeing each other on some weekends when we're not in the field. How cool is that?"

"Sounds like we all have much to be thankful for," Jim piped in.

The rest of the car ride was quiet as they all enjoyed the ride into the Poconos. An hour later, they arrived at the cabin and unpacked the car.

"How about you and Scott take the room on the left and we'll take the one on the right?" asked Cate.

"Okay," said Lori, conflicted about how she felt about sleeping together with Scott.

After plopping their suitcases in their rooms, the four walked onto the porch and looked at the scenery in front of them. "Wow, this is beautiful! I had no idea this part of New York was this terrific!" Lori said.

Scott replied, "I love the lake. It's so peaceful, and it's great to be away from the stress of West Point. Thanks for inviting me. I know this'll be a great weekend."

"Yeah, Jim and I came here in January and had the best time. I forgot I was a cadet, and the only bad part was driving back to Woops on Sunday night. This place is timeless and makes me forget the stress in my life. I'm so glad you both decided to come and share the weekend with us."

"I'd like to walk around the lake. Is that possible?" asked Lori.

"Sure, let me grab my camera and we can all stretch out and go for a walk," Jim said.

The two couples walked around the small lake and took pictures of each other and the lake and woods, enjoying the freedom and thrill of being on their own, away from the academy. Lots of laughing and walking hand in hand added to the specialness of the day. When they returned to their cabin, Jim said, "I don't know about you guys, but I'm getting hungry."

"Yeah, me too," said Scott, and Lori and Cate went into the kitchen to start making an early dinner.

"You weren't kidding," Lori said, "This hot dish is great!" after tasting Cate's casserole a while later.

"What's a hot dish?" Jim asked, surprised at Lori's words.

"Cate's specialty veggie dish is a hot dish," answered Lori matter-of-factly.

"I've never heard it said that way before. Where're you from?" asked Jim.

"Duluth, Minnesota, and we say hot dish for a casserole. In fact, I'd never heard of the word casserole until plebe year. Where're you from, Jim?" asked Lori, quite interested.

"I was born in Milwaukee, Wisconsin, but moved to Fort Bliss, Texas, when my dad joined the Army as a private. From there we lived in Grafenwoehr, West Germany, followed by Fort Lewis, Washington, and the Presidio in California. My dad's final assignment was Fort Riley, Kansas, and I went to ROTC at K-State and I got my math degree there. I'm an Army brat and attended six different schools in twelve years. I like moving and meeting new people. I guess it's in my blood."

Scott replied, "That's so cool. I went all twelve years to school in the same place in Kansas. My dad was a carpenter, and we never moved."

"I've lived in Duluth my whole life, too. I never knew how big the US really was 'til we drove to West Point in our station wagon. My dad's a window washer, and he loves his job, even though my mom kept asking him to finish his college degree and get a more prestigious job. I guess the main thing is you like what you're doing and treat people honorably."

"I totally agree!" said Cate. "I have no military service in my lineage that I'm aware of. My ancestors were gold miners and settled in Paradise, California. It's a great small place to be from. I have wonderful family memories of our small community."

"I'd love to go to California one day," Lori said.

Jim poured more wine, and they all drank another round with their steaks and salmon. Not used to drinking so much, Lori started feeling very happy. "How about starting up the fire, Scott? I'd love to watch the flames as we sip our drinks."

"Great idea! I'm on it," he said. As Scott started a fire in the fireplace, Lori, Jim, and Cate got up from the table with their drinks and moved to the living room. Jim put on *The Best of Bread* album to create a romantic mood while Cate sat in the loveseat. Lori sat on the couch and Scott joined her after starting the fire.

After sipping her fourth glass of wine, Lori was a little dizzy and feeling no pain. She was drunk and very unguarded. Scott was sitting next to her and he rubbed her leg. Lori laughed and whispered in his ear, "Hey, Scott, you're so nice."

"You make me so happy, Lori," he told her, and they started making out right there in front of Cate and Jim, who were oblivious, and doing the same.

Twenty minutes later, Jim interrupted the kissing session by saying, "Cate and I are moving into the bedroom, and I hope you have a good night."

"Okay," Lori said. After the others had left the room, she said, "Uh, Scott, you think we should move to our bedroom?"

"Yeah, sure," Scott said a little too fast. He pulled her up from the couch and they walked into their bedroom. Lori was having trouble walking to the bedroom.

Scott had enjoyed the day with Lori and didn't want to move too fast or take advantage of her. They both undressed and put on their PJs. They brushed their teeth, goofily smiling at each other. Lori jumped into the queen bed, and Scott slid in behind her. They cuddled and kissed, and Scott was tempted to go further, but he loved Lori and he didn't want to spoil the evening. Lori quickly fell asleep as Scott held her in his arms.

The next morning, Lori woke up with a headache, and she was surprised to be in bed with Scott. Not sure of what had happened the night before, she lay there trying to recall the evening's events. She remembered brushing their teeth together, but that was the last thing she remembered.

She watched Scott's chest move up and down and the peaceful smile he wore as he slept, then she crept out of bed and looked out the window. It had snowed two inches overnight, and it looked like a winter wonderland outside.

42

WEST POINT, SPRING BREAK, MARCH 1980

LORI, TRISH, JULIE, AND Reggie went to Fort Lauderdale, Florida, for spring break. They drove in Trish's new Honda Accord, with all four women taking turns driving to their destination on the beach while singing to songs on the cassette deck. Upon arriving at the hotel and looking at the ocean from the fifth-story balcony, Lori exclaimed, "Wow! This view is fantastic! I'm so excited about swimming in the ocean. All we have is lakes back home."

"Don't think you'll be swimming in the water; it's pretty cold," Reggie replied.

"Oh, I'm going in, even if only for a minute. Look at all the waves!"

Trish smiled widely and said, "This is cool. I've lived most of my life in Salt Lake City, and I haven't seen the ocean like this, either. Six nights here is really going to spoil me!"

Julie chimed in, "How 'bout we unpack and go for a walk on the beach? I'm stiff from the long marathon drive down here and need to stretch out."

"Great idea!" Lori said. "I say forget about unpacking. Let's just grab our cameras and get out there!"

"Okay," said Julie, laughing. "You're really excited about this, aren't you, Lori?"

"Yeah. I'm not from Destin, Florida, like you. How many times have you seen the ocean?"

"Oh, probably every week of my life, more in the summer. We lived less than a mile from the beach. This sand isn't as white as the gulf side, but it'll do," Julie replied.

Trish said, "I can't tell the difference between sand. This sand will do just fine. Let's go!"

The four Sugar Smacks left their two-bedroom suite, took the elevator down to the lobby floor, and walked out the back door facing the beach while passing the outside heated pool. "Nice pool!" Reggie said as they walked on the wooden pathway to the beach. "I could get used to this lifestyle."

"No kidding," Trish replied.

When they got to the water, Lori took off her tennis shoes and socks, pulled up her pants, and walked into the water. "You're right, Regg! It's cold, but it feels great, and these waves are so much fun! I love the warm sunshine."

The other three friends took off their shoes and joined Lori in wading in the surf. They then started walking south on the beach. After walking about a mile, Trish spotted a beach hut with some picnic benches on the sand and said, "How about stopping for a beer or drink and a burger?"

"I'm in," Reggie replied. "I'm really thirsty, breathing in all this salty air."

They all ordered burger baskets and beers, sat down on the picnic table, and drank their beers while enjoying the ocean view. "Let's have a toast," proclaimed Reggie as she lifted her beer bottle. "To friendship, fun, and sleeping in!"

"Hear, hear!" said Trish as they clinked their bottles together.

When their burgers and fries arrived, Julie asked the waitress for another beer.

Lori bit into her cheeseburger and said, "Oh my goodness, this burger tastes so good!"

"Just 'cause you're hungry," Trish said. "These fries are great too! Not as good as the fries in Germany, but almost as good."

"I don't see any mayonnaise to put on the fries, so I guess we're not in Germany," Lori replied. "I wonder how Anne and Maura are doing? Maura wrote last month and said they moved to Fort Bragg and she was scheduled to go to jump school this summer."

"Anne was the best sponsor," Trish said. "We were lucky to get two good ones."

"Sounds way better than my summer training, sweating to death at jungle school and being a supply sergeant at Beast," Julie said.

Reggie added, "Last summer, I went to Fort Ord for my CTLT. My sponsor was this MP lieutenant who wanted nothing to do with me. He did the bare minimum, I guess, like show me where the BOQ and O'Club was, and helped get my CIF issue. Other than that, I never saw him."

"Yeah, Trish and I lucked out. We spent six weeks as third lieutenants in Germany and then spent seven days in Paris seeing the sights. I thought the whole summer was a vacation instead of work, and it flew by. If the Army is anything like Germany, I'm sure I'll enjoy being an officer in a few months."

"What I think is weird is the guys seem to think being a good leader is all about being in good physical shape. For example, I did well at jungle school because I made all the runs, but the other gal and the four guys who fell out of the runs received poor performance ratings, even though they were smart and good decision makers. Seems unfair and narrow-minded," said Julie.

"You're right, Julie. It's the same way at school. It's such a macho place, and no sign of weakness is allowed. I wonder how West Pointers adjust to the real world after they graduate. When they actually get to have a social life and not wear their dress gray uniforms every day, how do they adjust?" Trish asked.

Julie chimed in, "My brother graduated four years ago. He said some grads adjust well and some don't. The ones who give West Point a bad name are the ones who are too idealist and treat their subordinates like they're incompetent plebes instead of trusted teammates. Yelling, being inflexible, and brown-nosing the boss are the grads who have not learned what it means to be a true leader."

Reggie said, "Wow! What happened to our fun afternoon of drinking and beach walking? I say we head on back to our hotel, unpack, and go to the grocery store. I can't afford to eat out every meal like you rich firsties."

"Sounds like a plan," Lori said as they got up and started walking back the way they had come.

At the grocery store, the four friends loaded their shopping cart with breakfast food, sandwich items, pasta, vegetables, ice cream, soda, and beer.

Lori also bought a few Ziggy cards to send to Willow. That night before going to bed, she wrote in one of the cards.

Hi Willow!

You'll never guess where I am right now. I'm in Fort Lauderdale on my first real spring break. We took a road trip in Trish's car along with Reggie and Julie from the basketball team. We're in a hotel suite with a balcony on the beach for six nights! The Atlantic Ocean is fantastic! So much bigger and better than the lakes at home. I collected a couple of shells and I hope you like the three I've put in this envelope. The weather is sunny and 72 today.

Enough about me. How's your pregnancy going? How's Jeff doing as a soon-to-be dad? How're our friends from high school doing? Say hi to your folks from me when you see them.

Miss you, Lori

THE FRIENDS SLEPT IN until 8:30 the next morning and had some cereal and orange juice, and Trish and Julie drank some coffee before figuring out what they wanted to do that day. They agreed to go for a long walk on the beach for a few hours, followed by lunch in their hotel, culminating with a movie.

"This is the life," Lori said from the backseat of Trish's Honda. "Sleep in, check out the ocean, eat great food, and catch a movie. I could get used to this."

"Don't get used to this. Being a 2LT is lots different, and there won't be much free time, I'm sure," Trish added.

"Well, Maura and Anne seemed to have lots of three-day weekends to take us places and relax. They didn't seem overworked to me," Lori replied.

"I think we caught them at a good time. I'm sure they worked many weekends and nights and pulled duty officer as 2LTs before they were our sponsors."

"You're probably right," Lori said. "Speaking of duty assignments, where are you two going after graduation? I got my first pick, Fort Bragg, North Carolina."

Julie replied, "You're lucky, Lori. Since my grades aren't too good, I got stuck with staying in El Paso, Texas, after I finish the Air Defense Artillery Officer Basic Course. I'm okay with that. Lots of my friends are in the same boat and got ranked Air Defense Artillery. You must have done well in school."

"I did okay, top half of the class, but only two MPs got to pick Bragg for their first duty assignment. I'm happy because that's where Scott is going and they have lots of platoons at Bragg."

Trish said, "I wish I were going to Bragg. I got orders to South Korea for a year after my basic course. I guess they need lots of logisticians to help with property accountability. I never expected to go to Korea as a 2LT. I hope it's like Germany. I loved Germany."

"Don't think it'll be like Germany, Trish. The cultures are very different. I love traveling, so I'd be happy with either overseas assignment," Reggie said. "So glad I'll be a firstie this fall. I can't wait to be a lieutenant and be a part of the real Army."

"You'll get your chance soon enough. I loved the Army compared to all the stupid rules at school," Lori said.

"Me too!" echoed Julie. Looking at Reggie, she asked, "What're ya doing this summer?"

"I got selected to be a squad leader at Beast. How crazy is that? After that, I'm going to air assault school. Should be fun!"

"Oh yeah! I loved summer training. I've heard air assault school is tougher than airborne school, but you're in great shape, Reggie. It'll be cool," Lori said.

Reggie replied, "I can't wait to graduate and start working. Academics are killing me. That's why this week is so great. No classes, no papers, no WPRs, no marching, no uniforms, and no formations. I love it!"

"Yeah," chuckled Trish. "Now what movie did we decide on?"

"*Moonraker*. Sounds like a fun James Bond movie, and you can't go wrong with James Bond. He's got the coolest gadgets, weapons, and vehicles," Julie said.

"I don't care for all the sexism with his skimpily clad ladies, but the action scenes and plot make up for the blatant sexism," Lori added.

"True enough. I never even thought about James Bond that way, Lori. I think Sean Connery is a looker," Reggie said.

"Well, Roger Moore is the new James Bond in this movie," Lori said.

"What? How can someone else be Bond?" Reggie said.

Trish interrupted, saying, "Okay, we're here! Don't forget to lock the doors. Don't want my new car stolen on leave while we're watching the movie."

43

WEST POINT, APRIL 1980

WEARING HER SOFTBALL UNIFORM, Reggie jogged up to Lori who was waiting in across from the library. Smiling like the Cheshire cat, Reggie said, "I got the best news yesterday!"

"Oh yeah?"

"I got a letter from the dean saying the academy had changed the regulations on cadet pregnancy. There are now various options when a cadet becomes pregnant. The Dean also closed my separation proceedings. I know I was not the only cadet who became pregnant, and I think my dad's lawyer was instrumental in the change. I'm so happy, I could float right now."

"That's fantastic news! We oughtta celebrate!"

"Good idea. We will this weekend. I'm so happy!" They walked in silence for a few minutes toward Buffalo Soldier's field across from the Thayer Hotel. "So tell me again, what were you doing last Saturday night?"

"I'd have to swear you to secrecy."

"Yeah, right. Let's hear it."

"I'm serious, Regg. You have to promise not to tell anyone before I tell you," Lori said.

"Uh, okay. Who would I tell anyway? You're my best friend. It's going to be lonely here next year without you, Lori."

"Well, how about Dan the man? He has a crush on you, and you know it."

"I know, but having a boyfriend and having a girlfriend are two different things. I can't tell him all my feelings like I can with you. I don't have to stroke your ego like I do with him. Girlfriends are the best," Reggie said.

"I agree. We had the best time last month on spring break with Trish and Julie. I never laughed so much in my whole life as I did the night of the bonfire. Julie is super funny when she gets drunk."

"You got that right. So spill. Where were you?"

"I was with Scott."

Reggie interrupted, "I knew it! You were supposed to meet us in Ike Hall for sodas."

"Sorry, Regg. This was a spur-of-the-moment event. I was heading out the door to meet you at Ike, and Scott came over in his sweats and said tonight was initiation night."

Perplexed, Reggie asked, "Initiation night for what?"

"I was inducted into the secret mole society."

"What's that? I've never heard of it."

"It's an old West Point secret; that's why you've never heard of it," Lori answered.

"Okay, so what is it and how did you get involved?"

"I'm not sure how or why or when it started, but Scott was inducted in his yearling year and he kept it a secret from me until right before Christmas. There's seven guys in the society, and I'm the first and only woman. They only allowed me to join because they like Scott so much."

"Okay, so what does the group do and why is it secret?"

"Well, from what I can tell, they love exploring the steam tunnels underneath all of the buildings. That's why they wear sweatpants and go at night, under the cover of darkness, so no one sees them going into or coming out of the off-limits areas."

Reggie impatiently asked, "Okay, so what happened at your induction?"

"Not much. After I changed into my sweats, Scott took me to the entrance of one of the steam tunnels and we walked a few blocks underground in the tunnels until we arrived at a small dark room. In the room, I met the members of the mole society. They had a few candles set up, and they officially welcomed me into their club. We then celebrated by drinking a mole potion laced with tons of alcohol. It was actually a really fun time. I was tipsy and I had no idea how we maneuvered through the tunnels, but we came out in the basement of Thayer Hall."

"Wow, that does sound lots more exciting than drinking with the gang at Ike. What happens if you get caught?"

"Don't know, but I'm sure we'd have huge slugs and spend months walking the area—not something I want to do this close to graduation. Perhaps that's what makes it so exciting and dangerous," Lori said.

"I see the team on the bleachers," Reggie said, pointing to the softball team a block ahead. "I guess CPT Smather is going to smother us again with his ideas on how to keep our winning streak going."

"Yeah, but it could be worse. We could have a losing record and he could be counseling us on what we need to do better. Come on! Let's jog up there, or we might be late and have to run laps."

ON SUNDAY NIGHT, LORI and Cate were in their rooms, bummed at being back for another week of academics. Lori felt this depressing feeling every Sunday night, knowing she had another hard week of studying. Reggie knocked on the door, entered, and said, "You guys ready for some Tony's pizza? I'm starving."

Lori replied, "Sure, Regg. I'd rather have some Heavenly Hash ice cream, but pizza sounds good too. You fly, I'll buy. Cate, you want a calzone or pizza?"

"I'd love a pepperoni 'zone and Coke tonight since I didn't have dinner. I'll pitch in with the cost of course."

Lori said, "Whadda you want, Regg? How 'bout splitting a sausage pizza with me? I haven't eaten either, and I'm getting hungry."

"Sounds good, Lori. I hope it's not too crowded at Tony's tonight. See you in thirty minutes!" Reggie replied as she grabbed a few bills from Lori and Cate and headed out the door.

Alone with Cate Lori asked, "So what's new with you and Jim?"

"We're doing great. We went into the city this weekend and had a grand time. We stayed in a small hotel, went out to dinner, saw a Broadway play, and took the horse carriage around part of Central Park. It was magical."

"Aren't you afraid someone might see you and write you up?" Lori asked.

"A little. I figure there's a small chance we'll get caught but a better chance we won't. We're willing to take the chance to be together. In another six weeks, I'll be a lieutenant and it won't matter anymore."

"True, but I'd hate to see you get slugged now, so close to graduation. They might even take away your dream assignment to Hawaii. That would be awful."

"Yes, but right now I'd risk a lot more to spend my time with Jim. We're madly in love. He finally got orders to the 25th Infantry Division at Schofield Barracks, Hawaii. Since I'm going to be in the MI brigade, we hope to live in a small town called Mililani, not far from post."

"When will you get to Hawaii?"

"I think around November. It'll be a tough six months at Fort Huachuca, but I plan on going to Hawaii for a few long weekends and Jeff will try to take a weeks' leave and visit me in Arizona if he can."

"Any wedding plans in the future?" Lori asked boldly.

"We're talking about it now. I'd love to get married on the beach with our families there. It's not practical and will be very expensive, but I think it'd be a wonderful way to start our lives together. How about you and Scott? Has it gotten serious yet?"

"Well, I really like Scott, but I'm not ready to commit to such an important decision yet. I think Scott is ready, but he knows I'm not. I turn twenty-two in July, and I think I'm too young to get married. Since we're both going to Fort Bragg after our officer basic courses, we'll have plenty of time to figure it out when we get together."

"Good plan. You'll both be invited to my wedding next year, so I hope you won't be in the field when we tie the knot on the beach."

"I'll try my best to be there, Cate. You know how it worked with Willow. I'm still torqued off that I couldn't be her maid of honor the Saturday she got married."

"How's Willow doing?" Cate asked.

"She's due this summer with their first baby. I'm getting excited for the whole family. Jeff is super excited, and I know he'll be a great dad. I plan on taking some graduation leave and visiting everyone back home in June."

A few minutes later, Reggie came into the room with a large pizza, a brown bag, and three bottles of soda. "I got lucky; only two cadets were in front of me, and then ten more cadets walked in. I got the last sausage pizza and pepperoni calzone, so that's why I'm back so soon."

"Great timing! I'm starving," said Lori.

"I am now, smelling the pizza!" Cate said as they started eating with smiles on their faces.

That night, Lori wrote Willow a note in another Ziggy card:

Hi mother-to-be!

So glad you are feeling better and your courses are coming to an end. Glad your pregnancy is going smoothly and you and Jeff have painted the baby's room a yellow color for a girl or a boy. I am finishing the last month of courses and I have been writing papers every week for my various electives. It's been tough keeping up with our busy softball schedule. We've had another winning season to date, which is cool. Sorry this is so short, I've got to write another paper tonight! Love, Lori

44

WEST POINT, 29 MAY 1980

GRADUATION DAY FINALLY ARRIVED. One hundred and nineteen women had entered the academy on July 1976, and sixty-two women graduated and were commissioned as 2LTs on 28 May 1980. The Honorable Harold Brown, Secretary of Defense, was the commencement speaker. At dinner the night before graduation, Lori and Scott's families had met each other, and this morning, they were sitting together in the Michie Stadium grandstand for the ceremony.

As Lori and Cate walked up to the stadium one last time, Cate commented, "It's wonderful it's sunny today. Some days were so bad, the thought of graduation was the only thing that kept me going."

"Yeah, me too, but what I'm really proud of is that all of us made it and our West Point experience is *finally* over!"

Nodding in agreement, Cate wistfully added, "I wish we could have sat together." Cate reached out and hugged Lori. "You've been the best roommate Lori!"

Grateful for her friends expression of friendship and appreciation, but uncomfortable with the show of affection, Lori gave her a hug back and laughingly replied, "I like the cheap seats. All you star men and women in the front row have to sit at attention, while I relax and hide in the crowd.

Cate acknowledged that truth ruefully adding, "Yeah, but how cool is it, that the next time we see each other, we'll both be grads?"

Lori gave Cate a huge smile, exclaiming, "The coolest ever!"

THE CADETS, WEARING THEIR full dress over white uniforms, marched into the stadium to the endless repetition of "Pomp and Circumstance." Lori sat down in the middle of the huge block of folding chairs on the football field, but it was hard to absorb the enormity of the moment. Her feelings were swirling around like a tornado. The Honorable Harold Brown's comments were unimpressive and as meaningless and politically correct as the three previous graduation commencement speeches she had heard. *This graduation is different. They said we'd never get in, and then when we did. They said, we'd never make it to graduation, but we did, and now we're here to stay!* Lori choked up at the thought of all the harassment, stress, and intense training she had managed to endure. She was proud of her accomplishment.

As her classmates' names were announced and they went on stage to receive their diplomas, Lori felt a strong bond to her classmates and especially her friends, who had helped her get to this day. While walking up to the stage to receive her own diploma, Lori scanned the stadium stands for her family, but she was unable to find them. As her name was announced, she proudly marched on stage, shook hands with General Goodson, and received her diploma. Walking back to her seat, Lori smiled as raised her diploma tube high over her head thinking, *I've done it!*

Thirty minutes later, when Lori heard, "Class of 1980, dismissed!" the whole field erupted as the new graduates jumped up, hollering and yelling and throwing their white caps high into the air and then shaking hands and hugging their classmates. Children who had gathered at the end zone were allowed to run onto the field and gather the caps. Members of the press corps descended on a few of the women for interviews.

Lori found Scott on the field. Grinning from ear to ear, they hugged and congratulated each other, oblivious to all the activity and noise exploding around them.

Lori spotted her and Scott's families approaching them on the field. Lori's dad gave her a huge hug, "We are so proud of you, honey. You're going to have a wonderful career, I just know it."

"Thanks, Dad. I wouldn't be here today if it wasn't for your and mom's love and belief in me."

"We wouldn't have missed it for the world. I had to see it with my own eyes."

Lori's mom chimed in, "Lori, you've set an example for so many young women to come. This day is one of the highlights of my life. We're so proud of you and your numerous accomplishments!"

"Thanks, Mom; good parenting and genes had a lot to do with this. You are the best parents I could ever wish for!"

"Hey, what about me?" Christa said. "I want to congratulate you too!"

"Shut up, Christa," Joe said. "It's not always all about you. Congrats, Lori. I'm happy for you. You're lucky you don't have to look for a job like I'll be doing next year; pretty cool."

"Thanks, Christa and Joe! You're the best!"

Lori felt a tap on her shoulder. "Congratulations Lieutenant! Maura exclaimed as she gave Lori a big hug and added, I never doubted you'd make it and I'm so proud and happy for you and your family!"

Surprised and happy to see Maura, Lori exclaimed, "Wow, I'm so glad you made it, thanks for the nice graduation card, but I sorta got the feeling you thought you wouldn't be able to make it."

"Well, you had enough on your plate and I didn't want to burden you with the worry that I might not make it through Jump week and if that were the case, I'd have been recycled and wouldn't have graduated in time to be here."

Noticing for the first time, the shiny silver airborne wings on Maura's chest, Lori yelled, "Oh, Wow! I didn't know you were going to airborne school!"

Maura chuckled, "Yeah, well neither one of us had a lot of time to write letters and I never got around to telling you that my next assignment is at

Fort Bragg, but I have to be airborne qualified to take the position branch nominated me for."

Lori exclaimed in disbelief, "I can't believe it, I'm going to Fort Bragg too! Looking at Scott and her family, Lori suddenly realized they'd never met Maura. "Hey everyone! This is Maura, my sponsor from CTLT that I told you about!"

After the introductions were done, Maura pointed out that Trish and Anne were walking their way. "I see Anne found Trish and her family."

Beaming with joy, Lori screamed, "You didn't tell me Anne was here too! What a great surprise!"

"Yeah, we thought it would be great to see both of you on your historic day. Waving to Trish, who had just joined the group, Maura added, Congratulations, both of you!"

Hugs and introductions were shared with Trish and her mom, brother, and Anne, before Mr. Nelson loudly interrupted, "I suggest we meet at the designated picnic site along the Hudson River in an hour. I'll have the charcoal revved up and steaks on the grill ready for barbequing."

"Sounds great! Anne chimed in. Maura and I'll stop by the Class VI store after we change and pick up some beer and wine. Can we get anything else?"

Mr. Nelson ignored the slightly disapproving look on his wife's face and announced jovially, Sounds great! This is a celebration and no celebration would be complete without a bit of beer and wine!"

It's about time, thought Lori as she smiled at all her friends and family before heading to her barracks room to change for the BBQ.

CPSIA information can be obtained
at www.ICGtesting.com
Printed in the USA
FFOW03n1858060318
45513684-46273FF

9 781457 539114